Narrow Highway

By

Michael Mikus

Disclaimer

"This is a work of fiction. Names, characters, places, and incidents either are the product of the author's imagination or are used fictitiously. Any resemblance to actual persons, living or dead, or actual events is purely coincidental".

Contents

Dedication

To my children, Jeremy, Nicholas, and Elizabeth;

To my brothers, Richard and David;

And to those who believed in me,

who upheld me—

and even to those who questioned me,

who thought I was crazy.

This is for you.

I'm still here, and the journey is far from over.

Note from the Author

I wrote this book because it was easy to place myself in the mind of the main character, Henry Boyle, having worked previously in Law Enforcement. I believe it to be the first step to educate, as well as entertain readers that there is something terribly wrong with the institution of our government—not the system, but the warped people inside it willing to sell themselves to the highest bidder, regardless of how it affects innocent people looked upon as puppets, whose strings are controlled by the dark forces who disguise themselves as light bearers for the hope of tomorrow. I also believe that I am the one to write the book because its theme of deception has captured my soul.

CHAPTER 1

The Manhattan skyline shimmered against the dark malevolent night. It breathed like a mythological creature standing above its glorious kingdom. It called to the daring and the adventurous to cross any of its spectacular bridges, roped in inverted arcs glittering in a swaying series to connect each passageway to the island.

But from the shadows of its Midtown Tunnel, as if spitting out a vile abscess, Trina Igan emerged driving a 1984 Buick Skylark covered with sun bleached spots and various dings and dents. The battle scarred vehicle, unsuitable for the 'Emerald City', had escaped from the mouth of this ungodly metropolis.

The dark exterior was the one good thing about the car, because it didn't show the dings and dents as much from previous altercations. Walmart paint covered them to a degree, but standing back to take it all in—the spots and the dents and dings could still be seen bleeding through like malignant scabs. Duct tape patched the seats and dashboard; a piece of plywood served as the floorboard for the driver, so that her feet would not drag across concrete. The windows had to be cranked; the side vents were busted; the seats were stuck; the ceiling cloth hung awkwardly, secured with more duct tape.

And the only things missing, to add to its underworld character, were bullet holes and a cracked windshield. Trina hated the car, but she exercised a state of grace because her boyfriend, Victor, said it was what they needed to cover their ambiguous flight. And the best thing they could do is represent themselves as average, middle class people enjoying a well earned vacation. But looking at the car, it was difficult to assume that they were anything but below average people, struggling to survive in a world about to swallow them whole.

She struggled to emulate the social sub-class, having come from a wealthy Connecticut background. She resolved herself to do the best she could all for the sake of love.

CHAPTER 2

From the Tunnel she connected to I-495, also referred to as the Long Island Expressway, and maneuvered her way through lanes of traffic for hours, first to the left and then to the right, in what seemed to be an endless array of back and forth lane changing. Her only amusement was to glance, every now and then, at open fields, suburban neighborhoods, and stretches of pine forest.

But the black white segments of the dividing lines had become hypnotic, causing her to drift too far into other lanes of traffic where the blast of oncoming car horns caused her to swerve into another lane. And once in that lane, horrific sound blasts of eighteen wheelers coupled with additional horns jerked her back into the safety of her proper lane with a white-knuckled grip frozen on the steering wheel. Then she stared deadpan at the grey asphalt stretching before her like a concrete river, thankful she was in the far right lane, where it was less likely to have a collision.

Victor slept through it all, head down, resting like a dead man. It was time to pull over, not only for their own well-being but for other motorists as well. She knew that Victor didn't feel good, but she wanted him to wake up. She reached over to nudge him.

"Victor. You need to wake up. You've got to keep me awake. I can't do it anymore. Wake up." She nudged him again. "Wake up, baby!"

She began to rouse him and, finally, he lifted his head to gaze at the snake-like highway.

Clearing his throat, he asked, "Where are we?"

"I don't know. I haven't seen an exit sign yet. I need to pull over. I can barely think. I almost had a," she looked at him, starting to doze again. "No, baby! Don't go back to sleep, okay? You've slept enough. I need you to talk to me."

Looking over at her, then back at the highway, he said, "Ok." He sat up and rubbed his eyes with his right hand. "Can you make it to the next turnoff?"

"Yes. I'll drive slow."

Victor nodded, then slumped against the door and window again.

She fixed her attention on the road, but before she could look for any signs, red and blue flashing lights appeared in the rearview mirror, spilling onto the surrounding areas to swarm her vision in a collective strobe of light.

"Fuck!" she said, with a stern sense of impatience.

This time she shook him hard to rattle his head. "Wake up, Victor! Victor! You have to wake up! We've got trouble!" she said, still shaking him hard.

He struggled to wake up through his morphine induced slumber. "Alright, ALRIGHT!" He saw the flashing lights all around him.

"What do I do?" she asked.

"Well. Pull the car over," he said, wearily.

She spoke with a sense of growing trepidation, slowly turning her head to look at him. "But what else do you have in the trunk? He's going to look there."

"He won't look there."

"How do you know?"

"Just pull over the car! Do it now!"

She pulled over the car and put it in park. She didn't like being talked to like that, even in tense situations. She sat with her hands in her lap.

"Turn the car off," he said.

"Why?"

"Because he will tell you to!!" he said, raising his voice even higher.

She turned off the car while checking her side mirror. Then she asked, "What do I say when he comes?"

"You just… answer questions," he said, waving his hand, searching for the answer that was not obvious to her.

"But the rifle!" she said, slapping her hands against her thighs. "He'll look in the trunk! What else do you have back there?" she said, raising her voice.

"Nothing! He won't look there!" he said, sternly.

Determined, she said, "Really. What else is back there?"

"He won't look there. It's okay," he said, trying to be patient.

She watched Victor withdraw his gun hidden in the sling. He pulled back the slide of the Beretta, easing one into the chamber. Then he replaced it in the sling, his hand on the grip ready to fire. He gave her a weak smile and said, "You'll be fine." Then, pointing above the visor, he said quietly, "Get them ready." He assumed his position, pretending to sleep.

His calm, cool demeanor was what she needed. Her stomach, fueled by a streak of adrenaline, was calm now. Her mind had cleared in a miraculous surprise like light entering a dark room. She reached above the visor to withdraw what the officer needed, but looking at them she said, "The address is wrong… my name isn't right."

He tried raising his left hand to reassure her, but he replaced it quickly, wincing with pain. In a tired, labored voice, he said, "We just got married. You haven't had time to change them. We're on our honeymoon." Then turning to her, he said, "Okay?"

She nodded and watched the officer get out of his car and proceed in what seemed to be a slow motion gait. She could hear his boots crunch against the gravel.

As the officer neared, her heart pounded in her ears and she wondered how they would ever get out of this. What else did Victor have besides a rifle in the trunk? She didn't want to go to jail, and if the officer looked, Victor would start firing to eliminate the problem. She wanted to scream, but that was out of the question.

Then she heard Victor whisper to her, "You'll be fine. Just be calm."

The officer was at the side of her car. At a glance, he seemed large and imposing, nazi-like. He tapped on the window. She lowered it.

"Evening, ma'am. License and registration, please."

The officer noticed she had them ready and was grateful. She handed them to him through the window. She was deep-breathing from her diaphragm to appear more relaxed. The last thing she wanted was for the officer to search the trunk.

"Did you know you were weaving all over the road back there, and I clocked you at 75? The limit here is 65. Are you aware of that?"

She lowered her head and said, "I guess, it just got away from me. I do apologize, officer," she said, looking up and giving her best effort at a smile.

"Have you been drinking, ma'am? Or taking any unusual substances that would impair your ability to drive?"

"Oh, no sir. Honest. I don't drink or do drugs. You can check me out if you like."

The officer smirked and stood there assessing the situation. There was no smell of alcohol coming from the car or cannabis. Using his flashlight, he looked in the backseat, but saw nothing. So, he bent down and flashed the light at Victor, leaning against the window like he had been sleeping.

"What's wrong with him?"

She looked over at him, then back at the officer.

"Oh, he just had shoulder surgery. He's been sleeping."

"What happened to his shoulder?"

She thought for a moment.

"He was shot in Afghanistan," she said, rubbing his leg. Then with a hurt look in her eyes, she continued. "They shipped him home to me soon after. He had one operation, but then he had to have another," she said, holding back the tears, her voice quivering. "It upsets me so much I can hardly sleep," she said, placing a hand on her forehead.

Sympathizing with them, the officer said, "That's what those .50 caliber rounds will do. They don't leave much."

Then she reached over and nudged Victor, saying, "Wake up, honey. Say hello to the officer."

Victor raised his head slightly and gave a lazy salute that the officer returned.

"Thank you for your service," the officer said.

"We just got married," Trina said, giving a weak smile, still holding back her tears.

"Newlyweds, huh?" he said, smiling. "Where are you headed?"

She looked through the windshield. "Well, we've never been to Long Island. So, we thought we'd come out here and see what it's like. We don't have a lot to spend. So just checkin-er out."

The officer looked at the car, chuckling to himself. Then, looking down the highway, he said, "Oh, it's a beautiful place. You're going to see a lot of wonderful things. The beaches…"

The officer's radio squawked. He answered it, listened for a minute, as Trina's heart was still racing and Victor kept his hand on the Beretta inside his sling. Finally, the officer said, "10-4. I'm 10-19." He gave the license and registration back to her.

"I got another call. You lucked out here, lady. Anyway, congratulations."

He tipped his hat to her, then jogged back to his car, got in, and sped away with his lights and siren flashing.

They sat there looking around at things they normally didn't. Trina exhaled loudly, and Victor lifted his head above the dash to watch the flashing lights shrink down the interstate. Several minutes passed as they realized how lucky they were and how horrible it could have been.

Looking at the plywood at her feet, she said, "That was close. Thank God."

"You did well," he said, trying to place his hand on her thigh, but it still hurt too much. He was wide awake now.

"Could you feel me shaking?" she asked. When no reply came, she asked, "What else did you have back there? Really, baby… besides, the rifle?"

"I'll show you later," he said, looking out at a field stretching into darkness.

She paused, realizing she was right all along. "I knew there was more back there. A big surprise, I hope?" she said, sarcastically.

He wanted to respond to the remark, but decided to let it lay.

As she drove, they listened to the noise of cars and the heavy metal breaking sound of transport trucks as they whissed by with back drafts and short periods of calm in between. They talked about how fortunate they were to have found each other in such an unorthodox way. And Victor restated his feelings for her that completely overwhelmed her again.

It was dangerous to continue the way they were traveling. And although the beat up Buick was good cover, they needed a place where they could think and get to know each other better. They looked ahead and listened to the sounds of the night as the highway stretched before them.

"Okay! I can't take this silence! You need to talk to me!"

Victor looked at her and said, "Sure, baby. What do you want to talk about?"

Chuckling, she said, "Oh, you act so casual about it."

"What?"

"Women love to talk. Don't you know that? It's soothing to their souls."

He raised his head to look at her, then whispered softly, "It's just that I'm so tired."

He snuggled as best he could, leaning partway against her, then he said, "And you're the most beautiful thing I have ever seen."

Then it was quiet again. And Trina drove with a smile.

CHAPTER 3

Victor was involved in a gunfight that took place in Trina's 6th floor loft apartment at 169 Mercer Street in Manhattan. Two CIA field operatives were killed. Victor took one in the shoulder as he dove and rolled to come up shooting, killing each one through the heart; two shots, two dead! The agents shot first making it self-defense, but who was going to believe that?

Detectives Boyle and Genesco were tied back to back in chairs. Victor dressed his wound in front of them, stopping the bleeding with cotton balls stuffed in the exit wound and using the cotton balls again with super glue to cover the front. He then injected himself with morphine and replaced the syringe in his medkit kept in his bag. Having finished, he talked to the detectives to try and buy the time needed, so that he could help them track the real killer who had terrorized Grand Central Terminal. And in order to do that, he needed time for his shoulder to heal

The case that drove Victor and Trina to Long Island was the Grand Central Killer case that was in the hands of Detective Boyle. Victor pursued Detective Boyle as the murders progressed with notes left on the bodies. The first note, addressed to him at the 37th Precinct, was purely an introduction, but after that when the initial reaction failed to peak Boyles' interest, he left them on each body knowing it was a surefire way to get them read and digested as evidence. Of course, Boyle thought the suggestions to help apprehend the real killer were preposterous, but Victor trudged on, refusing to give up the pursuit of clearing his name.

A task force composed of two NYPD Detectives, two operatives on loan from the CIA, and an FBI agent that no one really liked named John Westhouse was formed. Boyle's friend Dan Kearney was also used at times, but he was a retired FBI profiler shot in the knee and through considerable rehabilitation was able to walk again with a limp. His input was valued, highly respected, but only used when needed.

The case took its toll on Boyle and his Lt. Langley told him it was on hold and to pursue it only if a new development occurred. But Boyle figured what Langley didn't know wouldn't hurt him. He had been working with Detective Jimmy Gutierrez from the 9th Precinct concerning Javier Santiago who had given them the address of a girl named Trina, whose father owned the building at 169 Mercer Street where she lived and the two operatives were killed.

Trina was the girlfriend of Victor and the reason they wanted her address was that they thought she would lead them to him. They had discussed the fact that there had to be a getaway car and maybe one of Santiago's crew had seen a license number as they drove away. Boyle figured that the car used was the Buick Skylark. It just made sense.

After listening to Gutierrez explain about Santiago's injured crew, Boyle agreed with his partner, Eddie Genesco, that they should interrogate Santiago again to see if any of his crew members remembered a license number from the scene of the car bombing, a place where Victor had taken a Louisville Slugger and laid out Javier's crew all over the sidewalk, including Javier. Then he proceeded to blow up Javier's custom '63 Chevy Biscayne with a little C4 explosive mixed in with a fire stoker shoved in the gas tank that blew the car up. Javier and his crew scrambled like crabs as the car burned to a crisp.

***

As Boyle and Guiterrez pulled up to Santiago's address in a neighborhood known as Alphabet City, they noticed Santiago was outside 'kickin it' with his bros, who were still limping and hobbling, yet drinking and dancing to the music of Santana from a boombox. The song playing was 'Evil Ways' and several of them were dancing with their big-breasted, big-bootied 'chavas' having a spirited time.

Everyone stopped dancing in front of their building, but the music kept playing. "You want to talk to him or me?" Gutierrez asked Boyle.

"We'll both go, but you do the talking, okay?"

"Si mucho," Gutierrez said, smiling.

They both walked over to the crowd and Gutierrez motioned for Santiago to join them. He was glad they were playing Santana rather than some crazy sounding Cuban noise. They walked back to where the others were gathered by their cars and began the unique adventure of talking to Santiago.

"You know, this makes no damn sense to me, man. I am here having fun with my amigos and you," he said, pointing his finger at Gutierrez, "come to interfere with our celebration?"

"What celebration?" Gutierrez asked.

"Just being alive, bro!" he said, excitedly. "It's a beautiful day, the sun is shining, the sky is blue. What a beautiful country! We celebrate the day, man! We are alive on this beautiful, blue planet. You catch my drift, bro?"

Gutierrez thought for a minute, then asked, "What do you mean blue planet?"

"The earth, bro. It's what it looks like…from space."

"Oh, you mean outer space?"

"Si mucho," he said, then gesturing to the sky, he said, "Up there."

"You've seen it from there?"

"No, man. Pictures…the internet. They got beautiful pictures, man. The blue planet hangs on nothing in space. God hung it there," he said, placing one hand above the other.

Thinking again, Gutierrez said, "I'll take your word for it, but we got some business to take care of first."

"You guys should be out kickin it. Celebrating life!"

"Some of us have to work," he said.

"Then why don't you guys go do that? Stop messin with us. You could lock up your guns and badges and join us! Have some tequila, some cerveza!"

"Thanks for the invitation," Gutierrez said, walking him over to their cars. "But we need you to do something for us."

"Like what?" he asked, stopping.

"We want you to talk to your friends." He pointed at the others. "Those guys who just got out of the hospital and ask them if they remember seeing a car leave the scene where they got battered. Maybe they remember a license plate number. Do you think you could do that?"

"If I do that you got to offer them somethin'. Else they'll just say, 'Fuck those cops! We ain't got shit!'"

Gutierrez looked at Boyle, then Genesco and said, "What do you guys think? They got some pending charges, but nothing to get in a twist over. And they're not going anywhere in the state they're in. So we can pick them up whenever we need to."

Santiago overheard them and said, "Si mucho!. They ain't professionals like me. I ain't had 'em long enough," Santiago said.

"Well, aren't we the lucky ones," Gutierrez said, turning back to Boyle who smiled to himself.

They paused for a minute, then Eddie spoke up. "Tell them, if they can come up with one good license number, then we could soften their charges and perhaps make them go away. Don't promise it, just toss it out there as an incentive."

Santiago ran a seven man crew. He never took notes or wrote anything down for fear of leaving evidence. He was good at remembering numbers and didn't need any help from the detectives who had the case file there if he needed it.

He walked over to his crew members and turned off the music. Asking them to gather round, he asked them if anyone remembered anything from that day, making the incentive plain.

No one remembered a car driving away--some had head injuries with blurred memories and vision--until Tito Ramirez, a young protege, if you choose to call him that, remembered the car in question.

His injury was a broken arm and a busted knee. He managed to crawl the opposite way from the exploding car and remembered to focus on the license number, as the car drove past him. When he got to the hospital he asked for a pen to write down the number, hoping he could find out later who did this to them.

He kept the number in his wallet and when he was released placed it in the glove compartment of the car he now drove. He walked to his car, retrieved the paper with the license number, walked back and gave it to Gutierrez, a yellow piece of paper with ENZ-1560 written on it.

"That's it," Gutierrez said, turning to Boyle and smiling. As they started to leave, Gutierrez told Santiago, "If we get a hit on that number and it helps us out, tell Tito we'll work something out with him."

"What about me, man?" Santiago asked. "What about you?" Gutierrez asked. "What do I get?"

Gutierrez looked at Boyle, who smiled and said, "Pants with a zipper."

Santiago looked at him ashamed. "Aah, wow, man! That's really cold, bro! You still bring that up?" It referred to when they were on stakeout at 169 Mercer Street. And Santiago had to take a leak. So, Gutierrez got out and told him to piss in the gutter after unlocking his cuffs. Santiago bitched and moaned and said his 'lizard' was so big that he couldn't undo the buttons on his pants. Gutierrez laughing said that he wouldn't help him with his buttons, and if he ran that he would put one in his back. Santiago coaxed Gutierrez to come and undo his pants, but he wouldn't do it. The incident spread throughout the precinct and back to Boyle, causing him to mention it again; cops humor.

CHAPTER 4

On the way to the 9th Precinct the detectives still chuckled and poked fun at each other in reference to Santiago's difficulty extracting his 'lizard'. And Gutierrez added, "He even told me that he had no problem with the ladies, because they loved him. They referred to him as 'the King'."

They entered the precinct laughing and walked to the computer area in the back of the squad room to access the Domain Awareness System. Gutierrez sat at the computer where he operated the Vigilant Solutions System.

"This is the one I was talking about earlier. If we get a hit, it will mark the places that license number has been," Gutierrez said.

"Like a GPS map?" Eddie asked.

Gutierrez looked up at him. "Yeah, like that. Then we can put a map on the wall and put stick pins in the places it's been." He began entering the license number, looking to make sure his typing was correct. "ENZ-1560..." Then he tapped the enter key.

Then he turned around to Boyle and Eddie saying, "This thing searches about 2 billion records. Could be a few minutes. You guys need to hit the can, or coffee up?"

"Sure, Boxle said. "Thanks for helping us." Gutierrez nodded like it was nothing. "2 billion records? Jesus!" Boyle said.

"Best money the city ever spent, if you ask me. There's some privacy issues that the lawyers are dealing with, but that's only if it's abused."

"So you can do any lookup on this thing, even if it's not suspicious?" Eddie asked.

"That's what the privacy issues are about. But you have to admit it makes our jobs a lot easier," Gutierrez said.

Boyle's phone rang. When he looked at it, he saw it was Lt. Langley.

"I gotta take this. If you get a hit let me know." They both nodded. Eddie went to get coffee. Gutierrez looked at the screen awhile, then went back to his desk.

Boyle walked down the hall and seeing an empty room, he went inside for more privacy. It was an interview room and as he answered he sat down and put his elbows on the table.

"I'm sorry I didn't get back to you sooner, lieutenant, but it's been a little crazy."

Langley was hot. He could sense it before he spoke. "I don't care about crazy! Part of your job is to give me updates, which you have not been doing! I'm not happy about that at all!"

Boyle paused and looked away at the opposite wall, as he let Langley spout off about his lack of communication and sense of professionalism. He didn't need this now, but he knew Langley had a point. Dealing with superiors was an area for which he had little finesse, so he kept listening calmly as Langley continued to blow off steam.

"Do you think you run this department, detective? You think you're somebody special who can punch his own time clock? Make your own rules? I ought to just fire your damn ass and be done with you! You make my job a living hell!"

There was a pause. Boyle could hear Langley breathing while trying to regain his composure. He thought it was best to just wait. Then suddenly, as if it hadn't happened, Langley said, "Now, tell me what you have so far."

Boyle smiled to himself and proceeded to tell Langley that he thought Victor Enmerkar was no longer in the city. And they may have a possible license plate number. It failed to change Langley's attitude about how the case was going.

"I gave you some leeway, but I can see you're too close to this case! He was in the city and now you think he isn't? He seems to always be a step ahead of you."

"That's because he's not stupid, lieutenant. He still wants to talk to me. But he's careful. He wants it to be the right time." Boyle had still not told Langley everything that Victor had told him the day of the killings at Mercer Street.

"But you're not getting results! You're just spinning your wheels! How many others will he kill before you talk to him? What the hell are you waiting for?"

Boyle took the phone away from his ear as Langley paused to gather himself. He took a deep breath and said, "I'm taking you off this case, as of now! Report to me tomorrow and I'll see what we have for you."

"You can't do that, lieutenant!" Boyle rarely raised his voice to a superior.

"You watch me!"

"Who else are you going to put in my place? Think about it! One of those I don't give a shit detectives? Get real, lieutenant! He wants me! I'm the man! If you put someone else on this case, he'll start killing more people until you put me back on!"

There was a prolonged silence. Boyle took it as an acceptance that he was still up and running, so he proceeded to fill in Langley with information about the license plate number and the situation with the FBI, which seemed to appease him.

"So that's where we are right now, lieutenant. I haven't had time to talk to Westhouse, you know how that goes, or the CIA Ops, not that I'm in a hurry to do that either, but all good things come in time."

Langley took a deep breath, "Ok. Sounds like that license plate number could be a breaker." He paused, then said, "Does the 9th have that new software everyone's talking about? I forgot the name of it."

"Vigilant Solutions."

"Right, that's the name. We're in line to get it, too. But the Commissioner hasn't gotten the word from the Mayor's Office yet."

"Bureaucracy at work."

"Let me know what you get on that license number, and I mean, let me know."

"Gutierrez ran the number and we're waiting for it to come back. Did you know that database holds 2 billion records?"

Boyle heard Langley grimace through the phone.

"That's because it's nationwide. Ask him to narrow the search to the east coast. It would be quicker."

"Ok. How's the surveillance going at Grand Central?" Boyle asked.

"I called it off, Henry. We're way past 48 hours, and it seemed like a waste of time and manpower. So, I've got them working on other things."

"I wish I could tell you more here, lieutenant, but at least you can tell everyone that we do have a lead."

"Keep me updated. I mean it! You've bought yourself some more time, detective, so get some results!"

"Will do."

Boyle put his phone away. He was glad the call was over. As he walked back to the squad room. He saw Eddie sitting at the computer who looked up and saw him. "Nothing yet. I think we need to cut down the search."

Boyle leaned in to look at the screen still searching. "Yeah, how about the New York area? That would be---"

"Hold on. Let me kill this first." Eddie stopped the nationwide search, then turned back to Boyle. "Ok, the New York area..." Eddie typed as he spoke. "...that would be Manhattan, Bronx, Staten Island, Brooklyn, Long Island and..."

"Might as well include Jersey. They'll get pissed if you don't."

CHAPTER 5

The new search came up with several hits of the license number in the Lower East Side of Manhattan. Moving to a map on a wall, Gutierrez stuck push pins in every flagged location. A garage on Canal Street, several along the East River below the Williamsburg Bridge, and various other locations in the area, but the most consistent location pointed to the address of the Dreslin Hotel in Alphabet City.

Studying the map closely, Boyle turned to Gutierrez and asked, "What kind of a hotel is the Dreslin?"

"It's a flop house, really. You know, lowlifes...down-and-outers."

Boyle paused, looking at him, then asked, "Would you stay there?"

Gutierrez raised and looked at him. "Are you kidding me?"

"Would it be a good place to hide?"

Gutierrez looked again at the map, then said, "Now that you mention it...yeah" Then running his finger over to Canal Street, he tapped its location. "And that's where he takes the Skylark to gas it up, or get it fixed." Rubbing his chin, he looked back at Boyle and said, "I bet he pays that mechanic pretty darn well to keep his mouth shut. If I were you, I'd go there and ask some questions."

Boyle nodded. "Ok. Can I get a printout of that GPS sheet?"

"Sure."

Gutierrez walked over and pressed the print key, then pointed to the printer.

"It'll be up in a minute. What are you going to do now?"

"I guess I'll take this back to the task force and see what they say."

Gutierrez nodded. "FBI, huh?" he said, shaking his head. "If we had the manpower here, I'd go with you. But they've got what you need, unless you want ESU to jump in."

"No, no. That's too much. Low key is better."

"You know this guy better than I do, but I'd rely on them to help you. Sometimes you gotta do what you don't like."

Boyle nodded. Then turning to Eddie, he asked, "You ready?"

"I'm with you," Eddie said, getting up.

***

The Canal Street Automotive was located on Canal Street between Ludlow and Essex. It was an area where counterfeit goods and depressing ripoffs could be found at sidewalk stands raided frequently by the police, mostly just to push them on to resurface at another location. The building looked like most any facility set up to service cars except that it looked older and dirtier, as if stained with motor oil. Coats of white paint tried to cover the outside, but the stain seemed to bleed through. The inside was painted a dark green.

The service garage was built into the block in a semicircle with a driveway to enter and exit. They pulled up to the open door of one of the bays and got out. The hood of a gray Chevy sedan was raised. As they walked to the tool bench, the man under the hood saw them and said, "Be right with you. Give me a second."

He was adjusting something on the opposite side of where they stood and it obviously needed his close attention.

After waiting for what he considered a reasonable time, Boyle took out his badge and stuck it in front of his face. "Take a break," Boyle said, giving him time to read the ID.

The mechanic leaned up, placed his tools on top of the air blower, then grabbed a rag to wipe his hands. "What's going on, detective?"

"My name is Boyle. This is Detective Genesco. I need to ask you some questions."

"What about?" The mechanic was short, bald with thick black gray hair on the sides.

Full mustache. His face was puffy, as well as his body.

"We have information that you did some work on a 1984 Buick Skylark. The outside was pretty beat up. Do you remember that car?"

"I work on a lot of cars. Was this recent?"

"Fairly recent. If you worked on it you would remember it."

The mechanic paused. The name sewn on his shirt said Spiro. That settled it for Boyle. The man was Greek.

"You say it was beat up?"

"Yes. Badly in need of a paint job."

Spiro paused, wondering what to say, because the man who brought the car in asked me to work on the vehicle but not to mention his name. And, of course, he remembered the sizable bonus he received in cash to keep his mouth shut. So he asked Boyle with an economy of speech. "No. I don't remember it."

Boyle pulled out a picture from inside his coat. He placed it in front of Spiro's face. "Take a look. Does he look familiar?" Boyle watched his eyes intently.

Spiro paused before he asked, "What has this man done?"

"He's murdered four people. You've heard about the bombing at Grand Central?" Spiro looked at him nervously. "He did that?"

"Most certainly." Boyle learned in closer. "Now do you recognize him?"

Spiro shook his head and turned away. "No, no. I haven't seen him."

"Yes, you have! I have a GPS report that the Buick has been here several times. We can arrest you for interfering with a homicide investigation!"

"No! I didn't interfere with anything!"

"You've seen him and the car. I can tell by your eyes. Give us some information! Help us before he kills someone else! He's a maniac!"

"I don't know how to get a hold of him! I just worked on his car! I don't have an address! He just comes by when he comes by."

"Then you do remember him!"

"Yes, but he hasn't come by for a long time."

"What did you do for him?"

"I worked on the engine and the electrical system of the Buick. I made some modifications to it to give it more horsepower."

"What color was the car?"

Spiro laughed. "It's hard to say. Parts of it were sunbleached, others blue, some gray. Full of dents."

Boyle looked at Eddie. He took a deep breath and took out his card. "This is my number. I want you to call me if he comes back. It would help if you get an address."

Spiro took the card, looked at them both and said, "Yes. I will do that."

"If he wants you to work on his car, go ahead. Take the money. We don't want you. Ok?"

Spiro nodded. Boyle pointed at him as they left. "We'll be checking back with you, so stay alert."

Walking to the car, Boyle said, "We need to set up a watch on the place."

"I'll take care of it. Where to now?" Eddie asked.

"The Dreslin."

***

Arriving at the Dreslin, Boyle and Eddie were taken back by the graffiti-marked structure badly in need of a face lift. Walking in the front door, they noticed a few homeless people lounging in the lobby on the dirty furniture. Trash was scattered about the floor that no one seemed to notice.

"God, what a dump," Eddie said, looking around in disgust.

Walking up to the bulletproof, see-through window, Boyle saw the fat attendant sitting at a table with his back to the window, fat hanging down from his sides, eating something in a bowl with a large spoon. There was a hotplate, microwave and refrigerator underneath the table so fatboy wouldn't have to move if he needed something.

Boyle spoke through the drilled holes.

"Hey, you!" Boyle raised his voice to make sure the man heard him, but there was no response. So, he kicked it up a notch. "Hey! Fatboy! NYPD! Get over here!"

The man turned his head while still chewing, then put down the bowl and spoon, and got up with great effort that took him several attempts--he waddled over to the window and stood there looking at the detectives.

Boyle waited to see if he would speak. When he didn't he began introductions.

"I'm Detective Boyle and this is Detective Genesco." He extracted a picture from his jacket and pressed it against the glass with his palm. "Do you recognize this man? We have reason to believe he's staying here." Boyle kept his delivery cold and to the point, trying to keep his mind off the disgustingly fat man in front of him. His face was so fat and his eyes so buried in his skull that

Boyle couldn't tell if he was looking at the picture or just straight ahead.

"Show me some ID?" the fat man said in a weak, raspy voice that reminded Boyle of a sick animal that needed to be put out of its misery.

They both showed their IDs and badges by holding them up to the glass. The fat man leaned forward with a strained effort, and squinted his eyes to look at the IDs.

When he raised up, he said, "He doesn't live here."

"Look again fat man, because if you don't know, we're going to go through every apartment ourselves, which means you're going to give us a lot of keys. So think about that and take another look. I'll slide the picture through, if that will help."

The fat man gave no expression or indication that he would, so Boyle slid the picture through the money opening, then pointed at the picture. The fat man looked down at it, then picked it up to hold before his eyes, then said, "Try the third floor...maybe 327."

"Are you sure about that? He drives an old Buick Skylark."

"I don't know about cars. I just take money."

"He probably pays with cash, lots of it, in advance. Does that ring a bell?" Boyle asked.

The fat man paused, then nodded and said, "327," as he slid the key out to them.

Picking it up, Boyle said, "Alright, fatboy, but if this isn't the one," he said, holding up the key, "we'll be back for the other keys and call for extra help, which means you're going to get a lot more exercise."

Then they turned to look for the elevator.

Eddie said, "I'll take the stairs. You can ride. That way we won't miss him."

Boyle nodded, then when the elevator door opened he walked inside and pressed three. When the elevator door opened, Eddie met him and they continued down the spacious hall until they reached apartment 327. Boyle unlocked the door, they both entered, and were momentarily struck by the starkness of the room. Eddie walked to the bathroom, looked around, then turned to Boyle and said, "I'll start here."

Boyle nodded and began his search by opening the closet that had a shirt and a pair of pants hanging, a hooded sweatshirt, and an assortment of ball caps on the top shelf. At the bottom of the closet was a pair of what looked like army boots. Checking the soles they appeared to be worn.

Coming out into the combination living room/bedroom, Boyle paused to examine it, letting his eyes sweep the area to see if any place spoke out for him to investigate. Walking to the kitchenette, which was nothing more than a sink with a counter, upon which rested a hotplate, he opened the cabinets to see them empty, except for a few cans of peaches with the pull ring on top. He pulled open the single drawer on each side of the sink to find plastic forks, spoons, and knives he imagined were leftover from take out meals.

Moving to the bed that looked perfectly made, he pulled back the top blanket. It was pulled tight on each side, then checking the sheets, he discovered they were put on the bed using military corners. The only creases he saw were on the edge facing the room where it looked like two people had sat side by side. Lifting up the mattress, there was nothing underneath it, but he saw looking through the open springs a piece of paper on the floor. He dropped the mattress and extracted a pair of medical gloves from his pocket. After stretching them on with a few smacks, he got down on one knee and reached under to retrieve it, dragging it forward with a pen from his shirt pocket.

With the paper in hand, he got up and sat on the edge of the bed, unfolded it, and saw it was an application for an E-ZPASS, which was a cheaper and easier way of paying tolls going to and from Manhattan. The application was marked for the Queens Midtown Tunnel. There were areas on the application to fill in car information, including license plate number, model, and make of the car, which corresponded precisely with a 1984 Buick Skylark, ENZ-1560 under the name of Franklin Greene. Bingo!

Boyle called Westhouse who arrived in a black SUV with darkened one way windows in under 45 minutes. He came with two crime scene techs and some armed reinforcements to search the building's roof, staircases, basement, the exits, alleyways and all other ways of escaping under the wire.

Boyle met Westhouse in the hallway on the main floor after they explored the lobby and the rest of the building. "Hello there, Boyle. We got here as quickly as we could."

Boyle nodded. "Where's Caldwell and Billings?"

"On their way."

"Good." Then Boyle leaned in. "Do you really think all this is necessary?

"If he enters the building, he's ours. Completely surrounded. We'll stay back in the shadows so as not to discourage him." Then Westhouse laughed. "I just wanted to show you what we bring to the table. "

Westhouse noticed the fat man behind the glass and walked over to interrogate him. Boyle was impressed at the ease in which Westhouse moved in and around his attempts to evade him. He gave him the third degree and came up with more information about Victor

Enmerkar and he got him to admit his car was a Buick Skylark and that he paid his rent sometimes months in advance with hundred dollar bills. He used the name Franklin Greene to rent the room. Other than that, Westhouse hardly saw him.

After he was finished with the fat man Westhouse found Boyle and gave him the updated information. Then in a more serious tone, he stated, "Did you know that we ran that license plate number on the way over and---"

Boyle interrupted. "You have an LPR? Vigilant Solutions?"

"Our reading showed that he made several stops along I-495. Looks like he's heading towards Montauk."

"Montauk," Boyle said, trying to understand why he would go there. "Are you sure it's not a diversion? Maybe he ditched the car and paid someone to drive it there to throw us off?"

"It's possible, but I don't think so."

"Why's that?" Boyle asked.

"Just a hunch, Boyle. It may seem like it, but we don't know everything."

Boyle thought what an arrogant son-of-a-bitch. Then coming back, he asked, "Can I quote you on that?"

"No problem. Let's get that apartment dusted…what number did you say it was?"

"327."

On the way to the apartment Boyle showed him the copy of the application for EZ-PASS. Westhouse looked at it, nodded, then said, "Well, would you look at that. A confirmation! This, with his fingerprints, should nail him to the wall."

CHAPTER 6

We caught a break back there, honey. I kept thinking about the trunk."

"Always be calm...no matter what," he said, looking out the window at the passing countryside.

"Well, I guess I'm not there yet."

It was early morning and the sun was breaking on the horizon. Trina drove until the Manorville exit came into view. There was a truck stop just off the ramp with a Super 8 Motel. She drove to the renting office and parked the Buick.

Getting out, she said, "You can wait here, honey. I'll get the room. Do you want anything to eat?"

He shook his head and she went on. Getting out, he looked around the motel lay out that was rectangular in shape with a ninety degree angle and a second floor. He leaned against the side of the car, pulled out a pack of cigarettes and lit one up. He enjoyed smoking it until she came back with the apartment key.

"They gave me number seven. It's a lucky number," she said, smiling.

"Where is it?"

"It's just down there," she said, pointing. Then glancing at him, she said, "I didn't know you smoked." She could tell he didn't feel good.

"Strangely enough, it makes me feel better."

He turned to look in the direction she had pointed and said, "Down there?" "Let me get my bag." She opened the car door and retrieved her bag from the back seat. Then moving around the front of the car to meet him, she said, "How do you feel?"

"Fuckin great," he said, shuffling his feet.

"That good, huh?" she said, trying to be pleasant.

They walked slowly to the room. Victor was stiff from sitting so long, so she went ahead and unlocked the door, holding it open until he entered. He immediately went to the bed and laid down without taking off his shoes.

She noticed how comfortable he looked and decided to join him. She removed her jeans, pulled the curtains closed, and lay next to him. She tossed and turned mostly, but she did sleep some. Victor was out like a light. They laid that way most of the night, until Trina got up to take a shower. It was early, about 5 a.m. When finished, she put on fresh underwear and a bra from her bag, the same jeans and top, and went out the door with the key locking the door from outside.

Several minutes passed and then Victor woke and noticed that she wasn't there. His shoulder was growling, so he grabbed his medkit and injected himself with morphine. He sat there until the warm wave traveled through him. Then he checked the bag before putting it away and noticed his supply was low. So he called his friend Felix, who answered on the first ring.

"This is Felix. How may I help you?".

"Felix. How are you doing, man?"

"I'm doing well, Victor. Say, what's up with your overblown payments?"

"I appreciate what you do."

"But you don't have to do it."

"Is that what your wife says?"

"No, she's gone. I'm flyin solo now. How can I be of service to you?"

CHAPTER 7

Victor sat on the side of the bed for several minutes twisting his neck to loosen it, also his right arm. He rubbed his knees and lower legs to get the blood circulating better. It amazed him how strangely the body reacted to a gunshot wound. His thoughts traveled to Trina and how she would react to the things he had yet to tell her. He knew he loved her, at least he thought he did. It had been so long since his last romantic endeavor that he wondered if his judgment might be skewed from what the reality of this close encounter really was. But he needed her just like all people need someone. He hoped that he was not blinded to the fact that their age difference could be too great a chasm to cross.

His phone rang. He reached for it on the nightstand and answered. "Alonzo?" he asked.

"Yes. Is this Victor?"

"Speaking."

"Felix said I was to call you about a place to hold up for a few days."

"Do you have anything available?"

"I think we can help you out. Do you have anything against water?"

"What do you mean?"

"You know. With a beach. 17 Oceanside Lane. You can check it out. See if you like it."

"Oh, I'm sure we will. There's something else I need. Could you hook me up with a doctor to get x-rays for my shoulder? I want to see if there's any structural damage."

"Felix mentioned that. Why didn't he take care of it?"

"There's only so much he could do. I'm concerned about getting the use of my shoulder back. Full rotation, you know what I mean?"

"I do. But what you need is the x-rays first, bro"

There was a pause. Victor could feel Alonzo thinking through the phone.

"Let me make some calls. I can't promise you anything, but I will try my best to accommodate you. And I'll try to keep the cost down, because you are such a good customer."

***

Victor did not have to wait more than half an hour for Alonzo to call back. He barely had time to take a sponge bath in the bathroom sink. He walked back to where he sat before with a towel over his shoulder and answered his phone.

Victor saw it was the same number and dispensing with greetings, he asked, "Did you find something?"

"Yes. I believe I have what you need, bro. This man is a retired doctor, but not by choice. He was shut down, not for malpractice, but for criminal activity outside of that. So he works under the wire, like you. He still has a lot of his equipment. And this is your lucky day. He has a portable x-ray machine. If you need surgery, he can do that too. But let's hope not. Does that sound like what you need?"

"Yes, it does."

"Where are you now?'

"Super 8 Motel, junction of I-495. Manorville exit."

"Can you make it to his office?"

"Sure. Where is he?"

"Cedarville. He's in an old converted warehouse. It's just down 495. Won't take long. Can you go there now?"

He hesitated again. "Ok."

"I'll let him know you're coming and text you the directions. If you get lost. Call me."

They ended the call. Victor got dressed and collected Trina's bags, managing to put them in the backseat of the Buick. He found Trina shopping inside the truck stop boutique. She bought him two western style shirts plain in design with snap closures, a purple zippered sweatshirt with a strange but subdued picture on it, and some new underwear, T-shirts, and socks just in case he needed them. She tossed the bag in the back seat and they were on their way.

The Cedarville exit appeared in just a few minutes. Victor called Alonzo for some street names. Alonzo told him to go downtown to Main Street, then cruise until they found Clinic Avenue. Then take a right and keep going until some industrial warehouses come into view. They parked the car across the street in front of an old warehouse building and waited as instructed. A man would come to escort them inside.

Victor took out a pack of Rothman cigarettes he had purchased earlier and lit one with the car lighter. He cracked the window to let out the smoke. Trina wanted to say something but she let it go.

Rolling her eyes, then looking around, she said, "This is creepy. Is someone coming?"

"Yes. He said they would be right out."

He looked in the side view mirror and saw a man approaching from across the way. Victor took out his gun and sat it in his lap out of view. He flicked the cigarette out the window to let the man know which side.

The man was white, middle aged, bald with dark rimmed glasses. He was dressed in jeans and a T-shirt that said Billy Joel In Concert. He couldn't read the year. When the man was close enough, he rolled down the window.

"Good evening. Are you, Victor?"

"Yes. You're the friend of Alonzo?"

"Yes, sir. If you would come with me please. The lady also," he said, bending down to smile at her. They got out and followed the man across the street and entered a door that opened to a hallway with several other doors unmarked. They walked to the end of the hall and entered the door to their left. It opened to an operating room that looked more like a storage room with only the basic necessities to perform medical procedures. The operating table was in the middle of the room with a plastic shower curtain-like material that closed all around. They saw monitors and a few pieces of equipment that looked like they belonged in an operating room. There was a couch to the immediate left by the door, where the doctor asked them to sit and remove their jackets if they wished.

"Do you have a name?" Trina asked.

The doctor smiled. "Yes, but for our purposes here, names are not important. Just call me, doctor. I'm going to take some x-rays now, so make yourself comfortable." He smiled again and motioned for Victor to follow him to a corner of the room where the x-ray machine was located. He instructed Victor to remove his jacket and shirt. He removed the bandage and examined the entry wound and its place of exit. Then he asked him to stand in front of a panel. He pushed over the x-ray machine and asked Victor to turn several ways, while he took the pictures and changed the slides. Then going into a viewing room to judge their quality, he came out to where Victor was standing and said, "They'll be ready in a minute."

"How does it look so far?" Victor asked.

"Normal. But the x-rays will tell us what we need to know."

"How long have you been here?" Trina asked.

"At this place not long. I had a practice in Long Island City."

"What was your title there?" she asked.

"I was, and still am, an Orthopaedic Surgeon, but I no longer have a license. Please don't ask me why. I've resolved myself never to talk about it. So if you have questions concerning that, direct them to Alonzo." The doctor said, nodding. Victor acknowledged that he understood by returning the nod.

The doctor looked at his watch. "Those x-rays should be ready." He got up and went back into the room. When he came out he had a few examining x-rays in hand and waved Victor to come with him. He took them to a counter along the wall and clipped them underneath a fluorescent light that he turned on. Then he studied each one intensely.

Looking at Victor, he asked, "How is your range of mobility?"

Victor squinted his eyes at him and asked, "You mean, how far can I lift my arm?"

"Yes."

Victor showed him, lifting his arm to about a forty five degree angle from his side before the pain got to him and he lowered it, thankfully. His face was flushed. His breathing accelerated from the effort.

"That's not bad," the doctor said. He positioned himself behind Victor. He placed his left hand on top of the shoulder near the deltoid muscle, then taking his wrist pulled back on the arm. It was stiff and he tried pulling past the stiffness.

"Let me know when you're done, doc. That hurts like shit," Victor said through clenched teeth.

"I know, but if you can bear with me, I'll be done in a minute."

This time the doctor placed his left hand in the same place, on top of the shoulder, and standing behind him placed his hand under his wrist and lifted up. "Keep your arm straight as much as you can," the doctor said, as he continued to pull up on the arm. Although Victor was grimacing and clenching his teeth with a horrible look that made Trina look away, the doctor managed to lift his arm to about sixty degrees instead of the previous forty five.

When he released the arm, Victor closed his eyes and leaning over, let it hang loose at his side. Trina looked back and gave a sigh of relief that it was over.

"Ok," the doctor said, removing his glasses. "You're really very fortunate, because the bullet grazed your clavicle just missing your scapula and luckily went straight through. Your clavicle is still intact. We don't need to do anything concerning it. If the bullet had hit your scapula we would have a lot more problems to deal with. As it stands, I don't believe we need to do anything, except manage the pain, allowing six to eight weeks for healing, then begin therapy to get your full range of motion back. I can give you a list of exercises to do."

"Do you think I'll get back my full range of motion?"

"I see no reason why not. If you do the therapy. This is the area where most people fail, then they end up with locked shoulders and a nagging stiffness that causes other problems."

The doctor raised his finger, indicating to hold on for a minute. He walked to the counter where an out tray of xerox pages was located. And finding the right ones, he gave them to Victor. "If you do these exercises, religiously, you should have no problems. As your strength comes back you can add others. Just don't over do it."

"Alright. That's good to know."

"There is one final thing."

"Yes, of course." Victor motioned for Trina to open her bag to pay him.

The doctor noticed her and said, "Oh, no. Not that. Alonzo said that you've been so generous with your over payments that this one would be on the house. As long as it wasn't too much. All I did was take x-rays, and give advice. But I do want to advise you to let me stitch your entry and exit wounds, so that they will heal better. It will just take a few minutes," he said, gesturing to the table.

Victor turned to look at Trina, who was smiling and putting the money back in her purse. "Sure thing, doc. Let's get that done."

After Victor was stitched, they thanked the doctor and got in the car and tried to find 17 Oceanside Lane. Trina asked, "Are we going back to the farm house?"

Victor thought for a minute, then said, "No. I have something else in mind."

"Does it have a pool?"

"How about an ocean with a beach?"

"Are you joking?"

"No joke."

"Lovely. You can get a sun tan while your arm heals."

CHAPTER 8

On the way to 17 Oceanside Lane, they stopped at a gas station. She parked by pump 2. Victor gave her cash and told her to tell the attendant inside to turn on the pump. He also asked her to get a map and some disposable phones. He had a standalone GPS device, but it wasn't always reliable in more remote places such as this, so he wanted the map as a backup. He told her not to ask questions, just tell the clerk to turn on the pump, get the map, a few phones, then get out. Don't engage in conversation, just smile, look pretty and pay the bill.

He got out and opened the side flap to unscrew the gas cap. The clerk used the voice box to tell him he was ready to pump. He chose Super Unleaded and stuck the nozzle in and locked it in place. Victor stretched his legs, bending over slightly to test the effect it would have on his shoulder. He stopped and stood straight up, feeling the wave of pain sweep upward and knowing it was too early for that.

He walked to the side of the building and back just to move around a bit.

When he returned the nozzle clicked off. He replaced it in the pump and screwed the gas cap on. Trina came out. They got in the car. She still drove and Victor sat on the passenger side. He noticed the attendant standing at the window by the cash register looking out.

As she pulled out to get back on the road, he asked, "You didn't talk to him, did you?" Victor asked.

"No. I just smiled like you said. He was just looking at my ass, that's all."

"Did he ask you anything?"

"He asked about the phones."

"What did you say?"

"I just ignored him and kept smiling," she said, glancing at him with a smile. "Good."

"Did you get a map?"

"Yes."

Victor indicated the bag she brought. "When we stop, see if you can activate one of them. Open the back, take out the SIM card, and the battery."

"Why?"

"When the police get your number, and don't kid yourself, they will, they can trace you from its location. So please remove them. That's why I said to get a few phones. We can use them, then destroy them if we have to."

She looked at him and smiled, nodding her agreement.

The sign was just ahead of them, so she turned right onto a partially gravel-paved road with cracks that continued through a wooded area. The winding road curved and twisted around trees that shadowed the sunlight until it opened into a clearing upon which stood a simple blue, two-story clapboard house whose back faced a decline toward the ocean. The house was trimmed in white and looked well kept with a fresh coat of paint and a carport on the side. There was, what looked like, a barbecue grill resting upon a tiled patio in the back with plenty of firewood stacked neatly against a fence.

Trina parked under the carport. Victor got out and gave the house a walk around. He stopped at the wrap-around front porch to look for the pet rock he was told possessed the key. It was painted white, to blend in with some other sun bleached stones, and held a secret compartment for the front door key. After searching for a minute or two, he finally located it, removed it, replaced the stone in the flower garden, and opened the front door. Then he walked through the house to open the side door to help Trina unload their few belongings that included the rifle from the trunk.

Once inside, Trina turned to look at him. "Now, will you tell me what you're hiding in the trunk?"

Victor looked around the kitchen and through its windows to the great ocean. He looked back at her and said, "Sure. Come on."

She followed him out to the carport where he opened the trunk. First, he pulled up the carpet to reveal a hidden compartment that when opened revealed a black bag. He pulled it out, unzipped it, and told her to have a look.

She leaned over to pull open the sides and saw the money secured neatly with thick rubber bands and stacked neatly to conserve space. "Well, I'm glad you had it concealed in a hidden compartment. How much is there?"

"I stopped counting at $300,000."

She didn't blink or give an expression different from her normal beautiful smile. "Is that everything?"

He smiled and opened another concealed compartment behind the backseat. When he opened it, he pulled out a larger rifle in a zippered case.

"What do you have in there? A cannon?"

He rolled his eyes at her, as he unzipped the case and pulled out the pieces.

"This is a sniper's rifle with a convenient stand that I purchased for long distance shooting."

Picking up the long black scope, she asked, "How about a demonstration?"

"Come up on the deck."

Victor carried the few pieces of the rifle and Trina brought the zippered case. He sat the pieces on the patio table and began to assemble it, showing her how easy it was. She observed, changing her position for a better view when necessary, and didn't change her expression once. It was like she was memorizing how the pieces fit together, so she could use it when she had to regardless if Victor was present or not.

Having finished the assembly, Victor adjusted the scope and started to look at things far away. Trina was eager to have a look and asked him. "Are you going to let me see?"

Victor stood up and moved to the side. "Of course."

She bent over and assumed the position to shoot, knowing there was no magazine loaded. She looked at some trees across the way, a considerable distance, and saw the veins in their leaves. She stood up quickly and said, "I think I understand better what you do."

"Not all of it, sweetheart. Are you really sure you want to get involved in this? There's still time to back away and lead a normal life."

"No," she said. "That life is like walking around dead."

"You exaggerate. Come on. Let's look inside." She walked through the patio door and Victor took apart the rifle, placing it in its case with the stand, and followed her inside.

*****

After putting their belongings away and checking the bedroom to see if it had sheets and blankets, Trina checked the bathroom shower to see if it met with her approval. While she walked through the house, Victor walked outside to a path that he assumed led down to the beach. There were wooden planks embedded in the sand to stabilize the walk. He stepped lightly, as the path curved around a dune, until he reached the bottom that opened wider to encompass the vast expanse of the Atlantic.

The beach was deserted. The sand was undisturbed as far as he could see. Looking to the left and then the right, he saw that the banks of the dunes were thick enough to practice shooting. He was glad that he brought the silencers just in case someone was close enough to hear the shots.

He stood there captivated by the ocean, watching it slapping onto the beach, reshaping it slowly with each new set of waves. Perfect, he thought.

"Hey there." Turning around he saw Trina. "I was wondering where you were."

"Just looking around," he said, with a wave of his hand across the ocean expanse. "The waves are just beautiful," she said. Then she removed her shoes and rolled up the legs of her jeans and ran down to the water wading through the waves to leave her footprints in the sand. She turned to him and smiled, then continued the playful wading, skipping back when the waves came too high and returning with them on their retreat in a joyful dance, marking the beach with each new attempt. Victor waved for her to come. She trotted over to him and said, "I just love this place."

"Good. This will be our work area," he said, turning and gesturing to the dunes. "Any objections?"

"Nope. Bring it on," she said, flicking water in his face. Wiping it away and smiling, he said, "We start tomorrow then."

CHAPTER 9

Agent Westhouse had called ahead to make arrangements for a group of rooms to be reserved at the Beach Front Motel located close to Montauk, a short distance from the beach. He had dispatched Caldwell and Billings with a Ford Econoline surveillance van to set up temporary headquarters at the motel, a quiet out of the way place to conduct their work. Everything was in place when they arrived at the motel that had an empty parking lot. It was prearranged that the rooms would be unlocked and the keys would be inside on the nightstand for all four rooms; 4, 5, 6 and 7. So, Billings drove up to number 7 and parked in the gravel driveway where weeds had popped through here and there.

Getting out and walking to the door, he opened it and then walked inside. There were two double beds with a nightstand and a lamp on each side, a bureau, and a TV with a rabbit ears antenna. A lounge chair with a wooden frame and removable cushion was near the window. A small table was also there to be used for writing or as a coffee table.

Billings came in at that moment carrying the laptop. He stopped, looked around, then back at Caldwell. He turned on the water faucets in the sink to check the water. Then he did the same with the shower which checked out. He noticed some mold in the grout between the bathroom tiles, but thought nothing of it. The tub was clean, free of scum. No one had stayed there in quite some time.

The TV was a Zenith Chromacolor II with silver knobs and a pulldown compartment to adjust color, picture quality, and contrast. Adjusting the rabbit ears, he turned the channel dial, but he could get nothing to come in. Then, noticing an outlet closer to the window, he moved the TV closer to the window.

He tried it again, saying, "Well, we can get PBS on channel 53. The others are just local jazz from across the Sound."

"I could use a drink. What do you say?" Caldwell asked. "You read my mind."

Traveling back on 27, they noticed the 7 Eleven that they passed on the way in. When they pulled off the road to park in front, Billing's phone rang. It was Agent Westhouse.

"Yes sir. What can I do for you?" Billings answered, in his most professional manner. "It's not what you can do for me, it's what I can do for you."

"Alright," he said, glancing at Caldwell.

"I've come upon a license plate number with the help of Detective Boyle, and running it through our sophisticated LPR system, we came up with an address that may be useful to you and Caldwell."

"What is it?" he asked, wishing Westhouse would get to the point.

"We believe it's for the Buick. The new address that came up is 17 Oceanside Lane, which is close to the motel, I believe."

"17 Oceanside Lane," Billings repeated. "Alright, sir. Caldwell and I will check that out right away."

"If it becomes too much just isolate them. Then call for backup. We will be there as soon as we can."

"Yes sir."

Billings disconnected the call and put his phone down. "What is it?" Caldwell asked.

"That was Westhouse. The Buick is at 17 Oceanside Lane."

"How did they locate it?"

"They found the plate number and ran it through."

"And that came up? 17 Oceanside Lane."

"That's right," Billings said, writing down the address. "Now, all we have to do is find it."

Having collected a few sandwiches, some taco chips, and a six pack of beer, they walked to the counter to pay.

"This is the best we can do, I guess," Caldwell said, taking out his card.

After the counter attendant rang up the items, he asked, "You fellows having a party tonight?"

"No. We're just hungry and tired of driving." Billings said.

Placing the bottles in double bags, the attendant said, "You guys must be from the city."

"How'd you guess," Billings said, smiling.

The attendant started to laugh. "If I don't know you, that's where you're from."

"Yeah, first time out this far. Say...you wouldn't happen to know where 17 Oceanside

Lane is, would you?"

"Sure. It's just up 27 a few miles. There'll be a sign on the right to tell you."

Billings thought for a minute, then asked, "You know we're staying not far from there, and I didn't see any sign."

"You didn't go far enough. Just keep going east until you see it. And if you see the ocean you've gone too far."

***

After eating a sandwich in the van, they decided to converge on the address. About a mile or two past the motel turnoff, the sign for 17 Oceanside Lane appeared. Pulling in, Billings stopped the van and asked, "Lots of trees…thick undergrowth. Are you ready?"

Caldwell was eating taco chips and offered some to Billings, who shook him off. "Yeah. Let's do it," Caldwell said, brushing the salt from his hands. Then he reached in the back for his Glock 19. He checked the magazine, then put one in the chamber, checked the safety, then placed it on his lap.

"Get mine ready," Billings said.

Reaching in the back for Billings's weapon, also a Glock 19, Caldwell checked the mag, put one in the chamber and checked the safety, putting it on the console between them.

"Safety's on," he said. Then continuing, "There's bound to be a clearing up ahead. If you can turn off to park somewhere, we should approach on foot."

Billings nodded, as the trees spread into an opening just ahead. Then parking the van within the tree cover, they got out and stretched their legs, relieved themselves, then Billings grabbed a pair of binoculars on a strap that he placed around his neck. They took out two assault rifles and hooked their arms through the straps to carry on their shoulders and walked along the curve of the semi gravel road interspersed with spaces of hard packed earth that sprouted clumps of grass. As they walked in silence, their guns in hand, the sound of the surf was heard with the mingled chirping of migratory birds. The musical 'chur-a-lee' song was heard as they stepped forward.

The house was now visible. They could see the Buick parked alongside underneath the car port. He pulled a monocular from his pack and looking through it noticed the license plate had been changed and made a mental note of it. They were still inside the tree covering.

"KNZ-5181. He changed the license plate," he said, looking over at Caldwell.

Caldwell nodded, writing it down in his pocket notebook. "He must be getting ready to move."

Billings saw no signs of life. He motioned to Caldwell to continue walking along the edge of the tree cover until it crossed into a series of dunes covered with foliage. From there, looking through the monocular, they could see behind the house, but there was no sign of life.

"Maybe they're down at the beach," Caldwell suggested. "Let's see if we can crawl down there," Billings said, smiling.

Like slithering snakes---rolling in some places---they made their way to the beach. It was deserted. They walked close to the dunes in case they had to duck and hide, stepping over driftwood, remnants of old beach parties. Lonely shells decorated the sand, an occasional plastic bottle stood out like a sore. Then Caldwell heard voices, and looking up the beach he saw two people, one of them was bouncing up and down in the crashing waves. They were laughing and playing like children. He tapped Billings' arm who raised the monocular and when focused on them, he saw who they were.

"It's them," Caldwell said, still looking through the monocular. He saw them get out of the waves naked, grabbing their clothes and running into the dunes out of sight.

"Let's see if we can get closer," Caldwell said.

Maneuvering their way through and around the dunes, walking up some and sliding down others, after a few minutes they heard some shots. Thinking they were close enough, they crawled up a dune and looking over the top lying prone on their bellies, they saw the girl firing her gun at a target secured against an opposite dune. She emptied one magazine, then reloaded and fired again in rapid succession until it was empty. Then they both walked to the target to check the bullet spread.

"I only see one gun," Caldwell said. "And he seems to have plenty of ammo in his pockets."

Billings looked over at Caldwell. "He's training her. That's why they're out there." Caldwell nodded. "Well, he has good taste. I'll say that for him."

They watched and listened as best they could, as Victor took out a black marker and tore off a piece of cardboard from a sunbleached box next to the remnants of a campfire. He drew a series of concentric circles on it with a bullseye in the center, and walked with it to the opposite dune where he secured it with a stone and strands from an inkberry shrub.

Walking back, he took the Beretta and handed it to Trina.

"Ok. See if you can remember some of the things I've told you."

She removed the magazine, checked it---then she looked at Victor and smiled. She shoved it back with the butt of her hand and pulled back the action releasing a round into the chamber."

"Good," Victor said. Then continuing with a pointed finger to the opposite dune. "Now, see if you can hit the target."

She raised the gun and with one hand closed her left eye at which time he stopped her. "No! Remember what I said about your grip, stance, and breathing?"

"Oh, yes. I almost forgot."

"No, you did forget, because I told you, And you didn't do it!"

She smirked, then positioned herself, feet apart shoulder width, left hand over the right hand grip, she lined up her shot taking a breath in, letting out half of it, then gently squeezing the trigger--- but nothing happened.

She looked at him with an open mouth, a big question on her face. Then she remembered. "Oh, shit! The safety," she said. "God, I'm so stupid."

"Don't be sorry! And don't ever forget again!"

Billings was watching through the monocular, then pulled back to tell Caldwell what happened. "I don't think she's very good at this," Billings said, handing the monocular to Caldwell. They both got a kick out of watching their social interplay and kept watching for more. Peaking over the top of the dune they were careful not to blow their cover by raising their heads too high.

Now, Trina was angry. Because he was too abrupt with his answer. She quickly assumed the stance, aimed and emptied several shots at the target. Releasing her finger, she stopped and repositioned herself in a readied stance to fire again, glaring at him. He raised his hand to indicate to her to stop firing. He walked to the target and saw that all the shots were in a scattered pattern all of which were practically in the bullseye.

He walked back to her and said, "Good shooting. Was it because you were angry?" She took a deep breath and looked around and said, "Yes."

"Good. Remember that emotion, how it sharpened your vision. Can you do it again?"

"Of course."

The target practice with the Beretta went on like that with Trina scoring high marks with Victor. She went through several magazines only missing the bullseye when she didn't concentrate. Then Victor decided to put some movement into the practice. This time, he asked her to reload her magazine and have the Beretta ready to fire at her side by walking left to right, turn quickly and fire.

Victor looked at her sternly and said, "Do you understand what I'm asking you to do?" Victor asked.

"I think so, but not really."

He stopped to think for a minute, then asked, "Have you ever seen Dr. No? Or any of the Bond films?"

"Yes. Who hasn't?"

Nodding his approval, he said, "At the opening, when he comes walking across the screen, he suddenly stops and turns to fire into the camera. Do you remember that?"

She looked at him strangely. "You want me to do that?"

"Yes."

Pausing, she thought of a pleasant comeback. "Which movie did you like best, if you had to pick one?"

Smiling, he said, "Goldfinger. That was easy,"

"So then you like your women golden? Is that what you're telling me?"

Smiling, he said, "No, but that part was good. It was the girl's name. An unusual name."

She started laughing. "What's so funny?" he asked.

"You really don't remember her name?" He shook his head. "No."

"It was Galore...Pussy Galore. Remember?"

"Oh, yes. How could I forget that?" Victor said, laughing. Then he gave her a hug.

She continued the walking-stop-and-fire exercise, practicing it until her coordination and eye contact enabled her to hit the target consistently with dead accuracy.

After that, he explained the dive and roll exercise, first without the gun keeping her hands in front ready to fire. She performed the exercise until she was tired. Then as she was catching her breath, he gave her the gun but with the magazine removed.

"Well, you might as well leave it in. It's no good without it."

"Get used to the roll with it first. I don't want you to shoot yourself."

She frowned, then positioned herself and performed a perfect roll coming up in the firing position. He told her to do it again. She did. Again, again, and again. She got up, walked to him, and stuck out her hand.

"Give it to me."

He noticed the resolve in her eyes, then placed the magazine in her hand. She smacked it into place, positioned herself, performed a perfect roll to come up shooting. Victor raised his hand and walked to the target to check the spread. He had an idea where the last spree hit because he could see the target jump. When he got close enough to see, he saw four shots in the bullseye, because that's how many she fired the last time.

"Ok. Enough of that. Let's move to the rifle."

Trina said she was tired so they left it for another day. They walked farther up unto the beach and Victor scanned the line of dunes that ran north and south as far as he could see. Caldwell and Billings lowered their heads when his vision came close to their location.

Victor sensed something wasn't right. There was no one else on the beach. No tourists or anyone exploring the beach who had rented other beach houses or was taking a relaxing stroll. He looked, quickly, back to the dunes, realizing that they were good cover for anyone wanting to focus their rifle sights on them.

Billings and Caldwell lowered their heads to escape his stare, then peaked over the dune to get an idea of what they were doing.

Suddenly, Victor said, "Time's up! Let's go back!" She frowned like a little girl, but then came to him. "What's the rush? Do you need more sunscreen?"

"No. We should go back."

"Why? I'm having fun."

"Just get your things. Come on."

She obeyed his command seeing the look in his eye. So gathering her things spread out on the beach towel. She put her things back in her bag and draped the beach towel around her so that the word YANKEES read across her back. Then they walked back to the beach house together, as Victor kept looking over his shoulder at the dunes.

"Did you think someone was watching us?"

"I don't know, but it's best to be safe. I'll come back. Check it later."

"Check what?"

"The dunes."

She stopped and looked in that direction.

He grabbed her arm and pulled her forward. "Keep walking and don't look back," he said, putting his arm around her. "We're lovers, ok? So, let's project that image."

She kissed him on the cheek, but glanced back with her eyes. They walked arm in arm back to the beach house. Trina entered first, then Victor paused at the door, turned around, and looked out at the ocean. Then he brought his eyes to the dunes again.

Billings checked the angle of the sun and saw there could be no reflection from his monocular, so he focused on Victor's eyes as they covered the ground. He was confident that their location was not detected.

Finally, Victor turned and walked into the house, closing the door behind him.

Looking at the sun, then to the ocean, and back to the house, Billings said, "I think it would be wise to wait until the night."

Nodding his head, getting more comfortable in the sand, Caldwell said, "I agree. Let's wait until tonight."

CHAPTER 10

The moon hung like a giant spotlight casting an elongated tail that glistened as it stretched to the shore. The ocean was calm. No breeze blew in and the air was empty and dead.

Waking up from a nap, Caldwell asked, "How are we gonna play this?"

"Well, we're at a disadvantage with the moon again. Whenever you want it to be full you don't get it, and when you don't want it, you do."

"Ain't that the truth."

"We can lay flat, coming in serpentine."

"Serpentine?"

"You know...zig-zag," Billings said, motioning with his hand.

"What do you think he's got inside? I wouldn't put it past him to have a grenade launcher."

"No doubt."

"We should try to get him outside"

"Do you have an idea?" Billings asked.

They paused, looking at how the moon lit up the back of the house. They could almost hear each other thinking.

"What do you think he's doing in there?" Caldwell asked.

"Puttin' it to her, I imagine. Wouldn't you?" Billings asked.

"Hell, yes." They paused again. Then Caldwell said, "How about the grill? We could start that up, get it smoking really good. Then he's bound to come out."

Billings nodded, thought about it more, then said, "We could get him in a crossfire."

"And he wouldn't stand a chance," Caldwell said.

"What if she comes out first?" Billings asked, looking at him. Pausing, Caldwell said, "Don't shoot her." He smiled at Billings.

They set about gathering dried grass and bits of driftwood, leftover from abandoned campfires several of which had paper, styrofoam cups, and other combustibles to ignite. They gathered the stuff by taking off their shirts and placing the items inside like a sling carried by the corners. When they had enough, they moved toward the house low to the ground, stopping in intervals to lay flat and waiting to hear any sound. Approaching on each side to look in the windows for a visual of them, their eyes just above the window sills--they had no luck. The lights were out and the window that appeared to be the bedroom was too dark to identify, except for what looked like the form of two people sleeping covered with blankets.

Billings gave Caldwell the nod to start the grill, and much to his delight he found a yellow and blue can of lighter fluid left to the side. Billings lay prone about twenty yards away in the sand with the door in his sights to give cover for Caldwell, who was in the process of laying a good foundation to ignite the coals with the additional firestarters soaked in lighter fluid. He had a lot of experience in starting fires in the military, so when he was sure he was ready, he looked over at Johnson, gave a thumbs up, that was returned by him, then struck a match that he tossed on the grill that gave a low 'whoosh' sound as it burst into flames. He grabbed his rifle and ran out into the sand, assuming the same prone position as Billings, who was on the other side of the house out of sight.

The fire burned, and burned, and continued burning as both men waited for someone to come out, or a light to go on in the house. Smoke rolled out of the grill when the Styrofoam caught flame and the driftwood only added to the smoke filled air. The waiting seemed like an eternity. Billings took out his phone and called Caldwell. No answer. Maybe his phone was on silent, as well, and he just couldn't hear it or feel it vibrate.

He waited another minute or two, then getting up in a crouched position moved toward the grill ready to fire at the first sight of

Victor Enmerkar. Then coming around the corner to the opposite side of the house, he saw Caldwell bound with his arms behind his back and tied to his legs at a ninety degree angle resting on his stomach. His mouth was stuffed with a rag, and he was groaning something unintelligible.

Crouching low again, Billings moved toward him slowly sweeping his rifle along the top of the dune behind. And when he was almost upon him to ease his pain, he felt a rifle butt smash into the side of his head. Lights out! Caldwell groaned even more. He dragged them both by the collar closer to the house.

Trina opened the back door dressed in her panties and a NYU t-shirt carrying flex cuffs in her hand. "I hope you didn't hurt him," she said.

"He's just unconscious. He'll come around soon, but he'll have a real headache." She gave him the flex cuffs. "I hope that's enough."

He took them and said, "I'll make it do." Then he stopped and looked at her in the moonlight. "You look awfully cute."

"How's your shoulder?"

"Thank God for morphine."

She blushed. Caldwell was semi-conscious and couldn't help but notice her. "I'll secure him, check the other one. Then we'll try to get some sleep. Ok?"

"Rest maybe, but I don't think I can sleep," Trina said.

"You want to get started then? We can't stay here anymore."

"Who else is looking for you?"

Victor paused, then said, "Probably the FBI."

"What does that mean?"

He glared at her and spoke with a suitable imagery she could understand. "It means we need to walk carefully and cover our tracks." Then he looked at her hard again. "There's still time for you to get out of this. Go back to Mercer Street. Tell your father. He could hire a lawyer to clear you of any culpability. Then, I'll just disappear."

"Where would you go?"

"Away from here. I know a lot of places."

She was quiet, surveying the men on the ground. Then she came back saying, "I've come this far, so I might as well stay." Then she got up. "I'll make some coffee. Are you hungry?"

"Just a sandwich. Can you put out the grill?"

Victor watched her glutes move in perfect symmetry on her way to the grill. He was torn between the right thing to do and what he had to do. He wanted to keep her safe, but he knew there were no guarantees. He knew when the morphine wore off his shoulder would scream.

He secured Billings and let him lay in the sand, so that he would not be a threat when he woke up. He went through his pockets and found keys to a vehicle. Taking a flashlight from his pocket he walked toward the tree covered road in search of it, and was surprised when he discovered it to be a surveillance van. Opening the back, he looked inside--some of it he knew how to operate, some of it he didn't. At first, he thought it was a CIA surveillance van, but looking through some of the compartments he found a manual with an FBI logo on it.

Why are these guys working with the FBI? he thought. Unless, the CIA had requested it? That would seem to make better sense with them in an FBI van. Now, he not only had the CIA after him, but the FBI and the NYPD as well. Things were getting more interesting.

He closed up the back of the van, got in the driver's seat and started it up to drive to the back door of the beach house underneath the carport.

Trina fixed ham and swiss sandwiches on rye, a salad for herself in a container, placed them in a paper bag, and brought out two mugs of freshly brewed dark roast coffee to the lounge chairs on the outside deck. They decided to leave the sandwiches for later and sipped the coffee, feeling the initial caffeine sting with its penetrating surge through their tired bodies.

"I think that coffee is so strong it would give you an erection," Trina said.

"I don't need coffee for that, " Victor said, sipping away.

"I've noticed. Sometimes, I just touch you and boink," she said, pointing her finger into the air.

He looked over at her. "What's your point?"

"My point," she said, getting up and slithering toward him in a seductive way, "is that there is no point." She straddled him sitting in the chair. "I love you and am prepared to go anywhere with you."

"Anywhere?" he asked, looking deep into her eyes for a sense of doubt. "I'm all yours."

"What will you do if they kill me? Call up daddy?"

"That won't happen. You're too careful."

"If I was too careful, you wouldn't be here." Pause. "You don't want me here?"

"Yes, but the problem is that they will catch up to us. I want to clear my name. I don't care what they say, I'm not a murderer."

"I know. You're a killer, and you did it for the United States--- the old red, white and blue," she crooned.

He pushed her back by the shoulders. "That's not funny!"

"I was only joking."

"You don't joke about that! Not with me!" he said, getting up.

"I'm sorry, but you never joke about anything. Why don't you smile for chrissake?"

Victor took a deep breath, then said. "I'm sorry, but now is not the time. Nobody knows what a patriot is anymore!"

"Ok! I get it," she said standing up also.

Eying her with a glare that soon softened, he said, "No. No, you don't."

There was another pause. Then she struck a pose with her hand on her hip. "Would there be anything else, sir? Pussy, perhaps?"

"Go put some clothes on," he said, smacking her forcefully on the butt. "We have work to do."

The smack pushed her forward a few steps, then she turned on him holding her butt, saying, "You didn't have to do that!"

CHAPTER 11

They sat in the lounging chairs, talking to each other cautiously until early morning. It amazed them both how their anger surged, then disappeared as quickly as it came. It must be love, Victor mused, because he didn't know what the fuck else to call it.

When the dimness of dawn first appeared above the ocean, Victor loaded the agents in the van, thinking that someone would come looking for them. Then he decided to park it in a more convenient place. They packed their belongings and in the Buick and Victor drove the van followed by Trina in the Buick. She was confused as to where they were going, but decided to keep quiet.

After he dropped the van off at the Beach Front Motel, he got in the Buick with her, and they both decided that breakfast was what they needed instead of sandwiches. So they drove into Manorville and settled for a Denny's Restaurant, pulling up in front of its huge front window. Getting out, Trina came around the car to assist Victor if he needed it, because his shoulder was hurting. All she did was hold the door open for him.

When they entered the restaurant, a waitress seated them in the back next to the men's room because it was very busy.

The waitress came with menus and a coffee pot. They turned their cups up and she poured. "Hi, my name is Carrie. May I take your orders?"

"Yes," Victor said. "I'll have the breakfast special...whatever it comes with... hash browns, wheat toast," he said, looking up at the waitress, smiling.

"We do have sourdough bread this morning," she said, brightly.

"Excellent. Sourdough toast," he said, closing his menu.

She looked at Trina, who was flipping the menu pages. She quickly closed it. "Yes. I'll have that."

"Ok. Should be up in a second," she said, picking up the menus. Then she walked away, stopping to assist other patrons.

A middle-aged man noticing Trina's beauty walked into the door jam, bumping his nose on the way to the men's room. She burst out laughing, unable to control herself. It reminded her of 'The Three Stooges' comedy acts. She continued watching the man hold his nose, as he, finally, entered the men's room.

It was just what they needed to break the ice of their ordeal.

When their breakfast came, Trina ate quickly because she was very hungry and couldn't remember the last time she had eaten. When finished she noticed Victor was not eating and was deep in thought. Trina finished her sourdough toast and asked him "Are you going to finish your toast?"

"No," he said, pushing the plate closer to her, then continuing his deep thoughts. She put more butter and blackberry jam on a slice and ate it slowly. Victor lit a cigarette and studied her closely, as he flicked the ashes on his plate.

"Does smoking help you think?"

"I suppose so. Why do you ask?"

"My dad used to say it helped him think. He smoked cigars. Cubans. He had a large humidor, temperature controlled."

"Sounds like he was a connoisseur," he said, exhaling smoke in a fine mist.

"Oh God, he had every kind of cigar imaginable. He even had those black stogies. We have to sell the Buick."

After a pause, the sound of her fork was heard against the plate. Then the contour of her face changed into a wrinkled mess as she spoke quietly with an exaggerated, frantic tone.

"You know how I love that Buick. Can't we keep it? Please? I love it so much." Then she assumed a more solemn expression, taking another bite of the sourdough toast.

"Are you done, now?" he said, with narrowed eyes.

"I have to amuse myself some way," she said, munching away on the remnants of Victor's breakfast. "What kind of car are we going to get in place of it?"

"I don't know. Something...inconspicuous."

"How about a Mustang?" she asked, brightly. "A nice red one!"

"It's not exactly an everyday car."

"Why? There's lots of them around."

"They draw attention. We don't want that."

She slapped the table. "Well, fuck 'em, then! Let's get a granny wagon and be done with it! But make it a Mercedes," she said, pointing at him.

"I like to pay cash, you know," he said, rolling his eyes. "How much do you have?"

"Enough, but I need to go to the bank."

"What bank do you use?"

"Chase. There's a branch in town. I thought I remembered passing one."

"You don't have an account here."

"Not at that branch, but I'll open one."

"What name would you use?"

Thinking of names, he finally said, "Franklin Greene"

She looked at him oddly. "So I'd be referred to as Mrs. Greene?"

"Would you like to be?"

"Is that question what I think it is?"

He reached over to touch her hand. "I don't think our hearts have bonded yet. Not enough time. But it may be an option later."

She thought for a minute, then said, "You're so romantic. But don't bother. I have my own account."

They decided it was time to leave, but they had not received a check. So they walked to the cashier's station after Victor left a tip on the table placing it under a coffee mug. The place was beginning to empty, but other customers waiting to be seated stretched in a line by the main door. Their waitress was behind the cash register and was cashing out customer checks. So they stood in line until it was their turn and Carrie saw it was them. When they didn't give her their check, she looked through her apron and found it.

"I'm sorry. I usually place the checks down when the meal is served, but it's been so crazy today. Did you want to look at it."

"No. That's alright," Victor said. "Was everything fine, sir?"

"Please don't call me, sir. I might get used to it."

She looked up and smiled at him. "Ok. How was your breakfast?"

"Best one I've had this morning," he said, continuing to smile and hoping she would do the same. He gave her a twenty and said, "I left a tip on the table."

She rang up the check and gave Victor his change, as he noticed her dark hair, tied back in some kind of a roll, looked like it was about to let go with an avalanche of strands, some dangling to the side of her face. She possessed haunting brown eyes with an olive skin tone suggesting Mediterranean descent. He guessed early thirties, but the time spent waiting on people could be seen around her eyes that looked tired and bored from saying the same old things day after day without a change of the repetition in sight. She could be quite lovely, but for this day from Victor's viewpoint, she looked beautiful in an ordinary way.

"What are you folks up to today?" she asked, standing aside for another waitress to use the register and pulling a strand of hair behind an ear.

"Car shopping. Do you know anybody who has a good one for sale?" Trina asked.

"What kind are you looking for?" Victor forced a chuckle. "A good one."

"I hear you."

"I want a Mustang, but, you know…" Trina gestured with her eyes at Victor. "It has to be just right."

"The waitress said." Then to Victor. "You should let her pick it out."

"Then I'd be broke," Victor, said, playing the husband role.

"You know, my brother has a Mustang for sale...kinda beat up, but it runs like a champ."

"Really? What year?" Trina asked.

"It's an older one...'73, I think. 4 speed, Hurst shifter." Then she looked at Trina and said, "That means a clutch, if you don't know. Some people don't even know what a clutch is today. Can you imagine?"

"Isn't that the extra pedal on the left?" Trina asked. "Yeah, that's it, honey. Have you ever driven one?"

"No, but I've seen pictures."

"What color is the car?" Victor asked.

She laughed. "You know, I can't remember. My brain is so frazzled. It's been painted a few times. Let me think." They waited as she thought, then, "A dark blue, I think. And it has one of those...what do you call it?" She indicated a downward slide with her hand.

"Sloped back?"

"Yeah, yeah. Razor back. That's the word I was looking for. Think you might be interested? He's letting it go cheap."

"That's what most people say until they quote the price."

"Well, if you're interested, it's parked by the bank going out of town. He has his number on the windshield. I can call him if you want, and he can meet you there."

Victor paused, amazed at her persuasive abilities. Trina hugged his good arm and without saying anything he knew she wanted to look at it. "Sure. Tell him to meet us there."

"Ok," she said, then picked up the phone and dialed his number. As it rang, she looked over at Victor. "He's out of work right now, so he should answer."

As they waited, Trina rubbed her breasts against Victor's arm, which caused him to pull away slightly. It was a hazard, having a girlfriend in his line of work, but it was a risk he was willing to take, having gone over it in his mind many times.

"Dwight? It's Carrie. There's a guy here who wants to look at the Mustang." She paused, then continued. "A guy and a girl. I was telling them about it. They want you to meet them there."

There was a pause as she listened and kept rolling her eyes.

"Well, put some pants on and go down there and meet them. You're never going to sell it sitting on your ass all day." Another pause as she listened, then "Alright. I'll tell them. Bye." She hung up. Then looked up at Victor. "He said give him about 15 minutes and he'll meet you there."

"Ok. You said it's parked by the bank? Which one?" Victor asked. "Chase. You can't miss it. Good luck! Hope it's what you want."

CHAPTER 12

They drove to the location of the Mustang, which was parked in a vacant lot overgrown with grass and weeds, and over populated with realty signs and political advertisements close to the sidewalk. Victor pulled into the bank parking lot and waited. Trina kept checking her watch to make sure the guy was on time. While she waited she kept playing with Victor's earlobe trying to smooth the hair around it,

"If I had a pair of scissors, I'd trim that part around your ear. It keeps sticking out."

"I cut my own hair," he said flatly.

"Really," she said. "How do you get the back of it?" she asked, running her fingers through the back as if checking for lice.

Victor brushed her hand away gently, then said, "I just reach back and cut it. When you do it enough you get a feel for it."

Still inspecting, she said, "You do a really good job. Looks professional."

He looked at her and smirked. "I mess it up sometimes, then I get out the clippers and take it all down."

"All of it?"

"Yep."

"Michael Jordan?"

"Yep, only he looks good that way."

She leaned back imagining him with a buzz cut. "I bet you'd look good that way, too."

He looked at her smiling. "I bet you would, too. Only, down there." He pointed to the area between her legs.

She grinned. "Do you think?"

He nodded, looking toward the Mustang.

"Well mister, I don't suppose you have any shaving cream?" He shook his head, chuckling, while still watching for the guy.

"We'll have to stop and get some if you want to see a bald snatch."

He turned quickly to her. "Where did you learn to talk like that?"

"I just think it's funny," she said laughing. "I wonder if I'll have to put on after shave, too?" she asked, bursting into laughter again and pushing him, playfully, with her arm unable to contain herself.

Victor shook his head and looked toward the road, saying, "That must be him."

A Ford Ranger had driven up and parked along the street. What looked like a middle aged man got out and started looking around. When he heard a car door shut, he fixed his eyes on the parking lot, as Trina and Victor had started walking through the grass to the Mustang.

The guy was medium sized, well built, like a weightlifter---huge arms and shoulders, hardly any neck, giant hands, and a plethora of tattoos that covered his arms like sleeves. Victor wondered what the rest of his body looked like. It was probably covered with intricate designs of hidden meanings different to each. He hoped he would get an opportunity to see them, even if he had to ask, because people with that many tattoos weren't shy about displaying the work.

His head was shaved, and he wore a full black beard that outlined his face in a U to give him a rough appearance. It was obvious to Victor that he had been through alot, so he was careful with how he talked to him.

Reaching the Mustang the guy stuck out his hand and said, "How ya doin. I'm Dwight Taylor, and this here is Matilda."

While they shook hands in a firm, impressive grip Victor said, "I'm Frank Greene, and this is Trina," he said looking over at her, then back at her again to make sure she got it.

"Looks like you got quite a vehicle here."

"351 BOSS Mustang. The end of the line for Ford muscle cars."

"Looks like she's about ready to retire."

"That's just the outside, but she's got it where it counts." Dwight took a moment looking her over again. "Yeah, she's seen better days, but man, she's been a good work horse of a car. That's why I call her Matilda."

"Matilda? That's a strange name for a car. Why'd you call her that?"

Dwight paused a few moments to gather his thoughts. "That was the name of the first woman I ever dated. She was older and, man, she educated me on the wonders of womanhood, if you know what I mean. Right there in that front seat," Dwight said, nodding at Trina, who smiled back at him.

"Sweetest lady I ever met. An airline stewardess for Quantum...that's Australian. Then one day she just took off."

"On that big gray goose in the sky," Victor said, indicating with his hand, the taking off of a plane.

"You got that right. Whenever I drive it, it's like making love with her all over again. But you're not here to talk about that." He paused for a moment, then continued, "So Carrie served you both breakfast, huh?"

"Best one I've had today."

"And the only one," Dwight said, laughing again.

"Tell me some more about your car," Victor said. Aside from his physical presence, Victor noticed something unusual about this man. But he couldn't finger it.

"Yes, sir---"

"Call me Frank," Victor said, throwing up his hand.

"Ok, Frank. I've had this car since high school. Did most of the repairs myself."

"You never had anyone else work on it?"

"Well, some things, you know. You have to take it to the dealer when it's under warranty. That's what it's for."

"I see. But most of the engine work you've done?"

"That's right. It's the only work I've ever enjoyed. Ever since I can remember it seems like I've had a wrench or a ratchet in my hand. A lot of it was self-taught. I'm one of those freaks that read car manuals, then I jump in and try to figure it out. Then some of it is knowing the right guys to ask questions to. And working in body shops here and there."

"That's amazing. Carrie said it's been painted a few times."

"Yeah, and as you can see I got behind on that."

Victor nodded. "And you called it BOSS...something?" Dwight pointed to the name on the side by the front wheel. "It's a BOSS 351, and it has 390 horsepower."

"Damn! You could pull a train with that!"

"That's right. I don't know how familiar you are with muscle cars, but it was one of the best Ford ever built. And if I could get cute for a minute, 'If you must have speed, she has what you need.'"

Victor smiled at the rhymed couplet, then Dwight continued. "Now, I could give you a big sales pitch about what a fantastic car she is. And I've done that some already, but you can see how she is...the body sucks, looks like it's been through the war, but it's what's under the hood that's impressive ... and it's a 1971. Parts aren't easy to get, but you can still get them, and it's a classic, a piece of history, only 1800 were made, and I still use it, because she's got it where it counts."

"Like Matilda?"

Dwight laughed. "You bet. It just depends on what you're looking for."

Victor tried to feel him out some more, walking around the car. Then noticing his arms again, he asked, "You know, that's some great artwork you're carrying. Where'd you have it done?"

He paused, then said, "New York City."

"Where in the city?"

Dwight paused. "Rikers Island." Another pause. "You heard of it?"

"That's a big time prison." Victor looked at his arms again, then said, "Looking at all that, you had to do a good stretch."

"Twelve years."

"You don't say. Mind if I ask you what for?"

"You a cop?"

"No."

"Are you here about the car?"

"Yes. I don't mean to be rude."

They paused looking at each other. No one looked away.

Finally Dwight said, "Manslaughter."

"Really?"

"I got lucky."

"How's that?"

Dwight spoke quickly and raised his voice. "He didn't die! Now are we done with the interrogation? I need to sell this car. Are you interested?"

"I think so." Victor knew right then, this is a man not to be pushed. "Good. You want to get in it?" Dwight said.

Victor took the keys, not wanting to rile him anymore, then he got in and sat behind the wheel, reaching across himself to close the door with his right hand. The front bucket seats were plush, but cracked and needed leather treatment. The Hurst shifter was chrome plated and everything on the dash and speedometer looked clean and untouched by the onslaught of time, except for a few blemishes that could not be buffed out. He opened the glove box and saw the original owner's manual. Closing it, he turned back to Dwight who reached in with the keys.

"Start her up. You know how to drive with a clutch?"

"It's been awhile, but it'll come back. Look, I'm sorry if I got too nosy with you. I didn't mean anything by it. "

"It's a touchy subject. Don't worry about it."

Then Victor said, "I'd offer to shake your hand, but I'm still recovering from the first time."

Dwight laughed again. "Yeah, I get that a lot. Don't know my own strength."

"That's for sure," Victor agreed, laughing again to keep the big guy happy. The last thing in the world he wanted was to get this guy angry at him.

Continuing in a pleasant tone, Dwight said, "It's in first gear now. Push down on the clutch to start it. Once you do that, then you can put it in neutral, but she'll roll...not here, but on the pavement. So always put it in first when you shut her down. Then you can step off the clutch."

Victor nodded and inserted the key in the ignition, then pushing down on the clutch started the engine that broke into a 'VA-

RROOOM' sounding roar, growling louder each time Victor pressed on the accelerator that put a wide smile on both their faces. He then sat and listened to the engine idle---no vibration, just a steady purr that waited, patiently, for the driver's foot to press down.

Victor looked out the window and nodded at Dwight who nodded back, then he came over and leaned in. "Like I said, it's what's under the hood that counts." Dwight thought for a minute, then asked, "Do you like coffee?"

"Sometimes, I live on."

"Why don't you follow me to the farmhouse and we can talk more about the car. I'd like to show you what she can really do. It's not very far. Just a few minutes."

"Okay. I believe we can handle that."

"Good. I'll drive this and then she can follow me in yours. You can drive my truck," he said, tossing the truck keys to Victor.

CHAPTER 13

Detective Boyle had barely put his head on the pillow, when his phone began to vibrate across the nightstand. It was early morning and he didn't know where he was for a minute. Seeing the light of his phone, he caught it before it vibrated off the nightstand.

Clearing his throat, he answered, "... this is Boyle."

Westhouse, full of enthusiasm, said, "Grab your socks and scratch your crotch! We have a new development."

"Give it to me," Boyle said, yawning and still trying to clear his eyes.

"The LPR on our vehicle has a new reading for ENZ-1560."

"What's the location?" Boyle asked, writing the number down on a notepad kept on the nightstand.

"The Beach Front Motel."

Thinking for a moment, Boyle said, "That's where you sent Caldwell and Billings to set up a base. You lied to me, you son-of-a-bitch!"

Boyle had snooped around, talking to some of the other agents wanting to know where they were. It was a new agent who slipped up to reveal they were on their way to the motel to establish a surveillance center. He had carefully designed his questions to make it seem natural.

"Can't get anything past you, detective. I admire that. And no, I didn't lie to you. I said they were on their way. I didn't say where."

"Same thing, asshole. We're supposed to be on the same team. If you lie to me again, I'm done with your sorry ass." Boyle started to hang up.

"Wait, wait! Don't you want to know why I called?" Slight pause. "I can't wait."

"We're all making a mad dash there, as soon as I hang up. I believe our CIA friends have done well."

"Why's that?"

"They obviously have the Buick with the plate number in question. I've been trying to call them, but no one has answered. Would you care to join us, detective?"

Boyle rubbed his forehead. "Where's the motel?"

"It's off of 27. When you get to Manorville stop and ask, if you need to. Does your phone have GPS?"

"Of course."

"Good. Put in 'Manorville' or 'Oceanside Lane'. You might get some strange readings out there, but you'll find it."

"Got it." Boyle hung up.

It was Boyle's favorite time of the morning just before the sun came up. He moved quickly to the kitchen and using the Keurig this time put in a container of dark roast, slammed the lever and pushed brew. Then he hopped in the shower--hot water first, then gradually turned it to cold, waiting as long as he could to revive himself. Coming out he dried quickly and dressed this time in jeans and a muscle shirt. He put on his best athletic shoes.

On the way out, he grabbed his NYPD windbreaker that he really didn't like, because it advertised who he was. He preferred an incognito status. But he was in a hurry and it was easy to find.

Once in the Charger, he pressed the speed dial for Natalie's number and listened to the rings on his way uptown. There was no pick up and the call went to voicemail. After waiting for the recorded message to finish, a call came in that when he answered it was Natalie.

"Hello, it's me. Where are you?" she asked, her voice sensuous, though peppered with sleep.

"On my way to Long Island."

"Without me? Who do you think you are?"

"I'll tell you after I get there."

"What's going on?"

He paused, then said, "We may be getting closer. That's all I can say."

"So the guy you're looking for is on Long Island?"

"Looks that way."

"Well...he knows where to go, if he wants to relax." Pause.

"I wanted to tell you where I'm headed."

He heard a long intake of breath with an exhale. "Don't be gone long, lover."

Once he was on the Long Island Expressway, Boyle decided to air out the Charger to test the engine, which he hadn't had an opportunity to do in a while. If he were to engage in a high speed chase, he wanted the engine to perform at its best without any sputters. But before he did that, he took out his phone to call dispatch.

"911. How can I help you?"

"Hey, Delores? Is that you?"

"Good morning to you, too, Henry. Been awhile since I've heard from you."

"I know. Duty calls."

"What's up?"

"I'm on 495 heading to Manorville."

"I'm in Manhattan."

"I know, Delores, but I need a favor, hon."

"Hon? What's that supposed to mean?"

They had a previous relationship that ended abruptly, because Henry was too busy to call her back. Most of his relationships had ended that way---married to the job.

"Look, I know it's been awhile...and I should have called you, I admit that."

"Keep crawling. I like it."

"My schedule is just unbelievable. I don't sleep. I eat on the run...it's...it's just hard to keep up with everything."

"How does that apply to me?"

"I hate asking you--"

"No, you don't! As long as we're being honest, let's keep it that way."

"Ok, sorry," he said, gathering himself. "I know you're upset with me."

"You don't know the half of it, Henry," she said, raising her voice.

"Ok, I'll start again. You've heard about The Grand Central Killer?"

"Yes," came a stern answer.

"I'm on my way to Manorville from a lead I just received from the FBI."

"You hate the FBI," she said with venom beginning to form.

"So don't you, as…I remember and most of your superiors."

"The FBI…go on."

"Dolores, may I call you that?"

"You already have."

"Yes. This could be a break in the case. I've got to get there quickly."

"Drive safely."

"That's just it. I drive this Charger. Remember?"

Pause. Then came her quick reply that sounded, as if it were snapped off. "Yes---"

Hearing nothing else, he continued. "I haven't tested it for a while…you know, step down on the gas to blow out anything built up in the engine. I need to run at top sufficiency."

"Yeah…"

"It's just a friendly request, Dolores, for old times sake." Another pause. "Is that all you want?"

"Would it help if I said I'm sorry?"

"No," she said, then after a moment, "But, since this is an official request, putting all feelings aside, I'll put out a BOLO for Long Island to leave you alone…but it ends at Manorville. You got that?"

"Manorville. Got it. I appreciate it, too!"

"I bet you do!" There was a pause that filled the line, then came, "Take care of yourself, Henry."

"I will. Thank you."

Boyle waited a few minutes, then when he thought it was tight enough for the BOLO to be received, he stepped down on the gas and leveled off at 100 miles per hour, which didn't seem to be much of a problem for the engine, so he kicked it up at increments of 10, until he leveled at 120 mph. Continuing that way, he slowed down to 100 mph, then increased another 10, while listening to the engine or to see if he felt a vibration from the tires. But all was well. So he set the cruise control at 100 mph until he reached the turn off to Manorville, saying to himself, Thank you, Dolores.

CHAPTER 14

Pulling over to get some gas, Boyle stopped at a service station with a huge Texaco sign that he saw from I-495. Underneath the constructed canopy for gas pumps, he used his card to select Super-Unleaded and in placing the nozzle in the car tank, he pulled back the catch to let it secure and fill it up. Looking around, he didn't see much but an ordinary town that could have been Anytown, USA.

Lots of trees and plush green grass, houses begging to be updated and lawns that needed manicuring were everywhere. Rusting road signs in need of replacement lined each side of the roads, and kids riding bicycles making quick-stops at the station reminded him of a childhood he never had. It was a far cry away from his usual police routine in the city.

The nozzle catch released, Boyle completed the card transaction, took the receipt and placed it in his wallet. He walked inside and up to the counter. The woman behind it was so overweight that it redefined the word. But her personality was full of joy, which made up for it.

Seeing him, she asked, "Can I get something else for you ?"

Boyle pulled out his badge and ID, then said, "I'm here on official business. Have you heard of a place called the Beach Front Motel?"

She shook her head, saying nothing.

"I need some directions. Can you help me?"

She swallowed hard, trying to get it past her layers of double chins.

"Charles and Margaret haven't done anything wrong, have they?"

Boyle leaned in. "Who are they?"

"They own the place. They're elderly, but they still get around Ok...slow, but they do alright. Not many customers, you know."

"Ok. How do I get there?"

"Just follow this road here," she said, pointing outside.

Boyle repeated her gesture indicating the road that his car was pointed toward. "The one that I came in on?"

"That's right. It's 27. Follow it all the way out of town, until you come to a sign on the left that says, 'Beach Front Motel'."

Boyle nodded. "Good. That should be easy enough to find."

"The sign doesn't light up anymore. So if you go at night you might miss it."

"I'm going there now. I won't miss it."

***

The motel sign was easy to find. He turned left where the arrow indicated, then continued with trees on either side that moved into a hollow. After a short distance the trees opened up to reveal the spread of the motel rooms with the FBI surveillance van parked in front of number seven, the license plate number ENZ-1560 in view. But no Buick.

Sensing something wrong, Boyle pulled his Glock, and pulled the action back, releasing one into the chamber, then keeping it in his right hand, he used his left to steer the wheel, backing the Charger, so that the passenger side gave cover to the slide door of the van. He thought about calling Westhouse to get his ETA, then thought better of it. Whatever was in the van, if anything at all---or maybe someone was in the rooms, he could certainly handle it. And there were no other cars.

Getting out, he stopped and just stood there. Listening. Hardly a sound, except what nature supplied and cars sounding off from the interstate. He pulled his badge and raised it high calling out, "NYPD! ANYONE HERE?" No response. Silence. The area surrounded by trees, isolated, forgotten by the town.

He moved around the back of the Charger toward the motel and knocked on number seven. No answer. He tried to open the door. It was unlocked. With his gun ready, he checked the inside that looked undisturbed. The bathroom, behind each door, and checking the other rooms, all were empty. He knew something was wrong.

Turning back to the van, he approached the side door cautiously, crouched low, glock ready with a two hand grip. Taking a deep breath and standing to the left of the handle, he reached to grab it and jerked open the door with his back against the van. He heard no movement inside. Then swinging around to face the inside, adrenalin pumping, blood pounding in his ears like a frenzied drummer …it all came to an abrupt halt.

Boyle dropped his arms, feeling like a deflated balloon, and lowered his head. Rubbing his brow, he didn't know what to say. In front of him sat Caldwell and Billings lashed to the swivel chairs, where the FBI agents operated their surveillance equipment. They were faced toward the door, bound with nylon ropes, duct tape and flex cuffs---gagged, heads hanging down to their chests. A piece of cardboard left on their laps leaning against them read:

'I WANT TO TALK TO BOYLE ONLY!'

He is a persistent son-of-a-bitch! I'll give him that! When is it going to stop? With his phone he took a picture of the sign with them in the background. He didn't like these fellows, but it didn't matter.

Something left him every time an officer lost his life in the line of duty. He took a minute to gather himself to continue processing the scene. Then he thought he heard some faint breathing. Then jerking his head as a groan came from Caldwell, who then started to move his head slightly. Caldwell squirmed in his shackled seat beginning to wake up. The two, finally, opened their eyes and looked around, as if to ask, What the hell happened?

Deciding to release them from their bonds, Boyle started to step into the van, but without warning, like an unexpected surprise, he felt the pressure of a gun against the back of his neck. He froze, keeping both hands in front of him.

Then he heard, "With your left hand, remove your gun and toss it behind you."

The man stepped back. Boyle did as he was directed. This time he heard, "Now, the ankle."

Bending over he took out the .38 snub and tossed it behind him. Billings and Caldwell were still groggy, and began voicing muffled groans from mouths still stuffed with their handkerchiefs.

"Turn around," the man said, stepping back a few paces.

Boyle turned around to face Victor Enmerkar. He wasn't shocked because this was his MO. He hadn't seen him since the time on Mercer Street, when he and Eddie Genesco were tied up by the two previous CIA Ops that Victor killed. Because they were about to kill him and Eddie, his partner, then blame the murders on Victor, whom they thought were hiding in the loft apartment.

Victor had saved his life. He was grateful for that, but he had a job to do. He could see he was getting around despite the shoulder wound. He really didn't know why he was here. His mind began thinking of when to make a move, possibly hitting the injured shoulder seemed to be his best move. But he decided against it.

Instead, he said, "Let me untie them."

"Just leave them. I gave them something to relax, " Victor said, motioning for Boyle to move away from the van. Then he walked to close its door, as Boyle eyed him with a deep concern, trying to understand his actions. "You're just going to leave them in there?"

"For now. You can let them loose when I'm gone."

"How thoughtful."

"I think so. These replacements weren't much better than the previous two. I give them credit, though."

"For what?"

"They tried. Unsuccessfully, but they tried," he said, laughing. He turned slightly to indicate the area behind him. "I was standing back there in the tree cover just waiting for you to show up."

Boyle paused. "Why? Do you want to talk again?" he said, sarcastically.

Victor looked tired. A great heaviness came over him. He took a deep breath and shook his head to clear it. Then, he said, "Once you realize what's really going on, then you will understand my persistence."

Victor looked down at the guns, then he picked them up and stuck them in his belt, being careful of his arm that Boyle noticed.

He gestured toward the apartments and said, "Inside. We can talk there."

Boyle looked around after getting closer. "Which room?"

"Any...number, 7...that's a lucky one."

Once inside Boyle tried to shut the door. "No. Leave it open." Boyle left it as is, then stood looking at his captor.

"Sit wherever you want. I want this to be comfortable."

"Then point that somewhere else," Boyle said, sitting on the bed.

Victor lowered the gun, pulled out a chair and turned it toward Boyle with a view of the parking lot to his left. Boyle felt surprisingly comfortable and saw that Victor's demeanor had changed. He looked tired, obviously, from the ordeal he had been through that had yet to be finished.

"I see you're still up and around. Do you have plenty of morphine?"

"I'm not here for that," Victor said, raising his left hand with a grimace. "We don't have long. The rest of your crew will be coming. I need to reaffirm what we talked about on Mercer Street."

"Reaffirm what?"

"What we talked about! Our communication on Mercer Street! I want to make this right!"

"Turn yourself in! Then we'll talk about it!"

"Stop it! Ok? I'm serious about this! That's why I chose you!"

"You chose me?" Boyle looked surprised in a mocking way.

Victor knew it was the wrong choice of words. He looked exasperated. The first time Boyle had seen him that way. He looked around the room, through the door to the parking lot as if searching for the right words to use.

"You're a good cop, Boyle. One hell of a detective. Everyone counts with you. I respect that. I've been watching the news and reading the papers. They say a lot about who you are. And I read between the lines."

"Get to the point."

He paused, looking back through the open door. "Everything was up in the air last time we talked. I needed time to take care of some personal matters. Some of it I've done, but I haven't had time to rest this shoulder. Just a few uninterrupted days and I should be fine. And I wanted to touch base with you, again, to see if you'll give me that time so I can get the evidence I need. And that you'll also need to bring those responsible to justice."

Boyle tried to remember what he had said to him while he was tied up. "Do you mean, at Langley? Getting into the files at CIA headquarters?" Victor nodded.

"Yes. I still need time to do that. Will you give it to me?"

Boyle knew where he was going. He also knew what kind of man it took to take out two CIA Ops, while he was wounded in the shoulder, and then take him at gunpoint just to be able to talk to him. There had to be something to what he was saying.

"And if I say yes, you'll hop on a plane to South America."

Victor shook his head. "You're a hard man to convince. How am I going to get the evidence when I'm all the way down there?"

Boyle paused.

"I still think it's best if you turn yourself in."

"That's suicide! What the hell would my chances be then?"

"It's better than getting killed this way. Some glory minded fool will get a nervous trigger finger for you."

"I won't put myself in that place. I didn't kill those people!"

Boyle smiled inwardly as he could see what Kearney had said about him was true. That he wanted to come in. But here he was now in the flesh asking him for time to get the evidence. Evidence that only he could get buried in the secret files of Langley, Virginia. This was definitely the most bizarre case he had ever encountered.

"What you're asking me to do is to not be a detective. Do you understand that?"

"No!" he said, waving the gun at him, which Boyle followed with his eyes. "You're wrong! It's the height of what true detective work is. You'd be holding on to the facts, the hard reality of the case to finally arrive at the ultimate truth that no one can question. It's what we're all after. A release from this senseless death cycle that points to the fucking CIA!"

Boyle agreed with him, but tried not to show it. He scratched the back of his head and spoke quietly. "My hands are tied. I have to do my job."

"I didn't kill those people!"

Boyle nodded. "That may be true."

"It is the truth! Why else would I be here? Why else would I risk getting caught?"

Boyle laughed, shaking his head. "There's just too many unanswered questions."

"Give me time to answer them?" Victor said, almost stomping his feet.

Boyle couldn't believe what he was asking. "What the fuck do I owe you?"

"A chance like you give everyone else. Are you going to go against your own creed?"

"My what?"

"Your creed, man! Everyone deserves a chance! I've heard you say it many times! So what about me?" He paused a minute, then said, "Boyle, I'm tired. I don't want this anymore, and I've got a shitload to tell you. Will you help me?"

Boyle saw the deep concern in Victor's eyes, like he was pleading. Then he spoke frankly. "What the hell do you expect from me? I'm a police officer for chrissake!"

Victor took a step toward him. "Just hear me out. I gave you the short version on Mercer Street. Now, let me lay it all out for you." He glanced at the parking lot. "But I have to go. They'll be coming."

Boyle knew he was right, and if he was going to hear this man out---this was not the time to do it. He took out a card from his wallet and flicked it at him.

"That's my new number. Now get out of here. They'll be here in a minute." Then thinking about his guns, he said, "But can you leave me the guns? They're my favorites, and I like the way they feel." He looked directly at Victor. "Just take the bullets."

Victor smiled, then picked up the guns, removing the cartridges from the .38, and extracting the shells from the Glock's magazine with his thumb one at a time, collecting them all. Then, he did something that surprised Boyle. He opened the bathroom door and tossed them in the garbage can with a repeated clunk. "I'll be long gone before you reload. Shells are expensive," he said, opening his hands.

Noticing the card on the floor, he picked it up, looked at it and said, "So you'll talk to me?"

Boyle nodded, staring at him with a peculiar contempt.

"Thank you," Victor said. He exhaled with a sigh of relief, as if he had won a small victory. Then he walked to the door and looking out above the trees. said, "I know the FBI will be canvassing in Manorville. I'll watch for the right time. Give me ten minutes, ok?"

Boyle nodded again. Victor walked out into the parking lot and when he raised his hand, Trina came driving up in the Buick, while Boyle watched from inside the motel room.

When Trina stepped down on the gas pedal, gravel spun under the tires, some of it clinking against the van.

Boyle went immediately to the bathroom and reloaded his guns retrieving the shells from the garbage can. Then he walked quickly to the van, opened the side door and released Caldwell and Billings. They cursed, bitched, and complained, but Boyle heard none of it, as his mind was fixed on what Victor Enmerkar might have to share.

They both stepped down from the van stiff as boards, They began twisting and touching their toes to try and loosen up. Then Billings came up to Boyle and asked,

"Where the hell is Westhouse? He's supposed to be in charge, isn't he?" Boyle pulled a cigarette from a soft pack in his pocket and lit it. "According to him, he's in charge."

"He's on his way, isn't he?" Billings asked.

Taking a deep breath, Boyle said, "That's what he told me."

Pausing, stepping closer, Billings said, "You really don't have to tell him what happened, do you?" Billings asked.

Boyle gave him a cold look, then Billings came back with, "You're the boss, not Westhouse. Although we could work that out, too."

"I don't make deals. You guys need to take my advice and get into another line of work, because this isn't for you."

"Yeah, but...damn! He's one cagey son-of-a-bitch. One minute he's here, then he isn't. You don't even see him until it's too late. He slipped up behind us unnoticed." He paused to think a minute, then asked, "Could you put in a good word for us? That we really did try?"

Boyle eyed them. "The way I see it, he got the best of you. Just like he got me."

"Leave the man alone, Billings," Caldwell said. "We fucked up so admit it." Turning to his partner, Billings replied, "But the mission isn't over.

That's the point I'm trying to make. There's still time." Then, turning back to Boyle, he continued. "And if Detective Boyle could give us a break and not tell West house that would be even better."

Boyle considered the option, then said, "Explain to me what happened". He looked over at Caldwell. "This includes you, too." Caldwell got up. Then Boyle spoke to both of them. "If you're thinking about lying, forget it. Now's your time, so go for it."

Both men explained their hearts out. At times, Boyle thought they deserved an Academy Award for their reenactment of the siege on the beach house. At one point, he had to turn slightly to keep from laughing, but he kept it together, asking a question or two, here and there, that both of them answered together, until one kept quiet to allow the other to explain so Boyle could understand.

When they had nothing else to say, Boyle took his time watching them sweat in eager anticipation. Then lighting another cigarette, he asked, "How are you going to explain the switching of the license plate?"

"He switched it when we weren't looking. Sometime in the night."

Boyle nodded, then looked around and said, "Go clean up the mess in the van, and take that whiskey and beer inside."

They both practically got on their knees to thank him, saying that they owed him a favor whenever he wanted. Boyle explained to them that he wasn't interested in that. He just wanted them to think and make better decisions like calling for backup. There was no shame in doing that.

When finished with the cleanup, Caldwell came to Boyle and offered his hand. Boyle shook it, as Caldwell said, "Thanks, Detective. You're the one who's really in charge."

CHAPTER 15

Dwight Taylor was a difficult man to describe and even more complicated to understand. But some things just defy description, not that he was exceptional by the world's standards, but in comparison to its picture of success, he was just an ordinary man; a product of his environment uniquely defined just like the rest of its confused inhabitants searching for their own enlightened meaning. Dwight knew at an early age that he wanted to be a mechanic and move toward opening his own vehicle repair shop. But as John Lennon said, 'Life gets in the way while we're making other plans'.

The inciting incident that caused him, not only to fall from grace but to crash into something he never thought would happen, was that he caught someone quite unexpectedly and who he thought was his friend, in the act of intimacy with his first romantic go around. And to make matters worse, they were teammates on the high school football team.

Bombs exploded in his mind, resulting in a hot-fevered craze that caused him to confront his teammate under the football bleachers. Dwight said nothing, knowing he was guilty, and walked right up to the boy and knocked him out cold—a one punch knockout!

The boy was rushed to the hospital, where after a close examination, it was determined that his brain stem had been damaged causing further trauma to the brain. The boy recovered, but it was not a full recovery. Rehabilitation could only do so much. He was socially classified as 'slow in the head'.

The judge sentenced Dwight to twelve years for manslaughter. It was considered a stiff sentence for a first time offender. Dwight's father had no money for a lawyer, and his attempts to convince the judge for a lighter sentence were futile. Due to overcrowding and limited bed space, Dwight was sent to Rikers Island, where he learned how to survive by staring fear in its face. He fought so many fights that he was never paroled. Most of his time was spent on the weight pile where two friends stood guard for the duration of his workout. Outside of that, his time was spent in solitary confinement.

At present, Dwight lived with his sister Carrie outside of Manorville in the same one hundred year old farmhouse he grew up in. It was a classic, white clapboard Victorian with a three quarter wrap around porch decorated with gingerbread ornamentation. A red barn in the back was just as old, and it was sturdy with heavy cross beams supporting a loft that held various heirlooms and treasures from their family history that reached back before the Civil War.

There were gasoline signs like Texaco, Marathon, Shell, Phillips 66, and keepsakes so sacred that no one ever bothered to open them up, and not knowing what else to do with them, stored them in the loft. They never worried about thieves because Manorville was a small community. Nothing ever happened that was newsworthy, except what came from 'Gotham City', so most everyone depended on the local grapevine.

They knew that Dwight Taylor was a jail bird, that he was out of work, and out of hope with a bankruptcy pending. He hoped that he could sell the Mustang, so he and Carrie could get some breathing room from all the bill collectors and others eager to buy the house, wanting to know when they would be vacating the premises. The stress was unbearable.

***

All these thoughts ran through Dwight's mind as he led the three vehicle caravan off of 27 and onto a gravel road with corn fields on either side that belonged to their neighbors that he hardly saw except during harvest. Their land had been sold long ago when Dwight's dad died, and struggling to keep up on the mortgage and taxes, plus having to go to prison for a dozen years, coupled with not being able

121

to find a good paying job, made it seem like good sense to claim bankruptcy. They had to get out from under the suffocating pressure of trying to keep up. They were sinking into the quicksand of overwhelming debt.

They had yard sales when they needed cash. Prices were negotiable. But the one thing Dwight was aware of, more than anything else, was that the people were the most conniving, heartless, and downright cruel when it came to money. When he and Carrie had their backs to the wall with no way out!

Family heirlooms went for almost nothing. Antique furniture sold for a fraction of the price, because the people he thought were his friends cried and whined and complained about how little money they had, and how they couldn't afford to pay what he wanted, when in reality, they were just evil tight-wods pinching their money to see how far they could push someone to the limit.

One day, in the middle of a rather trying afternoon, scavengers came with their walkers and canes, and pursestrings pulled so tight it would take a miracle to loosen them. And there were others, who walked upright without assistance who were just as conniving. They were the hunters, who prowled and searched in the barn loft and shadows of the basement seeking what no one knew was there. They pretended not to care or want what they found, but offered a few dollars as an offering for the hidden treasures found. Then left quickly full of joy from what they stole from these ignorant people.

Dwight watched them and knew what they were doing. He was beyond hurt as he watched the priceless items that made up the composite of his family's hardworking, humble life walk away. He was numb, walking around not knowing what else to do, because he and Carrie needed money so badly. The people were like wolves circling in for the kill, slowly sucking their life from them. It seemed that they weren't happy unless they could snap off the blade once the knife was plunged. Then they walked away not caring to watch them bleed.

It got to the point where he couldn't listen to their whining complaints anymore. If anyone should be crying it was he and Carrie! They were losing their farm! But not to those lying vultures! So, determined to make a statement, he got up on the flatbed of a truck and started shouting at everyone to stop insulting him and to take their crummy nickels and dimes and to go home! When they didn't listen and kept on looking at things, he got down off the truck, ran inside the house to get his double barrel shotgun, stuffing extra shells in his pocket.

Then running back through the yard around the trees, like a patriot trying to protect the remnants of what belonged to his family, he climbed back onto the truck bed, and after opening the breach and loading the shells, he cocked back the hammers and fired both barrels into the air that resembled a sonic boom echoing off the barn. That got some attention! So he opened the breach, took out the empty shells, reloaded and fired again! That really got their attention! Carrie came running through the yard and jumped upon the truck with him in a show of solidarity.

Then he heard a voice shouting, "What the hell are you doin, you idiot?!"

Dwight saw who shouted the question. He pointed his massive, tattooed arm at him with the shotgun raised above his head in the other, and screamed back with a warlike cry, "YOU GET OFF MY LAND! NOW! ALL OF YOU! GO AWAY! LEAVE US ALONE!"

He opened the breach again, removed the empties, reloaded and fired again.

The people looked up at him like he was a crazy man. Some of them whispered to each other, mumbling things he could not comprehend. Then, slowly, shaking their heads, they put back what they held in their arms and the people with walkers, canes, and the hunters went back to their cars.

Soon the land was theirs again…for a time. It was quiet. They clutched each other in the entanglement of their misery and shame, hoping for relief as they wept bitter tears.

***

Soon after the shooting incident, the Suffolk County Sheriff came with some deputies and arrested Dwight for disorderly conduct and the unlawful discharge of a firearm in a public place even though it was his farm. Since it was a sale, they considered it public. The judge, having known his parents, was lenient and dropped the charges, but did impose a five hundred dollar fine, which Dwight couldn't pay---so he had to spend thirty days in the Suffolk County Jail.

When he was released, he came out relaxed and renewed to the fact that nothing could harm him anymore. His resistance to pain was, now, quite high. He accepted the fact that pain was a brutal teacher, drawing it close as a welcomed friend, reminding him that he was stronger than most and was able to endure whatever the world took from him.

And they could take what he owned, put him in jail---they could torture, even kill him! But they couldn't take away what was in his heart, the ability to see through their lies and the fact that people were unable to see that the world had deceived them. And they just went about their lives, as if they didn't care—truly defeated!

He didn't know how to expose it, let alone fix it. He was just one man. But he knew it was there, waiting to encircle them with a choking web of deceit. The tail of the monster had been exposed to him leaving a bad taste that would not go away. No matter how he tried to expel it.

Victor picked up on the fact that Dwight was a man of high principle. He treated people the way he wanted to be treated without any compromise in between—and that was rare. Seldom was he repaid for what he gave. It was safe to say that Victor liked him from the start.

CHAPTER 16

The two cars and Dwight's Ranger had pulled up to the old farmhouse. Victor noticed the house looked weathered but still stood proud. Dwight pointed for them to park along the fence by the barn. Then he got out and told them he would start the coffee. He disappeared inside the house, using the screened backdoor.

Trina came over to the Mustang and eyeing it closely said, "Well, the outside is ugly, but it has a better shape than that Buick."

"Ugly is good for us. If the engine is as good as I think, we'll take it. But let's see how it rides first."

"You're so smart. I wish I knew what you know."

"I've just lived longer. That's all. And believe me, there are some things I know that you don't want to know."

"We'll see." They kissed and hugged each other tight. They stood that way making out with each other for a few minutes. And just as their heat began to sizzle, they heard the screen door slam and heard Dwight's footsteps in the gravel.

Dwight smacked his hands together and said, "Ok. Are we ready for a ride?"

"Ready as we'll ever be," Victor said.

"Tell you what. I can tell you haven't driven one like this for a while. So why don't I show you what she can do first, then turn her over to you?"

"Fine by me," Victor said.

"Me, too," Trina agreed, feeling her face.

Dwight assumed his position in the driver's seat. Victor sat in the passenger seat up front, after trying to get Trina to sit there, but she insisted the back was fine. Dwight drove to an old stretch of blacktop off of 27 that was hardly used anymore, except by farmers driving their machinery. The road had dips and turns that he had used since his youth to run and gun the engine, and race when opportunities arose.

Dwight drove a little farther and then stopped the car. "The first thing I want to show you is how fast she goes from zero to 60, and how easy it is to use this Hurst shifter. It's not like driving passenger cars. That's why they call it a muscle car. It's got power." Dwight kept turning his head so that Trina could hear, then he said to her, "You might want to sit back and fasten your safety belt."

"Ok, if you say so." She leaned back and buckled up. Victor checked his belt, too. "Ok. Are we ready?" Dwight asked.

Everyone agreed. Then Dwight looked at Victor and asked, "Does your watch have a second hand?"

"Yes."

"Tell me when it gets up to twelve."

"Ok."

They waited a few seconds with anticipation. Then Victor said, "Go!"

Dwight stomped the accelerator that spun the tires, smoke rising from both sides of the back, and when the tires securely grabbed the pavement---the car jerked forward like the force of a rocket ship taking off--- their heads thrown back into the cushioned seats, then another jerk threw the car into second gear that rose the front end up slightly continuing the acceleration. Again, with a rocking shift, the car slammed into third gear to even out the ride.

And last, the fourth gear sent the car into what seemed like a blinding speed---as both Trina and Victor looked out the window to see the corn whisking by in a blur.

When the odometer reached 110 mph, Dwight turned to Victor and shouted, "Time." Then he eased up on the accelerator, and down shifted to third gear.

Cruising along, he looked over at Victor and asked, "What was the reading?"

"15 seconds...if I read it right." Victor's shoulder was throbbing from the force of the shifts.

Nodding, Dwight said, "Not bad for an old lady. My shifting is a little rusty, otherwise I could've done better... but, 30 mph in about 4 or 5 seconds, I'd say; 60 in 8 or 9; and 110 in about 14, 15 seconds." Turning to Victor he asked, "What do you think?"

Victor paused for a moment, then Dwight added, "Are you alright?"

He breathed deep, then let it out. "Couldn't be better. Impressive." His shoulder was still throbbing.

"I used to do jumps with this baby back in the day...like the Dukes of Hazzard. You remember that show? Only not as grand." Victor nodded. Dwight continued. "But I was young and stupid. This car's worth too much to risk that now."

"Yeah, don't do that to impress us!" he said, raising his hands. "We're already impressed," Trina said, leaning forward.

"She handles well on curves, too. There's a pond out here. I'll take you out around it and show you. Then you can grab the wheel," he said to Victor.

"Ok."

When they reached the farmhouse, Victor parked the car and was careful to get out, not wanting Dwight to see he was favoring his left arm. They got out and Victor looked at the surrounding grounds, impressed with the tree covered acreage and with the structure of the time worn barn. Perhaps this could be a home?

He saw something in Dwight that made him want to know more about him. He saw an opportunity to help a man who was down on his luck.

They went inside to have some coffee. Carrie was there, back from the restaurant. After exchanging pleasantries, she and Trina went on a tour of the farmhouse to let the men discuss their business. Dwight brought two mugs of coffee to the table.

"You want sugar?" he asked, indicating with his hand a bowl full of sugar packets, sweet & low, and stevia.

"No, just black," Victor said.

"That's the way I like my women," Dwight said. Then he explained. "Just kidding. There was a guy on the cell block who used to say that every time he got a cup. Amazing how things like that stay with you."

Victor sensed that this was the time to inquire about Dwight's history. He started slowly trying not to be offensive and to keep it matter of fact.

"How's it been since you got out?"

"It sucks, but thanks for asking."

"Seriously, I'd like to know...if you want to tell me. Are you adjusting alright?" Dwight paused. "I thought we were here to talk about the car."

"We are, but I thought it would be nice to get to know each other a little better."

"You sound like a parole officer."

"I'm sorry. Let me reassure you, I'm far from anything like that."

"So what's with the questions? I told you I was in prison, and the reason."

Victor threw up his hands. "I don't mean to be nosy, but I think we can help each other."

"You can help me by buying the car."

"Mister, don't waste my time. I've been straight with you. And I've been as nice as I know how to be."

Victor leaned in. "Yes, you've been more than cordial. But let me cut to the chase. And I don't mean to overwhelm you, but I'll go ahead and give you twice what you want for Matilda. Cash."

Dwight paused, looking around the kitchen, then back. "I don't know what your game is, but I'm not playing."

"Alright, then. How much are you asking"

"I was asking 15, but I ain't doing this. I just got out of prison, man. I can't get hooked up into anything. I'm sorry you came out here for nothing--"

"I'll give you sixty grand now. Cash. No strings."

Dwight stared at him. Dollar signs exploded in his mind, but he was used to con games. He decided to play along for the value of entertainment.

"Where's the cash?"

"Here."

"Where?" Dwight looked around, opening his hands.

"Outside."

"Outside?" Dwight narrowed his eyes.

"In the Buick."

Dwight started laughing.

"You're either fuckin nuts--"

"Or I'm telling the truth," Victor said, completing his statement. Then continuing, he said, "Come on. I'll show you."

They walked outside; Victor first, followed by Dwight who was cautious, not really knowing what was going on, whether this guy was a complete whacko or what. They walked to the back of the Buick, Victor took out the keys and unlocked the trunk, when Dwight stuck out his massive arm in front to stop him.

"Mister, if you're thinking about trying anything---"

Victor interrupted his warning by saying, "What do you think I'm going to do? Rob you? Come on! Give me credit for having a few brains, at least."

Dwight lowered his arm that looked like a tree trunk to Victor. "I guess you're right. Sorry."

"Frank. Call me Frank," he said, smiling at him. He noticed Dwight was almost smiling. The corners of his mouth were starting to turn up, evidenced by the spark in his eyes that were alive with hope.

Victor removed part of the carpeted floor to reveal a hidden space. He reached in and pulled out a black duffel bag. He unzipped it for Dwight to see the money.

Dwight looked inside the bag. His face remained stoic. Victor counted out 60 grand and laid it beside the bag. Victor looked at Dwight waiting for him to say something.

"I thought it would be bigger," Dwight said.

"You're thinking in terms of tens, twenties, maybe some fifties. Hundred dollar bills. Makes it easier to carry. So what do you think? Can we talk now?"

Now Dwight was smiling, not completely, but a middle of the road smile. "Yeah. Lay it all out for me. Okay?"

"That's what I've been trying to do." Victor zipped up the bag, replaced it in the hiding place, then smoothed out the carpet. He neatly placed the 60 grand in a plastic bag. Then seeing Dwight turn to walk back to the house, he said, "Here. Don't forget this."

He tossed the money to Dwight who felt it through the plastic bag, then asked, "How much do you have in that other bag?"

"You mean the black bag?"

"Yeah."

"I don't know, really. A good amount, though."

Dwight laughed to himself. "Yeah. Let's talk. We might have to get rid of the women though."

Victor thought. "Do you have any booze?"

"Sure."

"We could get them drunk. Then after they're asleep, we can talk."

"I'll have to send Carrie to the store. I'm out of beer."

Victor pointed to the bag of money in Dwight's hand. "Tell her to take Trina with her."

"We could barbecue, I guess. What meat do you like?"

"Couple of T-bones would be nice. That sounds good to you?"

"Hell, yes! I'll tell the girls to get anything else they want. Carrie usually eats salad," Dwight said, shaking his head. "I just can't do that. Some of it's ok, but she eats it all the time."

"Did you know that the strongest animal in the jungle is a vegetarian?"

"No. Which one?"

"The elephant."

CHAPTER 17

The girls grew tired and decided to hit the hay. It was determined that Victor and Trina were spending the night and when the boys were ready to sleep, Dwight would show Victor which bedroom to crash in. The boys chatted awhile, then started to get down to business.

The night was calm and the air was cool, as they relaxed even more to enjoy the warming flow of alcohol that ignited their minds, and spirit.

"Thank you for the money, Frank. I don't know how I could ever repay your kindness."

"It's a gift. Don't worry about it."

"But it's too much, though I am grateful."

"I'm happy to do it."

"But nobody does that. Why would you?"

"Because you need it and I can give it. And besides, I need to do something good."

"What do you mean?"

"I mean, you did the twelve years at Rikers, then you came out and had to spend another thirty days in the county, not to mention the pain and humiliation you went through. Our judicial system is definitely against us. So, I'm doing this not only for you, but myself as well."

"I…I don't understand."

Victor turned to look at him more. "Call it a chance at redemption. I just need to do something good."

Dwight took a deep breath and let it out. "There's more I need to tell you."

"Are you sure?"

"I need to tell someone I trust, or I'll go nuts."

"Tell me what?"

Dwight leaned forward resting his elbows on his knees, while looking at the ground. "Remember the sheriff and his deputies? The guys I told you about who arrested me?" Victor nodded.

"Well, they didn't like the judge's decision to drop the charges. They hoped he'd send me back."

"You paid your debt. What else did they want from you?"

"I don't know...but it wasn't enough."

Victor leaned forward in his chair and said, "Tell me what happened? Take your time."

Using his shoes, Dwight stirred the dirt at his feet. Then, looking up, he tried to find a constellation. Then, thinking he knew what to say, he started, but then withdrew. He got up and walked over to the grill, seeing that it was still burning. Then he looked up for another constellation but had no luck. He walked back and sat next to Victor who said nothing, respecting his choice to wait.

A calm interlude ensued, populated with cicadas singing, screeching songs that raised in volume, then lowered so as not to deafen surrounding ears. Unknowingly, they absorbed the peaceful serenity of the night. Then a terrorized cat defending its homeland screamed fits and yowled in a frenzied fight that circled in heat, then circled again to end in a separate peace, continuing the prelude to the tortured night.

Dwight cleared his throat and leaning forward began to speak. "One night, I was out here working on the car. My day job was at a vehicle repair shop in town, so after that I would come out here and work in the barn to relax...drink a few beers.

I took a break and went into the house for a bit. When I returned...I thought I sensed something strange outside the barn...a presence." Then he turned to Victor. "You know, humans are like that. We give off a kind of energy. You can sense it." Victor nodded and Dwight went on explaining.

"So I went to the door and looked around. It was dark, the overhead light was on, but I didn't see anyone. When I turned around…I stopped." He used his finger to point. "There was this man wearing a ski mask over his face. He was wearing coveralls, like the kind you step into and then zip up to protect your clothes. Then, I heard someone behind me. When I turned, he was wearing the same. Both men had clubs, baseball bats, or something. Anyway, a couple more joined them." Then he looked up at the stars again, thinking.

"There were five, or six…. no, five of them. Then they, slowly, began closing the circle—and there was no place to run." He took a minute to gather himself. Victor just let him talk, sensing it was what he needed. They looked at each other several times, looking away a little embarrassed by the nature of the disclosure. "I'd been in fights before inside the walls. At times like that you think… take out one, possibly two, then try to get one of their bats and use it on the rest of them, swinging three sixty like a helicopter, which is what I did. But they were smart. They let me swing until I was tired. Then they jumped on my back, took me down, and I knew that was it. When they started on my head, all I could do then was curl up and cover." He raised his hands to show his crooked fingers and oversized knuckles. "They used a sledge on my hands. They tried to pull my arms off, but…they didn't realize the strength of my ligaments…so they gave up." He paused to gather himself. "Then they just clubbed my head and kicked me, until I couldn't see—and I went out. They just left me there in the dirt. Carrie found me when she came home." He lowered his head to say, "Later, the doctor told me that my clothes were soaked in urine, so …they all had a go at it."

A fluttering noise above their heads made them search to find its origin, which was a pigeon trapped inside having lost its way. Finally, exhausted, the bird flew into the wall, falling dead to the dirt floor.

"I'm so sorry, Dwight. I had no idea," Victor said, reaching to touch his shoulder.

Then Dwight began to chuckle. Looking at a section of the barn he said, "Six months in a coma. Do you believe that? They fed me from a tube! They thought I was brain dead, and they asked Carrie if she wanted to pull the plug, but no...she refused to let me go. I don't know if she prayed or what, but…one day I just woke up," he said, with tears filling his eyes, as if he still couldn't believe it.

Then continuing, "I knew something happened, but I had no memory. It took another six months for that to come back.

Then he perked up and talked without the previous overwhelming emotion. He acted as if the ordeal he went through was second nature. Victor smiled at his change in nature and hoped he would shake it off to enjoy the evening. But he wasn't finished with his gruesome descriptions,. And it didn't bother him as much.

"My legs were broken, so I had to learn to walk again. I wasn't talking all that well, so the doctors debated on whether I had brain damage…until I said, "Hold on guys. My parents used to tell me that, so I don't think I've outgrown it. The nurses got a chuckle out of that. They kept teasing me, trying to cheer me up."

Then losing his smile, he got quiet again. The song of the cicadas continued, the barn creaked, a gentle breeze brushed the trees pushing soft air waves through the barn.

"Why do people do that, Frank? I never did anything to them. Who am I, that they would do such a thing?"

Looking up at the stars, he said, "You know, Dwight, I've asked myself the same question many times…out in the desert, where the Milky Way touches the sand and the stars and planets feel so near that you could…reach out and touch them. But to try and answer your question…I think that most of the time we're just lost in a big fuckin matrix. That's what some call this world. Others call it…well, they call it a lot of things, but what they mean is that its a big fuckin mess. I don't want any part of it, but I have to in order to live. Just like everyone else. But I'm not gonna lay down and die. Fuck that and fuck whoever tries to put me there.

"I read one guy's description that we're like mice running in a giant maze trying to find our way out... and then another guy said we're like puppets with a million strings attached, and when the puppet master pulls…we have to follow. So, who the fuck knows?" There was a short pause. Beers were sipped.

"Some say it's just confusion, the world I mean. And the only time we come close to understanding any of it is when we decide if something is good or evil."

"You mean, whichever?"

"I'm not sure about the good. It comes, it goes, and it never stays long for that matter. But, at least, we know it's there." He sipped his beer, thinking. Then said, "It's like a surprise…you know, happy birthday! Then it leaves to circle back and surprise you, again."

"So, we just wait for it, then? Is that what we're supposed to do?" Dwight asked, confused.

"Hell. We're never ready for it. If we were, it wouldn't be a surprise," Victor said, smiling. "But we learn to count on it so we can live. It's about the only thing to look forward to because we know it's coming. Ever hear of 'Murphy's Law'?"

"Yeah. How does it go?"

"If something can go wrong it will. Or something like that."

Victor took out a cigarette and lit it. He puffed it a few times, eyed it as many, then blew a smoke ring. "Look, I'm not any smarter than the next guy…" he stopped and threw up his hands. "I take that back. Because I've met some of the stupidest motherfuckers on the face of this earth."

"Me, too," Dwight said, nodding.

"And I know for sure there's a darkness out there that seeks to take us. If we're not careful, we'll become a part of it."

"Like criminals?"

Victor flung open his hands. "Maybe. There's always a maybe and a but." Then laughing to himself, he said, "It seems to me that if evil had a job, it would be to make you think it isn't there so it could sneak up on you." Dwight nodded, then Victor got up to stretch.

"Enough of that shit. Tell me some more about the BOSS." He walked to the Mustang to look it over.

Dwight paused, thinking about what to say. He took a deep breath and exhaled loudly. "There's one last thing I need to tell you...to get it off my chest." They looked at each other. Then Dwight asked him, "Are you ready for it?"

"Yeah, you'd better tell me." Victor was walking around the Mustang like he was inspecting it.

"I think you'd better sit down," Dwight said, looking over at him. His eyes were far away.

Having seen his eyes, Victor tossed his empty beer in the garbage, which made a loud clunk, and sat back down motioning for him to begin, knowing what was to come was not good.

Dwight spoke softly but with a solid determination. "When I was well enough to start working on the Mustang, to get reacquainted with it...the engine sounded awful, a high-pitched grinding sound like screaming metal. So, I shut it off, and began my inspection, wondering what in the hell was the problem, because I would never in my life leave a vehicle in such terrible condition. So, I took things apart, checking this and that...then I got a flashlight and crawled underneath and, surprisingly, found some grains of sand on the engine block.

"I thought, how in the hell did sand get there? Then, slowly, like a snake slithering up my spine, a cold fear grew inside me. I tried to shake it off, but it persisted like a predator, as I checked all the fluid openings, hoping that it would somehow go away. "

He lowered his head shaking it side to side, tears in his eyes, reliving the moment, he said, "Those fuckers put sand in the gas tank, the radiator, oil and transmission." His voice began to crack with an overflow of emotion. Slowly, his face took on the form of a wounded animal.

"I had to rebuild the entire engine from scratch!" Breathing heavily, he turned to Victor and exclaimed, "You know how impossible that is with no money and claws for hands?"

Then he pointed to the Mustang. "That's why I know that engine so well! It's a part of me!" Then, taking on the form of a wounded animal he said, "Nothing like kicking a man when he's down."

Victor didn't know what to do or say, so he put his hand on Dwight's shoulder. Raising his head, Dwight said, "You said you believe in evil. Do you believe there's a God?"

"I'd be a fool to say no. It just gets cloudy at times." There was a heavy pause. They heard their own heart's beating. "I'd like to ask you something, Dwight."

"What?"

"I've done some things in my life…things I'm not proud of, and I'd like to make amends if I can." Then he looked directly at Dwight. "Would you allow me to make sure that the Sheriff and his men or anyone else doesn't bother you anymore?"

"Good luck with that," he said, stirring the dirt with his shoe.

"From what you've told me, they'll probably be back to check up on you. We need to be ready."

"For what?"

"For whatever may come. We don't know what they'll do. Dwight, I can help you. You've been their victim long enough. I can help you overcome that."

"How?"

Victor leaned back stretching. "Ever hear of military surplus?"

Dwight looked at him hard. "What are you suggesting?"

Looking around, he said, "You've got the barn here, lots of acres, good points for clear sightlines. Would you object to having some more firepower at your disposal?"

A self-righteous expression covered Dwight's face. "Hell, no! I'm all for it! Just as long as it's legal. I don't want to go back to prison."

"Everything is legal," Victor said, smiling. "Bring it on then."

"Good." Victor saw the wheels were turning inside his head. "I think it's time I told you about who I am, where I came from...what I've been doing. And the plans I have."

"What's your story, Frank?"

"First thing...my name isn't Frank."

CHAPTER 18

Agent Westhouse arrived at the Beach Front Motel with some new members for the task force---versatile men who were like baseball utility players with the capability to play most any position. The van was parked parallel with the side door facing rooms 4, 5, 6 and 7. Individual laptops were taken inside and the portable transmitter, housed in a separate compartment in the rear of the van, captured wifi signals from all around. Outgoing encrypted transmissions were read only by those authorized to see them. In the same compartment was the mini-server and a large battery to power the surveillance equipment with a backup.

It was explained to Westhouse, at his request, how the license plate ENZ-1560 ended up on the FBI van. Caldwell and Billings were convincing in their explanatory cover up on how Victor had slipped away after they had him cornered at 17 Oceanside Lane.

Boyle backed their story, giving them the evil eye when Westhouse wasn't looking, by giving praise of their efforts.

The door to the van was left open, because the motel was practically hidden from public view, and the only way people knew of it was because of the sign with the arrow pointing down the road. There was only one way in and out. Trees were the only things surrounding them in a three hundred degree circle. They were the only residents at the motel, so their security could relax some.

Room chairs were brought outside for the group to sit and discuss their plans, options, and new info when gathered---or to just relax breathing the ocean air and to have a few drinks as they were doing now, making use of the whiskey and beer supplied by Caldwell and Billings.

Westhouse had called for air surveillance to accompany their efforts. The special single engine planes were equipped with cameras capable of searching a six mile area, much like Google Earth, to help pinpoint the Buick, but nothing had come from it yet. They were all a bit frustrated and were sitting outside trying to come up with a new idea, because it was obvious that Victor Enmerkar was still in the area.

"What do you think happened to the Buick?" Caldwell asked.

"He's ditched it by now. Forget about it," Boyle said.

"It may still show up," Billings said.

"Maybe, but it makes sense that he knows we're looking for it, so I wouldn't count on that. If it shows up at all, he won't be attached to it," Boyle said.

"You mean a different owner, or a new paint job?" Westhouse asked. "Right," Boyle said.

"He could have disposed of it at a junkyard...one of those car crushers. Or he could have torched it on the beach," Westhouse suggested.

"That's possible. But I don't think he'd do that there. Too easily seen. The smoke would draw attention."

"Yes, you're right," Westhouse agreed.

The utility agents were sitting outside the circle, but could still hear.

"What's stopping him from using the Long Island Railroad? He doesn't need a car, does he?" one of them asked.

"No, he doesn't. But the train would limit his ability to escape," Boyle said. "He hasn't done that bad so far," Billings said.

Westhouse placed his hands on his thighs and stood up. The agents followed by stretching. Some took out cigarettes that prompted Boyle to light up.

Then Westhouse said to him, "I want to talk to you. Walk with me."

They walked behind the surveillance van toward the treeline out of earshot of the others. Boyle had an inkling of what Westhouse was thinking, but went along with it as a good player.

"What can I do for you Agent Westhouse?"

"What really happened out there at the beach house?" Westhouse asked with his hands on his hips.

"I wasn't there. I can't tell you. "

"But that story you gave me. Is that the truth?"

"It's the truth of what they told me. Why don't you ask them?"

"Did you believe them?"

Boyle stood back and eyed Westhouse. "You question me?" Boyle paused, looking directly at him. "Be careful, Westhouse. I was beginning to like you."

"Same here."

"Then what the fuck is your problem?"

"I don't believe their story. I can smell a cover up a mile away. And you're part of it."

Boyle looked away, then back and said, "That would be your problem, wouldn't it? I mean, you being in charge and all."

"Don't test me, Boyle!"

"What are you going to do? Fire us?"

"I've considered it."

Boyle laughed. "You know, you're just fuckin stupid. Those men are the best link we have to him right now, because they've seen him. Up close and very personal. And just for the record, I don't like them. How they got to be field operatives, I'll never know. But right now we need them! If Victor Enmerkar is, in fact, this sadistic CIA assassin, did you ever stop and think why he didn't kill them or me? He wants something, you fucking moron! Stop trying to be in charge so much and start listening. You might just learn something."

Westhouse pushed down his anger. He wasn't used to being talked to in such a manner. "What is it that he wants? Do you know?"

Boyle took a breath to enable him to repeat it again. "From the start, he's wanted to talk to me. Why? I don't have a clue. But in the letters, and now he…" Boyle thought for a minute. Then taking a risk, he asked, "Can I trust you with something? Just you and me?"

"Of course. Why would you ask that?"

Boyle threw up his hand. "Don't worry about that. Can I trust you?"

West house paused, then asked, "Is it about the case?"

"What the fuck you think it's about, asshole?" Boyle wished he hadn't said that, because he saw Westhouse fuming. Then he changed his tone. "I'm sorry. I shouldn't have said that. But can I get your word? Cops honor? Forget the FBI, forget the NYPD. Just two cops working on a case? I believe it's important, and the fewer people that know it the better."

Westhouse toed the gravel. Then he said, "You have my word. Now, what do you have?"

"First, let me tell you what really happened, then I'll tell you the rest. But Westhouse, if you screw me on this, I swear I'll---"

This time Westhouse threw up his hand. "I won't! Just you and me, ok?" He offered his hand. Boyle accepted it and they shook.

"Let's walk farther away, and I'll tell you what happened at the beach."

***

CHAPTER 19

Sunrise at the Taylor Farm was a classic picture of old country living like what you see in magazines. The sun's rays sliced through the trees to light up the back barn where Dwight and Victor were still talking. The overhead light was still on. Dim light permeated through the doors, unnoticed, as they sat upon the hood of the Mustang. The beer was gone. They didn't want any more tequila. They were just talking and relating to each other, looking out the back door of the barn at the morning light as it slowly ignited the green countryside.

"The CIA... man, I never would have imagined that of you," Dwight said.

"Most people don't, which is good. I'm not exactly your fictionalized portrait of someone like that."

"You look more like a...well, just an ordinary fellow, until a person gets to know you."

Victor smiled. "Well, I'm sure some don't want to know me, and others are sorry that they do. Just your average boring dude, who gets shot in the shoulder. That's who I am."

He had told Dwight about the incident at Mercer Street, that he had killed two CIA operatives who were after him, for previous murders he did not commit. Dwight was trying his best to make sense of it all.

Victor had been inspecting the barn previously, looking for the best storage areas. Many thoughts, some wild, were running through his head.

"So what do you think about using this loft to store some things?" Victor asked, looking up in that direction.

"No one ever goes up there. What are you thinking of storing?"

"Ammunition, mostly...a variety of explosives, Semtex, C4 with detonators...some assault rifles, hand guns, grenades, RPGs, Claymores...I'm getting carried away. Sorry. I even have a bazooka, but it's a relic, not even sure it works. Oh, and I have some excellent military cutlery for close encounters. Or we could display them on the wall, if Carrie doesn't mind."

Dwight paused, looking at him. "Yeah, just your average boring guy. So tell me, who's going to come looking for you?"

"Right now, the FBI and the NYPD. Detective Boyle will try and find me unless I find him first. He agreed to help me prove I'm innocent."

"Of those murders you mentioned?"

"Those and a few more they're trying to stick me with." Dwight paused. "And you fixed your shoulder yourself?"

"I had a doctor check it out. I just did what he said."

Confused, he said, "But doctors report gunshot wounds. Which one did you go to?"

"I have a number that I call when needed. They sent me to someone who took x-rays. So, I should be good to go in a few weeks. He's a doctor. He just doesn't have a license."

"Are you sure he's a good doctor?" Dwight asked, smiling.

"I trust the person that referred me."

"And that's why you want to stay here?"

Victor looked at him. "That's part of it. But Trina and I have a beach house we rented. We can go back there if you want. I just figured we could help each other, Dwight. So what do you think?"

"Well...," he said, then taking a deep breath, "it's fuckin fantastic. I don't think I can turn it down. But don't you think we need to go to a lawyer, or somebody like that?"

"Depends on how far along you are on this bankruptcy mess."

"We haven't signed anything yet."

"Good. Then it's just between us. I'll help you get out from underneath those debts, but we can handle that tomorrow or whenever. I need to go to the bank and open an account. And Dwight," he said, putting a hand on his huge shoulder, "I want to help you get back on your feet so you can get back your self-esteem. Then we could fix up the place. Make it profitable. You always wanted to go into business, didn't you?"

"Of course, but that—"

"I can arrange to have your mortgage paid off, so the house can be yours free and clear. And you don't owe me anything. All I ask is that Trina and I can stay here for a while."

"Hell. Stay as long as you want. I just don't want to go to jail."

"We won't let that happen. We'll get everyone together to explain what's happened and what the future plans are. Okay?"

Dwight looked at him, then said, "Sure. Trina and Carrie seem to like each other. We have several acres back there. You could build a house back there if you wanted to. I'll even help you."

"Do you know how to build houses?"

"I can learn, just don't get too damn fancy."

"I see this place as a refuge," Victor said, looking out at the hills behind the barn. "If anything ever happens that causes us to defend ourselves, we would feel safe here and fight back to defend ourselves."

"You mean like a fort?"

"Maybe, but it must be something inconspicuous to fit in with what's already here." Then he got serious. "I'm tired Dwight. I can't keep up the fight much longer. I need to clear my name and have a place to rest and regroup. And if things work out, a home," he said, smiling, "that would be a wonderful thing."

"You have a home, right here." He offered his hand. "You want to shake hands on it?"

Victor looked at his huge hand, then asked, "How about a blood oath? Just to keep it organic."

Dwight looked at him questioningly. "You mean like the Indian tribes on the plains?"

"Yeah, but that's Hollywood. More than likely, they got the idea from the Norsemen, or one of those Scandinavian tribes moving down the continent."

Dwight thought for a moment. "The mixing of our blood."

"Blood brothers."

Dwight smiled. "You got a knife?"

They moved to the back of the barn that was open and looked out at the rolling hillsides. He stopped to view the availability of space and strategic areas that gave cover. He took out a Swiss Army

Knife from his pocket and opened one of the blades. He then took out a Bic lighter from another pocket and flicked it, moving the flame under the knife, while turning it on both sides.

"That should kill any germs," he said, then looking up. "Any words of wisdom?"

"Fuck no. I'm just glad we're friends," Dwight said.

"Blood brothers, here we come!" Victor made a small cut on his palm, then gave the knife to Dwight who did the same. They made sure their blood was flowing, dripping some of it. Then they looked at each other and shook hands to inaugurate the oath. Dwight's hand, although surgically repaired, was twice the size of Victor's and was hard as a rock.

"You understand I'm your silent partner, and if anyone asks where the money comes from, tell them it's an inheritance and if they keep asking, tell them it's none of their business."

"I got it."

They unclasped hands. Victor dabbed his hand with a handkerchief, then gave it to Dwight who did the same. They started walking to the kitchen to get some coffee, breakfast, and then some sleep.

"I want you to take that sixty grand and fix up the Mustang...not for me, but for you."

"But I thought you liked it?"

"I do, but I believe the Ranger is better suited to me. We could both use it. And the Grand Prix. If you need more money, we'll work it out. Don't worry about anything."

"Whatever you say. We're brothers now…different mothers, but still…"

"What color are you going to paint Matilda this time?" Victor asked, smiling. "I don't know. I haven't thought about it."

"If I could make a suggestion, how about 'Acapulco Blue' or 'Gulfstream Aqua'."

"You have thought about this."

"Then put flat black on the hood with a tan stripe down each side, and a BOSS 351 on the raised part of the hood. Also on the sides."

"Cool."

"It's just a suggestion."

"What if someone asks me about you? What should I say?"

"Tell them I'm your cousin and Trina is my girl. You took us in because of hard times."

"What about the money? Word is bound to get out."

Victor thought for a moment, then said, "Tell them it's an inheritance from a distant relative. And if you can't think of anything else, just tell them it's none of their damn business."

Victor went to get his medical bag from the Buick, and when he returned Dwight told him which bedroom to use. Trina was already fast asleep on the antique brass bed. He opened the bag to withdraw a syringe filled with morphine, and set it on the opposite side.

He sat on the bed quietly and removed the bandage on his arm. He loaded the syringe and injected the morphine. Then inspecting the bandage he put it back on to be replaced when he woke up.

When he was ready to lay down, she was on the wrong side for him to make use of his right arm. So he gently pushed her until she rolled over to make room for him. After he was comfortable beside her, he took a mental inventory of what lay ahead. His plans for the farm were working out. He felt good about helping the Taylors have a real life again, opposed to the defacement and humiliation of a bankruptcy that was always made public in small town newspapers. He believed the good choices he was now making would place him in a better light with whoever he met in the future.

As he relaxed into the first stages of restful sleep, his mind was interrupted by a nagging thought——his country had lied to him and was trying to kill him coupled with the whole sordid mess of Grand Central—how could he ever explain it to Boyle? His first reaction would be to arrest him. But if he could just talk to him in a relaxed manner, he knew he could convince him that he wasn't responsible for those ugly murders. He knew the question was in Boyle's mind, so he was halfway there. But the evidence from the CIA files would exonerate him.

Then going deeper in thought, how could a military coup be in the works to overtake the major countries of the world...a changeover to a New World Order? That would just be absurd, preposterous, he thought. And unforgiving! He tried to put his mind around it, but it was just too big of an idea. Maybe the CIA files would tell him more.

Continuing to relax, his mind drifted to a poem remembered from his early days in the Middle East, sleeping in a hole dug at the bottom of a sand dune. It surfaced clearly to define his feelings on the subject.

'Let me tell you my brothers and sisters of the pale
night, all of us are not born equal in this pretentious
world where nothing makes sense if you think for
yourself. We're dealt a hand in the Grand Casino, but
some say the deck is stacked. Maybe it is. I don't
know.

But there's something wrong at the edge of town.
There's a circus without a clown with a sign posted
HELP WANTED! I need a job, but I'm not qualified.'

CHAPTER 20

The next morning after breakfast, Trina walked outside with Victor to sit under the trees to the side of the farmhouse on the wicker furniture, now spotted by time, that belonged to Dwight's parents. Victor wanted to talk to her about going back to Mercer Street, because the thought that he had endangered her, dragging her out of the city stuffed in the Buick to fight the smothering traffic of the Long Island Expressway kept nagging at him. He thought that giving her another chance to change her mind might be beneficial to all concerned. Of course, she would have the option to return if she so desired. The sun had cleared the sky, and a cool breeze rustled the leaves on the ancient oaks,. So far, she stood firm in her decision to stay.

The sun had commanded the firmament by clearing it of all clouds to leave a high azure sky. And a cool breeze rustled the leaves on the ancient oaks, allowing patches of sunlight to decorate the ground. Trina stepped on the light patches looking up to let the sunlight embrace her face to make it even more beautiful. Victor stood back and watched her playfully step from one patch to another, as if crossing a stream when the distance allowed, and each time she looked up her face took on a heavenly glow of something he could not express.

When they sat on the wicker furniture, he looked around at the shaded area with the light patches, and it seemed that they were in a place far away from the trouble they had faced—a safe zone where nothing could harm them. Victor realized it was just the positioning of everything where they sat that compressed his emotions. He was glad that he was there to experience the scene, as simple as it was to some. But to him it was glorious.

Trina had an idea of what he wanted to talk about, but she wasn't sure. She watched him standing there several steps in front of her, looking around at the trees and then up at the sun coming through that lightened his face as well.

He was such an unpredictable man, and she had asked him previously to explain more of what he did for a living. She figured that was the reason they were there, but ever so curious, she asked, "Is everything alright, babe?"

Turning to her, he said, "Yes, of course. Isn't it wonderful? This place, I mean. I know it's just a country farm, but it's almost like…well, I don't have the words. It's just wonderful."

"I know. It isn't everyday that you get to walk on sun spots. I mean, how many people can actually say that?"

"Not too many, I would think," he said, still standing and looking up.

Looking at him curiously, she asked, "Are you going to sit? And what did you want to talk to me about?"

He walked over and sat next to her. Then he said, smiling, "I wanted to talk to you more about my previous occupation," he said, pausing to gather his thoughts. "I know you think I'm a spy, but I'm not really, although I do that kind of work from time to time. The real name of the game is intelligence work. And to satisfy your curiosity," he said, touching her knee, then continuing, "I'm a field operative and, yes, I'm trained to be an assassin. But most operatives are trained in that manner anyway. It's just that some show more proficiency at it so they end up carrying the label."

"Like you. You're very proficient."

Victor nodded and smiled. "So to answer your question, I need to lay some groundwork to help you better understand. You may not realize it, but the world is based on a sophisticated system of lies from its foundation all the way to the top," he said, lifting his arm and smiling to accentuate.

"No, that can't be," she said, wrinkling her forehead.

"Let me explain first. Then if you want to ask questions, that'll be fine." She nodded, agreeing to be quiet.

"Like I was saying, the government lies to us all the time. It's gotten to be a big mess," he said, shaking his head. "And it's to the point now that the only way you can tell when the government is lying, is when their lips move." She looked at him curiously, and he continued. "Yes! It's that bad!"

Then he paused looking at her and said, "That's a joke in case you missed it. But there's a lot of truth in it."

"Can we skip the history comedy lesson? You know, get to the good part."

Shaking his head, he said, "I'm getting there. Just trying to keep it light." Then a shadow moved across his face to change his expression. "As much as I hate to admit it, we've been sold a bill of goods without our realizing it. You've heard the saying, 'America, land of the free and the home of the brave?' In truth, it should read 'Land of the deceived and home of the controlled.'"

"Now, I know you had to make that up."

"No, of course not," he said, laughing.

Then before he could begin again, she said, "I think you should take up public speaking. There might be a future in it for you."

He turned to her, and he was not smiling. Not even a trace. "Do you want to hear this, or not? You just may benefit from it."

"I don't see how, but keep going," she said, waving her hands.

She agreed, sitting calmly, while focusing her attention on the barn. She wanted him to fast-forward to the good stuff, but she was content to let him talk. He was trying to remain calm to get through what he had to say.

"Okay," he said, then he continued. "I believe it to be true that most people are too lazy to investigate what's really going on. And history will back me up that the reason the government lies to us is to keep us in the dark so that they may benefit. And it goes all the way back to ancient times. They're still telling the same ones today, only they're updated to blend in with modern times. So, if you want to be fashionable, just pick one that's most attractive."

"Now you made that one up?"

"They've been passed down from the beginning!"

"The beginning of what?"

"Time!" he shouted.

"How could that be? When was the first lie, then?"

A little perplexed, he said, "You got me."

"Well, there had to be a starting point in order to keep track of them."

"Nobody's keeping track! The lies have become the truth! That's the whole point here! Just listen, please!"

"I am listening."

"But you keep asking questions! Just close your mouth and listen!"

"You can't talk to me that way."

"Your life could be in jeopardy!"

"Oh, please," she said, folding her arms and turning away.

There was a pause. So he continued. "Alright," he said, taking a deep breath. "People want to be governed. They want to be told what to do, because they're so used to the lies. They just want to go to work, come home, eat hamburgers, have intercourse, and continue this cycle of laziness until they die in the grasp of deception."

"Wow! That took a lot! How long did you work on that?"

He jumped up and pulled her to her feet."Just forget it," he said, looking away. "You can call your Daddy and tell him to come get you!" He started to walk away.

"No, no! I want you to tell me!"

"Then watch your mouth, because I will let you go! Don't think that I won't!"

"Ok!"

"Do you think you can shut up?"

"Yes," she said, grumpily.

"Good!" he said, getting in her face so that she turned away.

It was quiet for a minute, then he started to laugh ironically. "You know, I've heard that shit about 'the truth will set you free'…it may be true, but the path to understand it can cost you your life." Then he turned to her and said, "Because the people that control this world don't want you to know the truth. They've devised a clever system of deceit, and their whole purpose is to keep lying to you for their benefit until you die. Choking and squeezing you with lies until the end." Then he interjected again, "It's a world system, babe." He shook his head, then looked at her. "That's nothing new, but it may be to you."

"I think I've seen something like that on the television."

"That may be. But I'm sure it was quickly removed. They own the news media."

"Who are the controllers?" she asked.

"That's a good question. Some say its people like the Rockefellers, the Rothschilds, and probably some kings from the Arab countries. No one knows for sure." He took a minute to think, then said, "It makes sense to me that just a few people call the shots." Then he turned to her, raising his arms. "I'm talking above the Deep

State." Then lowering them, he said, "Hell, they could be anybody." Stopping to glance at her, he said, "I've met and talked to a few members of this 'elite world group'."

"You've met them?"

"I've met some of them who disguise themselves very well. They're very smart, pleasant and courteous…highly intelligent, but very evil! And they like me. They said I have nothing to worry about as long as I keep quiet. I can't tell you who they are, so don't ask. You're better off not knowing! If I told you, my life and yours would…cease to exist." Then he turned to her again and said, "Does that sink in?"

She nodded. Then asked, "Do they know who I am?"

"Yes. If they know me, they know you. Can you stay on top of it? That is, keep your mouth shut and do what I say?" he asked.

She sat motionless.

Leaning toward her, he said, "You asked me about the controllers. Do you ever think for one minute that they will tell you the truth? Hell no! They tell you what they want you to know! Wars are created to feed the economic systems worldwide, and they finance both sides!" Thinking for a moment, he continued.

"I remember reading a quote...someone in Europe, I believe...can't remember the name now, but it went like : 'If you can control a country's money, it doesn't matter what the laws of that country are'. Then looking back at her, he said, "That goes completely against our Constitution and the laws this country was founded on. And if you believe that the history books are accurate… well, you need to wake up."

"Our history books are wrong? " she asked. "Oh, hell yes!"

"How can you say that?"

"I've uncovered a board of directors who decide what history is to be written. It doesn't matter that much what really happens, they just bend and twist it to their liking. And that's all of history, from the dawn of the written word to the present. So, in that regard, they can control our knowledge also. And guess who's on the board?" She turned to look at him. Their eyes met, as he re-gathered his focus.

"It's to the point, now, that we expect people to lie to us, because it's gone on so long that we believe most anything. That's what we have today. A new world full of lies that reach back to when we first learned to tell them." Taking a breath, he continued.

"I'm starting to ramble. Sorry. But getting down to how this applies to your question, I want you to start expecting that people will lie to you---no matter who they are, no matter where you are. Then never accept what they say, unless they can prove to you, or you can prove to yourself that it's the truth. That's ground rule number one."

She moved to speak again, but anticipating it, he put up his hand again.

"The way you do that is to just ask simple questions: 'Can you confirm that?' 'Can you verify?' 'What do you mean by that?' I know it sounds silly, but they will help you get to the truth, and don't quit until you get there!" he said, pointing his finger.

"The main thing is don't believe everything you hear or read. You've heard that before, but now it's time to put it into action! You've been deceived long enough! So put it back on them!"

He paused to let it sink in. She was dumbfounded by the simple logic that had now become clear to her.

Then he looked over at her and asked, "I'm sorry if I offended you. That was not my objective. But does any of this make sense to you?"

She said nothing, but kept staring at the barn. He could see her mind working.

"So what you're saying is that almost everything I have learned is not what it seems to be?"

"Yes! It actually goes back farther than Shakespeare. He wrote in Hamlet: 'There are more things in heaven and earth, Horatio, than are dreamt of in your philosophy.'"

"My God, you know Shakespeare, too?" she asked, turning to look at him.

He smiled and fought back his laughter. "I've spent a lot of time alone. And when you do that you read a lot." He reached out with his injured arm, steadying it with his right, grimacing in the process, to put his hand on her leg. "I'm grateful you're here, and if you choose to stay, I'll protect you as best I can. Because I don't want to be alone anymore."

She took a deep breath, looked at him, then asked, "What gives you the right to say all these things?"

"Because I've done the research and I've touched it…the tail of it."

"The tail of the monster?" Turning to him, she asked, "How do I know that you're not lying to me now?"

"Because you can't make this up. It's too fuckin big! "

"I believe you, baby," she said, touching his hand. "I don't care about them. I care about you."

"Then believe what I'm telling you," he said, earnestly.

"I want to, but my God!" she said, putting her face in her hands.

"Listen to me. I don't want to hurt you, but you need to know. Your government cares absolutely nothing about you. They will lie to you through their teeth and smile while they're doing it. You're nothing more to them than a product with a dollar and cents value attached to your social security number. All they want is your money, to keep you poor and middle class, put poison in your food to make you die early to control the planet's population---so that they stay rich to control the earth. And the Constitution and the Bill of Rights will be tossed right out the window." A thought came to him that changed his tone.

"Did you know that a cure for cancer has been around since the 1950's?" She turned to look at him. Then he nodded.

"And did you know that Thomas Edison stole from Niccolai Tesla the plans for the entire planet to utilize free energy from its mother source? And you haven't heard a word about any of that until now, have you?"

Trina paused, grabbing her head again. "I need a break, ok?"

Victor knew she was suffering from information overload.

"It's a lot to take the first time. It's not for the fainthearted, that's for sure. Remind me to tell you about the Federal Reserve sometime; there's nothing federal about it, and there are no reserves."

Looking away, almost begging, she said, "Please, no more now!

CHAPTER 21

The FBI started canvassing in Manorville at the County Courthouse, where shops and businesses stretched around it to form the town square. Then, gradually, working their way out to the homes and businesses along its streets and avenues in all directions. They found it to be an exhausting effort going door to door, and the people were unenthused by their presence, thinking what in the world would the FBI be doing in Manorville. However, some showed excitement to think they would actually knock on their doors, as if they were special people picked from a file to be included in the investigation.

They asked eagerly if working for the FBI was like it was presented on television, but the agents avoided those questions, as well as the many offers for coffee to sit down and have a chat. Frustrated by the lack of a positive response, they began stopping people on the street to show the photocopy of Victor Enmerkar, asking if anyone had seen him.

Those that stopped to look at it, looked up at them like they were crazy, as if to say 'no one like that ever comes to Manorville'. Others just looked at them with empty small town simple expressions and turned to walk away. Wherever they mentioned the name of Victor Enmerkar it was the same thing all over again.

Later, on their final stop at the Manorville Police Department, as a courtesy to give a futile update of their efforts, and more importantly to inject in them a warning—the suspect, a known killer who was a CIA rogue assassin, probably using an alias---was believed to be in the area. All Captain Hennessey said was that they would look into the matter, which told the FBI that they were not concerned about such things outside the monotony of their daily routine. The photocopy given to them was push-pinned to a bulletin board and forgotten about.

Their only bright spot of the day was when they asked questions at Lenny's Furniture Emporium and accidentally discovered it to be a cover for a brothel. The madame asked Westhouse if he was interested in furniture or a girl. Westhouse showed her the photocopy and his badge whereupon the hostess asked him politely not to shut them down, gesturing to the back warehouse, because it would put them out of business. And they needed the income from the tourist trade to keep up their high profiles.

Taken back by the quick revelation Westhouse stood silent to let her continue. Then as a gesture of good will, the madame offered all of them a carte blanche for the remainder of the season, if they could just overlook the fact that they were ever there. Westhouse graciously declined the offer and told them their secret was safe with him. Then she offered to give him a good price on a sofa, but he declined that as well.

***

The agents grew frustrated by their inability to get even one facial recognition from anyone and were losing hope with their efforts. It was difficult for Westhouse to justify expenses for their time spent. And like the members of his task force, he was tired and frustrated by the lack of results.

So, he decided it was time to disband the task force, believing their time would be better served back at Federal Plaza. They packed up the surveillance van, checked out of the motel, and Caldwell and Billings drove it back to the city followed by Westhouse.

Before leaving, Westhouse shook hands with Boyle, wished him all the best, and told him to call when he got back to the city. Even though they were still on loan, Boyle cut loose Caldwell and Billings. He decided to stick around to give it one last shot to see if Victor would contact him.

CHAPTER 22

Several days later...

Boyle was still in Manorville trying to make himself visible in the bars and shops in an effort to get on the good side of the people as compared to the sterile, abrupt asking of questions that the FBI made famous prior to that. He had been sitting on the benches at the town square feeding pigeons and gulls, hoping to gain acceptance from the old timers talking about what it was like back in their day---World War II stuff. But he wasn't very good at it. Even though he was a Marine and a Gulf War Veteran, they didn't trust cops. And he couldn't blame them really. He didn't have the gift of gab needed for such things as that. He was too direct and aloof. And besides that, he knew that cops in general did not have a good reputation.

He had hoped to get some kind of response that would lead to a trail he could follow to find the Buick and better yet the location of Victor. He knew it was possible, so he moved on to another location.

At the high school he found a baseball diamond and watched some little league games. He talked to some of the parents, but still no one knew anything or acted like they cared. But if you talked baseball they were all in. He actually became interested in a few players.

A few fathers thought their sons had major league talent and the pitcher of the hometown team, a young black man, actually reminded him of Bob Gibson, the hall of fame pitcher of the St. Louis Cardinals during the 60's and early 70's. Baseball was a game he had always wanted to play, but it just never worked out that way. As a kid he listened to the Yankees on the radio. There was no TV at the orphanage, and he collected pictures from magazines when he could get them. Mantle, Ford, Gehrig and Ruth---the old timers were his favorites. And he fought to keep them, because what he learned to do as a kid was to fight for what was his.

And now, thinking back through the cases in his career, he knew the reason for his longevity was that he kept fighting for what was right, which didn't always coincide with the law or make him friends in the department. He had always questioned things no matter what they were, but something was not quite right about this one. He couldn't put his finger on it. Maybe Victor was telling the truth.

This case was the most bizarre, baffling, outrageously peculiar one he had ever been involved in. Just when he thought he might have something---it went south into nothing. He felt impotent as far as rendering any of his investigative abilities to help capture this Victor Enmerkar. He was the one in control. All Boyle had been doing was waiting, occasionally coming up with something, and he hated it!

***

The game he was watching was over now, and people started to leave. He realized he couldn't wait any longer to be contacted. Duty called, and Lt. Langley would be wondering when he would return to work. He wasn't on good terms with him anyway. He liked Langley more than any other lieutenant over him. He made a mental note to give him a call. So when he got back to the motel, as he was slowly packing his bag for the drive back to Manhattan, thinking if there was something he had overlooked that would help drive the case forward, he received the call he was waiting for.

The display for the call registered 'unknown'. So, he pressed the answer button and cautiously said, "This is Boyle."

"Hello, detective. Are you in a hurry?"

Boyle knew who it was. He answered a bit annoyed.

"I can't wait here forever. I have a job."

"I am sorry, detective. That was unkind of me, but I had to be sure that it would be just us. May I join you for a chat?"

Boyle shook his head at the irony of the statement. "If you're coming, do it now. I'll wait, but be quick."

180

"Good," Victor said. "Would you be so kind as to open your door?"

Boyle, a bit surprised by the response, pulled his firearm. The call was still active, the phone in his left hand, so he said, "If you're outside just come on in."

Boyle readied himself to fire waiting for the door to open.

"My God, I thought we were beyond such silly games," Victor said in a tired, easy voice. "I know this must be trying for you, detective, but if I had wanted to kill you, I could have done that the last time we met, but I didn't. It's vital that I talk to you! Now, please, open the door and leave your gun outside. I promise to return it."

Boyle sprung over to the side of the door with the handle, his back against the wall.

He reached over and jerked it open with his left hand and snapping his arm in a raised position to point the gun through the open door; he saw no one on the outer left side. Then swinging his body to the right side of the door and raising his gun in the same motion pointed it to the right side of the door, but he saw no one there. Then, stepping through the door, low to the ground, and checking each side, again, with quick jerks, arms extended. Then he relaxed his arms, as he wondered what was going on.

He heard his phone ring again that he had dropped in the heat of the moment. He saw it laying on the cement and walked over to pick it up. When he answered, a voice said, "Put down your gun, detective."

Boyle saw the red dot floating on his chest to indicate someone was aiming a weapon at him with a red dot laser sight. "I have you dead to rights. There is no escape for you, or any possible way you can take me. Please. Put down the gun. We've come a long way, and I don't want to shoot you now."

Feeling impotent, Boyle placed his Glock on the cement.

"You can be like a stubborn child, detective, but I admire it. Now, kick the gun farther away like a good boy."

Boyle kicked it away.

"Thank you. Now, one last thing. Raise your pant legs, so I can see if you have that snub .38 you like to carry."

Boyle bent over to raise his pant legs. He removed the gun and placed it on the cement and kicked it away. He waited, then said impatiently, "Well...come on, if you're coming."

The red dot disappeared from his chest, and looking straight ahead into the trees, he saw Victor Enmerkar emerge from the green darkness carrying a lightweight AR-15 semi-automatic assault rifle mounted with the red dot laser sight. It was not pointed at Boyle, but lowered and ready. The weapon was so lightweight and balanced that he carried it by the grip and could fire it using one hand. The few days that had passed had been good for his shoulder. The rotation of the joint had improved tremendously and all that remained was the pain that he managed with the morphine, but he needed less and less as time went on.

He wore shades, a cheap ball cap dark in color, a green zippered military style jacket, and thin leather gloves--the kind you could pick up a dime with while still wearing them. He sauntered up to Boyle, and stopped a few feet in front of him.

"I'm sorry we have to meet like this." He removed his hat to scratch his head. Boyle noticed he still had most of his hair. "It seems dramatic, I know. But it's my hope that we can sit down like mature adults and talk freely."

Boyle eyed him, then the rifle. "The AR-15 doesn't lend itself to that."

The edge of a smile turned up at the corners of Victor's mouth. "That's one thing I like about you, detective. You are aware of your surroundings."

"Not all the time. How much did the sight run you? $700?"

"It was a package deal. I try to bundle when I can. It's cheaper that way. I had a Black King at one time."

"What's a Black King?"

"The most powerful sniper rifle Winchester ever made. Supposedly, only ten! Most people think they're more legend than fact, but I'm here to tell you I won one in a high stakes poker game. It had the black walnut stock you read about, and I tested it at a mile. Man, what an exquisite shooting machine...luxurious! I've read that it's accurate beyond that, but who's got the time to test that far? Truth be told, I didn't use it that much. It was like royalty! I kept cleaning it all the time to keep it pristine. It just wasn't practical for me to use it. I kept it locked up most of the time, brought it out to show every now and then. I ended up trading it."

"What did you trade it for?"

"An arsenal, plus enough ammo to last me for God knows how long."

Their eyes locked trying to feel each other out. Boyle's mind was churning away trying to come up with a way to get the best of him, but now was not the time. He was in control as usual. It was his modus operandi.

In an effort to change his frame of mind, Boyle asked, "How's your girlfriend?" Victor paused and looked at him intently. "My what?"

"Trina, I believe is her name."

They locked eyes again for what seemed like a longer time than it was. "I want her left out of this," he said, with a stern look.

"Too late. She's an accessory."

"I know, but accessory to what? She hasn't done anything!" Victor said, raising his voice.

"Have you forgotten that this is all about you? Anyone that helps you, they become a part of it!"

"She's never killed anyone! She could never do that!"

"Do you know how many times I've heard that?" Boyle said.

"Well, you're hearing it from me now!" He paused, then said, "I wanted to talk to you about her. If all this should go south for me, can you go easy on her? She's just a kid. I haven't forced her to do anything."

Boyle just nodded, then said, "Is this that honest talk you wanted?"

"No. I just thought…" Victor looked away, then back at Boyle. "If I put down the rifle can we sit like men and have that talk?"

Boyle waited. The odds of taking him increased dramatically without the rifle, depending on what else he was carrying. Boyle knew that he probably was, so he went along with it, saying, "Yes."

"Do I have your word that you won't try anything?"

"Are you asking me not to be a cop?"

"I'm asking you to put it aside and listen."

Boyle eyed him closely, then said, "Well, you know, Once a cop always a cop." Then he added, "But we can talk."

Looking back, Victor said, "No weapons?"

"I prefer it that way," Boyle said, knowing that Victor's exotic fight training would give him the edge. Still, it would be his best chance to try and take him down, especially having been shot in the shoulder.

"Deal." Then he said,"But how far are we going to put them down?" They stood there looking at each other, trying to decide the distance.

CHAPTER 23

"Tell you what. Let's bring out some chairs, sit and breathe the ocean air," Victor said.

"You mean me, don't you?"

Victor smiled, and said, "When you're ready."

Boyle brought out two folding chairs, sat them facing each other under the canopy of the walkway for the apartments. Victor sat and leaned his AR-15 against the wall of the apartment. Boyle sat also. They got as comfortable as they could, trying to find the right spot on the chairs. Boyle could see his weapons on the other side of Victor still laying on the cement.

"How's the shoulder?" Boyle asked.

"Better. It'll be good as new in no time." Then he looked around and said, "Here we are Boyle. Just you and me. At last," Victor said, trying to begin easily. He took a deep breath and let it out. "It's a wonder this motel hasn't shut down. Who in their right mind would want to rent a room all the way back here?"

"The FBI," Boyle said, with an ironic smirk.

"You got me there," Victor said with a nod, then he came back with, "How do you work with those guys anyway? They're some of the most uptight assholes on the face of the earth. They can't do anything without getting permission."

Boyle nodded, leaned back and started to muse. "A wise man once told me, the best way to deal with an asshole, is to become one yourself. That way when the asshole looks at you, it's like looking in a mirror, so he sees his own asshole, and then he knows what to do."

"And so do you," Victor said, laughing. "I guess that's right. Words to live by."

The laughter died. Silence. No one knew where to begin.

Finally, Boyle asked, "What are you going to do? Keep on running?"

Deep breath, exhale. "I've already told you. Nothing has changed. And you know my background somewhat, so there's no sense going there."

"How extensive is it?"

"How do you mean that?"

"Are you really the badass killer people say you are?"

Pause. "I do have that reputation, but it's because of numbers, not reality. I don't deserve the celebrity status they've given me. But people are people. They love labels."

"What are the numbers?"

"I don't know."

"Give me a ballpark."

"Too many to count, and I never kept track."

"That's with the CIA only?"

"Yes...there, and some other contracting jobs."

"Blackwater?"

Victor smiled. "Among others."

Boyle paused thinking, then said, "Explain something...if you will. I never understood how the CIA gets away with killing people...sometimes thousands like the Phoenix Program during the Vietnam War. Some would call that murder."

Victor sat up straight and spoke as if reciting from memory. "Executive Order 12333 explicitly prohibits the CIA from engaging directly or indirectly in assassinations. That's the form that everyone signs when they first come in that says they will comply with the order."

Boyle shook his head.

"But it's bullshit! How do they get around it?"

Victor paused, studying Boyle. "Manipulation of paperwork."

"How so?"

"When a situation arises that necessitates killing, it's allowed for reasons of National Security...a generic reference that covers most everything they do illegally. The reports are written up accordingly. And there's a lot of them."

"Did you write reports like that?"

"In the beginning, but as time went on and the numbers went up, my reports were assigned to a secretary at Langley. I just wrote up notes, the specifics of what happened, then she massaged them to look right for those that would judge them."

"The 'Kill Count Secretary'. Was that her job title?"

Victor smiled, enjoying Boyle's dry humor. "Yes, in a manner of speaking."

"Because of National Security."

"Correct. It's all bullshit, like you said."

"But you kept going."

"I did."

"Why?"

"I believed it was for my country."

Boyle leaned forward. "Do you still believe that?"

He looked around, then back at Boyle. He spoke soft but firm. "No. Absolutely not. That's why I'm here."

"But why me? What is it that you want?"

Victor lowered his head and Boyle saw his expression change from cold hardness to a more empty expression. Like he was lost. "I don't know what else to do, really...I don't know who else to talk to. I don't trust anyone," he said, then turning to Boyle he said, "...except you. You're an enigma, a dinosaur in a world gone mad, because you live by a code."

A pause occurred after that. Birds chirping, the wind rustling the trees. "I just do my job. What kind of shit are you talking about?"

"It's like the Corps, brother. You don't leave anyone behind, and I'm asking for your help."

Victor changed the position of his chair so that he faced Boyle more directly.

"I know those notes probably freaked you out a little, especially the first. I was testing your mettle. You see, I go through periods of depression and it helps to write things out. The first one was just a description of how I was feeling, who I really am, actually. It just came out in a rush."

"Does this have a point?"

"When I was overseas, I would fill up the emptiness by writing journals...mostly, scattered thoughts to make sense and help fight the demons that came with loneliness. You probably think I'm nuts, and I may be, but I wanted to get your reaction because of what happened to me."

Boyle opened his hand and asked, "And..." Victor took a deep breath and shook his head.

"You're really going to positively think I'm nuts, now, but there's no way to say it better, than to just say it."

"Ok."

"I got suckered into taking a physical, where they gave me a sedative to knock me out. And when I was under, they drilled a hole in my skull and put an implant inside to control my brain."

Boyle nodded, looked around, wondering what to say. He checked his fingernails, pulled on his ear, tried to get something out from the corner of his eye, then finally in a matter of fact way, he said, "You got to do better than that. Some popcorn and beer would help, but Jesus, man! Come on!"

"Think about it! Would I go to all this trouble, putting my life in jeopardy, trying to get your attention, if it wasn't true? I'm innocent of those murders at Grand Central!"

"You've said that. What about 10th Street? Vernon Fahey! Remember him?"

"That one, too! They controlled my mind from a remote to see if it worked."

"What worked?"

"Haven't you seen The Manchurian Candidate?" Boyle paused.

"Yeah. Denzel Washington. So what?"

"It's the same thing! The CIA never stopped those MK-ULTRA programs. They wanted to see if they could control me as the perfect assassin, then erase my memory. Only this time with new updated technology."

"That's nice, but you killed those people."

"No! They killed them! They are responsible!"

"But you did the killing! By law, you are guilty!"

"What law? Show me the one that covers that!"

Boyle sat there silent, not knowing what to say or do. His reasoning was slowly taking over to understand what Victor was explaining, if it was the truth. And he fought hard to get rid of the thought. Victor relaxed and let him think about it awhile.

Then he said, "I know it's a lot to take in. You've never been confronted with it. I get that. But Boyle, I swear to you by all that's holy, this technology has been around since after the Great War, and they've been perfecting it, slowly, to do what I've explained."

"What do you mean, the Great War?"

"I'm sorry. World War II. We brought over Hitler's scientists who were working on that very thing. We put them to work, gave them immunity, and here we are. Operation Paperclip. You can look it up."

"Is that the CIA?"

"Who else?"

Boyle paused. "Have you killed anyone since?

Victor thought about the incident with the Sheriff, but he was innocent of any wrongdoing. So he answered, "No, of course not!"

"How do you know?"

Victor paused, momentarily, looking away to focus on what he was about to say. "Because when it happened before, it was like my thoughts came from somewhere else, and I had no control over them. It was like I was watching the whole thing from inside my body while it killed those people, but I was helpless to refuse. Then after, I had no recall of it until it happened again."

"What about the notes on the bodies? Do you remember writing those?"

"Not until after the last one. My memory started to come back to reveal everything and nothing has happened since then. So what they put in my head must have malfunctioned. I don't believe it's working any more."

"And you've had no episodes since then?"

"No!" Then, remembering the scar on his head. "Here! You can still feel it."

"Feel what?"

"The scar."

Victor started to lean down, but then raised back up realizing that he was putting himself in a compromising position, which he hated because he just wanted to talk.

Boyle smiled at him. "Don't worry about it. I'm still a cop. This could be evidence." Victor took out his Beretta, pulled back the action and released one into the chamber, then leaned forward so Boyle could feel the raised area and see the scar. Boyle knew that if he was going to take him now was the time. But he hesitated. Then he leaned back and looked at him.

"Thank you," Victor said. "For what?"

"Trusting me."

Boyle laughed sarcastically. "You still got the upper hand, asshole! You've had it all along!" Then, he laughed sarcastically and said, "So hell, you must be telling the truth! And frankly, I don't know what to do! This is way out of my league, and probably yours! You'd have to go up against a government agency capable of fighting wars on their own."

"I know."

Boyle paused. "That doesn't bother you?"

"What bothers me is letting them get away with it. I'm tired of hiding like a rat. I'd like to have some kind of a normal life. You mentioned Trina. She's a part of it. I just want the chance to be free of it. I'm tired of killing! I don't want to do it anymore!"

CHAPTER 24

Boyle sat there nodding his head. Although he didn't like it, he was growing to like this unusual man. And he had always liked unusual things.

"I don't suppose you have any kind of proof? So far it's just what you say. Not good enough."

Victor leaned forward. "I know who did it and where it was done."

Boyle raised his eyebrows. "Where? Who?"

"Brookhaven National Laboratory."

Boyle frowned, like he wasn't sure what Victor was talking about.

"It's that place on the North Peninsula. They do a lot of nuclear experiments."

Boyle nodded to indicate he knew the place. "That's why you're in New York?"

"Yes. Dr. Carl Emerson did this, and if he didn't do it, he spearheaded the operation. He's a microbiologist, a neuroscientist, along with being a surgeon. He's worked with the CIA developing a toxin extracted from shellfish to put on the end of a needle that when fired into someone will kill them instantly. Why a shellfish, I don't know, except that they must be highly toxic. That should be evidence enough. And that's recorded somewhere."

Boyle thought for a minute, squirming in his chair. Then he asked, "Do you have any idea where he lives?"

"I can find out. It should be easy enough."

"And you say he works for the CIA?"

"He's like a freelance contractor. He goes where the money is. And he's protected. We're talking NSA, and other agencies. And forget about going to Brookhaven. They're tighter than a Nun's cunt when it comes to getting inside."

Boyle grabbed his head and started rubbing his temples and neck. "Do you trust me enough to give me your phone number?" Victor walked over and handed him his phone.

"I have these throwaways, so it'll be changing here and there." Boyle wrote down the number. Victor stared at him.

"Does that mean you'll help me?"

Boyle looked at him hard. "I'll help anybody. Because everyone deserves a chance. But it's a matter of 'can' I help, not 'will' I help you. The operative word is 'can.'"

"Alright. Can you?"

"I'm going to try."

Victor looked hard at him. "And what exactly does that mean?" Boyle began to get agitated.

"It means I'm not a lawyer! I don't even know if there's a law concerning this!"

"But you could find out."

"From who? What would it be classified under? Murders because of mind control? Come on!"

"But there has to be someone! The DA, perhaps!"

"It would be better if you just give yourself up. Then we could seek a lawyer. They're easier to obtain then."

"I'm not coming in! They would kill me!"

"Who?!"

"The government! They want me dead! Don't you get it, man?"

"Then how the hell do you expect me to help you?!"

Victor paused, walked around a bit, then turned back and said, "You're helping me now...by just talking to me." Then like a groan from a dying animal, he said, "Do you know what it's like to walk in my shoes?"

Boyle was taken back. "Of course not."

"I never dreamed my life would end up like this." Boyle could see tears forming in his eyes.

"You made the wrong choices," Boyle said, quietly.

Victor turned quickly toward him, and said, "Thinking they were right! I love this country! But the hard part to swallow is that they don't give a fuck about any of us! Remember Kennedy?"

"Which one?"

"Both! But I was thinking of John."

Boyle paused, wondering where he was going. "Only what I've read."

"Do you believe Oswald killed him?"

"No. He was a patsy."

"Correct. So who killed him?"

"Kennedy?"

"Yes."

Boyle paused. "It was a conspiracy."

"Yes, but who was in the conspiracy?"

"I don't know...several, I suppose."

"Right again, and the conspiracy was carried out by several highly trained shooters like myself. And, you probably don't know this, but the kill shot was fired by the driver of the limo. They cut that part out of the Zapruder film, where the limo slows down, then he turns around and fires over his right shoulder into the President's head. Bob Greer, or Bill Greer, I think his name was, and then the whole cover up conspiracy rolled out from there."

"So, it was the CIA."

"Yes, with others as well."

Pause. Silence, then Boyle asked, "So, what's your point?" Victor paused, taking a long deep breath and letting it out.

"I'm not sure I have one. It's in there somewhere," he said, raising his arms slightly, then letting them fall. Then he spoke with a release of bottled frustration long overdue. "But I just need someone to talk to, Boyle. And you're it! I'm sorry, but there's no one else!"

Victor looked at him. Boyle noticed his emotions and nodded, recognizing the same intense feelings of loneliness and helplessness he had oftentimes felt.

Boyle broke the silence by asking, "Is it alright if I call you Victor?"

Victor nodded without looking at Boyle. His thoughts were lost in the trees.

"We need a plan. We can't come up with one here. I have a job and need to get back there. I'm also going to need some knowledge on how things are done on your end. I'm not promising anything, you understand, but we need to get rolling on this because it's huge, enormous, bigger than I ever imagined."

Victor had turned to him, clearing his eyes with his hand.

"Remember Mercer Street? I told you then I need to get into the CIA classified files. I believe the evidence we need will be found there."

"Why there?"

"Because it's where every immoral, illegal thing they do goes. It may not even be at Langley. They could have moved it."

They paused.

"So, that's the plan for now. I need to get in there."

"How are you going to do that?" Boyle asked, astonished.

"I'll figure it out," he said, the glow returning to his eyes, the sharpness of his speech reborn.

"Would you object if I asked Mr. Kearney to join us?"

"Is he that tall guy you meet every now and then...has a limp?"

"Oh, you do get around!"

"He seems very knowledgeable."

"How would you know?"

"I've listened to some of your conversations. But I need to meet him first."

"I'll set it up," Boyle said,

"We should meet soon while this is fresh on our minds."

"No problem. I'll give you a call."

Victor walked over to pick up Boyle's guns. Then he walked back and gave them to him. "Thank you." While they shook hands, he said, "It's not enough, but it's all I have now."

"Just keep your head low. We'll figure something out." Then Boyle laughed, unable to control it.

"What's so funny?"

"I never thought I'd see the day when my suspect became my partner."

CHAPTER 25

Victor had talked to Dwight before about getting rid of the Buick, because it was a calling card for the police to come and get him. They talked about obtaining a different car in a trade or sale, whichever worked out to be beneficial. Victor said the engine in the Buick was excellent and asked Dwight if it would be possible to lift it to be placed in another vehicle obtained from a salvage yard or comparable facility.

Dwight made some calls. The man at the Long Island Salvage Yard said that he had a 1984 Pontiac Grand Am with a decent interior, no engine, and that he would consider swapping it for the Buick frame. He said they had a tow service to bring it out and then pick up the Buick. That sounded like a good deal to Dwight, but he wanted to look at the Grand Am before he agreed. The man gave them the address and they drove to the site.

Dwight looked over the Pontiac and told Victor he should take him up on the offer. Victor asked Dwight if he could get the proper connectors and he said that he could. So, they made an appointment for the Pontiac to be delivered.

Dwight went right to work on the Buick to disconnect the engine from the chassis. Victor helped him secure a chain around the exhaust manifold of the engine that was connected to a manual hoist from Harbor Freight that he had kept in the barn. When completed, he lowered the arm to let the engine rest on the ground where it was covered with a canvas.

Once the man from the salvage yard came with the Pontiac, he took one look at the Buick and said they needed to negotiate a higher price because of the difference in the bodies and interior of the Pontiac.

The delivery man was the owner of the salvage yard. Victor took the guy aside and said, "I'll give you two thousand cash, right now for the Pontiac, and you take away the Buick. But crush it. Ok?'

"I was gonna do that anyway. It's all beat up and shit."

"And I want you to kill the paperwork on this, delivery and everything."

The man's name was Roy, short, rough looking, big hands. He looked at Victor quizzically and asked, "What are you talking about?"

"I got another five hundred. Will that kill the paperwork on this?"

"You're kidding me."

"I may need some more things later. Are we okay with that?" Roy hesitated. "What's your deal? Who are you?"

"Someone that I need you to forget about, unless I come see you again?"

"Look man, I don't want no strings."

"And there are none. If I want anything else you'll be paid. I'm not the Mafia or anything like that. And this is cash," he said, showing him the money.

The owner paused. "So, it's a one time deal?"

"Unless, I come to see you again, which may never happen."

The man took a breath, then nodded his head. Victor stuffed the money in his shirt pocket. They shook hands and Victor said, "Thank you."

Roy pulled the Buick on to the flatbed truck using a hook and chain on the axle controlled by a winch on the side. After securing the wheels of the Buick, Roy got in the driver's seat of the salvage truck and after checking the money to see if the amount was there, he drove away.

Victor steered the Grand Am into the garage, as Dwight pushed from behind until it was in position. Dwight surveyed the engine compartment noticing where the connectors would go, and he took measurements to make sure of a proper fit for the engine to be lowered in place. They agreed to start work on it the following day.

***

Dwight and Victor rose early the next day and carried their coffee to the garage to begin work. Confident that the Buick engine would fit the Pontiac, Dwight put the motor mounts in place and helped Victor push and guide the engine hoist closer, steadying the engine in preparation for its descent. Victor was careful to use mostly his right arm as he adjusted the hoist a few inches, as Dwight used a pry bar to position the engine, lining up the bolt holes. Then using a hydraulic jack and a wooden block, Victor raised the motor using his right arm, as Dwight eyed the holes for the motor mounts until they were lined up to what he thought was correct. He slipped in a motor mount and bolt. Not all of them fit perfectly, but he got two of the four into place, one on each side front and back.

As they worked on fitting the engine, they did not hear an unexpected visitor arrive. At the door opening of the barn stood the Sheriff of Manorville with a couple of his deputies. The sheriff looked around the barn, then came back to them.

"Hello Dwight. Looks like you're kind of busy. What might you be doing?"

Neither Dwight or Victor said anything because they were straining to get the engine to rest on the last motor mount. Finally, they stopped, knowing that a trip to the auto parts store was needed to get a few remaining items.

Dwight didn't say anything but just glanced at Victor. Victor stopped what he was doing, raised up and turned around to look at the Sheriff.

"Who's your friend there?" the Sheriff said. "I don't believe I know him."

The Sheriff's name was Floyd King---big, robust, cocky, authoritative---not particularly that good looking, but not ugly either. He smoked an offensive cigar that was cheap and stunk from what Victor could smell. Probably the two for a dollar kind, or whatever was on sale at the gas station because they were beginning to turn stale. He had a prominent belly, which Victor couldn't understand. How could you chase anyone with that thing in your way? And from the size of his stomach, it was obvious that he didn't chase anyone. He just told people what to do.

And there was an edge about him that Victor picked up on by the twang in his voice, a glorified air of superiority that even though he was a public servant, an elected official whose salary was paid with tax dollars---he thought his shit didn't stink as the common man's did.

"I said I don't know you, boy. What's your name?" Victor didn't say anything. Just looked at him.

Sheriff King looked at his deputies and smiled, then spit in the dirt. "What's the matter boy? Cat got your tongue?"

The deputies and the Sheriff laughed. Then Victor looked through his stare into the heart of a man he knew was uncomfortable in his skin, trying to be someone he wasn't.

"First of all, I don't appreciate being called, boy. I do not respond to that. Secondly, why do you want to know my name?"

"Because I asked you."

"Have I done anything wrong?

"I don't know."

"Have I broken a law?"

"I don't know."

"Am I under arrest?"

Sheriff King paused. "Not yet."

"You don't seem to know much. Do you, Sheriff?" Sheriff King smiled. "Who's your friend, Dwight?"

Dwight looked at Victor who nodded at him, then back at the Sheriff. "His name is Frank."

"What's he doing here?"

"He's a relative of the family. He's helping me get things in order."

"Well, that's good," he said, taking a few steps farther into the barn to look at the Grand Am, he said, "New engine. I remember you were good with cars. Is that for Carrie?"

Dwight looked at Victor who gave him the nod again. "No. It's for Frank."

"Really," he said, then looking quickly at Frank, then back at Dwight. "You're helping him out, I guess."

"You could say that."

"From the look of the hoist there, I'd say you're thinking about going into business."

"You could say that, too."

"I do say that. Maybe I'll bring my car someday. Have you, give it a tuneup? What's the charge for that?"

"I haven't got that far yet, Sheriff."

"No discount for an old friend?" the Sheriff said, with open arms.

Dwight wanted to scream! Rip his damned head off! He decided not to say anything. The Sheriff focused his attention back to Victor. "So you're a friend of the family?"

"What seems to be the problem, Sheriff? Why are you here?" Victor asked.

"Just making the rounds. Dwight and I know each other. We had an altercation in the past. He paid for his mistake. Just want to make sure he's doing the right thing. Help out if I can." Then he looked at Victor. "What did you say your name was?"

"I didn't."

The Sheriff looked at Dwight. "Frank Greene," Dwight said.

"That's with an 'e' on the end," Victor said.

The Sheriff smiled and nodded. "You boys take care." He and the deputies got in the car and drove away. Victor and Dwight walked to the barn door and watched the car kick up a dust cloud on the gravel road.

Dwight looked at Victor and said, "See what I mean?"

"Yeah," Victor said, watching the dust trail of the Sheriff's car.

***

As the Sheriff's car pulled out onto the highway, Deputy Beasley asked, "What's with the new guy, Frank Greene?"

"Beats the hell out of me," he said, looking at him in the rearview mirror. "Run a check on him, Dave. When we get back."

"How did he spell that name?'

"That was Greene with an 'e' on the end."

After arriving back at the police station, Deputy Dave Beisley ran the name of Frank Greene through their computer and came up with a long list of names, none of them were spelled with an 'e' on the end. No name had an address remotely close to Manorville or

Long Island for that matter. When the deputy brought the results to Sheriff King, he said,

"There's a lot of Greens out there, but nothing spelled with an 'e' on the end. Nothing close around here."

Sheriff King studied the computer report, chewing on his cigar. Then he removed it and placed it in a wooden ashtray carved from the ring of a tree cut by a chainsaw, sanded and then varnished.

"Reports don't tell us everything. I want you guys to start spending time out there."

"Why Floyd? What's the guy done?"

"Don't have a clue. But I saw something in his eyes. I didn't like it. So let's find out more about him. And the others also. I can't believe Dwight is squeaky clean all of a sudden."

"What am I going to say to them?"

"I don't mean you have to drop by. Just make your presence known. Start by parking your cruiser at the turn off road. Make them think you're trying to catch speeders. Just be there like a nuisance. You know, get them thinking."

"Alright, Floyd."

He picked up his cigar again. "And grab a pair of binoculars. Go back in the woods a stretch and see if anything unusual is going on behind that big-ass barn."

CHAPTER 26

Victor began the discreet process of shipping assault rifles, hand guns, and what seemed like an endless supply of ammunition, most of which was stored in the barn loft, until he knew what to do with them and where they should be stored. He placed them in the house, closets, and other strategic places to be grabbed when needed.

He had a few claymore mines, but decided to hold off ordering anymore until he saw how things played out. He wondered if it was the right move, but after thinking about it, he placed the mines in staggered intervals undetected with the human eye.

He also ordered a Super Bazooka, bought online with an advertisement for free overnight shipping, along with several rockets which were quite expensive themselves. He was anxious to try it out, but he knew it was way too clumsy for a close encounter.

But what he did know, specifically, was that he did not want unwanted visitors to surprise them, day or night.

***

The longer range weaponry Victor had shipped was disguised as car parts. He let it come by regular shipment, regardless of what the advertisement said, the overnight shipping was not free, and it was too expensive. What he ordered was an RPG-7 anti-tank rocket launcher. The RPG stood for 'Rocket Propelled Grenade' and was quite popular with different countries and used by a range of terrorist organizations in the Middle East and Latin Americas. Its maximum range was 1000 yards, and it was highly effective up to 200 yards. It was front end loaded with a pistol grip, trigger, and an optical sight. It could be fired inside buildings because of its small, back blast. Then it could be unhooked in the middle and secured with a strap to be carried over the shoulder. It was powerful, cheap, simple, and robust.

The most powerful weapons delivered were specialized explosives such as C4, a versatile explosive, putty-like in substance that can be pressed into gaps, cracks, and holes in buildings, bridges, and machinery. Highly used by the military, it was dependable for demolition, in anti-personnel weapons (remote explosives), and in terrorist attacks.

Also included was Semtex, another plastic explosive used for commercial blasting, demolition, and military applications. Both were packaged in various degrees of intensity, and marked accordingly.

What he was most anxious to fire was the M20A1B1 Super Bazooka anti-tank rocket launcher effective up to 300 yards. It could also be fired from the shoulder, the barrel easily disassembled into two parts for compact storage and a strap secured to be carried over the shoulder. Rockets were loaded from the rear. The only drawback was when it was fired, a dangerous backblast zone was created up to 25 yards. Outside of modern weaponry, it was the most destructive, handheld weapon from WWII that he had ever heard of that he could now hold in his hands. Undoubtedly, an antique, a collector's item, one he could have fun with.

When it came, he was eager to test it, because he had heard that it could destroy a car or truck, until all that was left were just pieces. He had yet to see that, and when Dwight told him there was an old truck rusting away in the back among the hills, Dwight agreed to go out there with him to give it a test firing. He was amazed at the sight of the weapon, how army green and heavy it looked. It was five feet in length. Dwight carried the rockets and Victor carried the bazooka by a strap over his right shoulder. They walked out through the fields and taller grass, around a tree covered hill, where other hills rose in a cluster forming a pocket away from the sight of the house.

Dwight pointed out the rusty truck, which seemed to blend in with the surrounding wedged into a hillside. Saplings and various weeds had grown around it, but the outline of the truck could still be seen.

"You want to test it, big guy?" Victor asked. Dwight nodded, not sure of what to expect. He had seen pictures but that was all.

Victor slipped it off his right shoulder, and with Dwight's help connected it in the middle, and raised up the sight.

"You mean it has a sight, too?" Dwight asked. "Oh, yeah."

"I thought it was just a big pipe that fired a rocket."

"Well, it is actually, but you have to aim it from the shoulder, line up the sight, then squeeze the trigger. Let me show you this," he said, taking one of the rockets. "It loads from the rear with an electric firing mechanism. I'll be the loadman. You have to connect the wire on the rocket to the ignition system." He showed him where it was and completed the task securing the wire. "Then just aim and fire. But let me caution you. If you ever load one of these monkeys, don't ever stand behind it—whatever you do."

Then he looked straight at him. "Let this be your warning, Ok? Stand back and away from it, because the back blast is nasty."

"No problem," Dwight said, criss-crossing his hands. "Ok. Hoist it up. Aim and fire. When you're ready"

Dwight picked up the five foot long rocket launcher and placed it on his shoulder. He played with the sight, adjusting it some, then he looked over at Victor, who was standing to the side. Victor nodded to give him the go. Dwight lined up the target and pulled the trigger, but nothing happened.

He brought it down and looked at it. "What did I do wrong?"

Victor smiled, then said, "The safety...on the pistol grip...I forgot to tell you. I'm sorry."

Victor came over to show him while he released it. Then he moved to his previous position and nodded again.

Dwight nodded back, raised it again to his shoulder, lined up the sight, took a deep breath, let out half of it, held, and fired.

The rocket sizzled in a straight line with a loud 'WHOOSH', exploding the rusty truck dead center to burst into a cloud of flames with bits of metal flying in pieces, including bits of the saplings, which was nowhere to be seen on ground level.

What remained of the truck was a low burning fire.

"HOLY JESUS! WHAT A SHOT!" Dwight exclaimed. Then laughing, he said, "UNBELIEVABLE!"

Victor looked at it, and said, "I guess, it does work at that, huh?"

"You want to try it?' Dwight asked, laughing in amazement, lowering to the ground.

Victor was hesitant, because he knew that just to get your hands on one of the rockets ran about two hundred dollars. They were expensive little devils. He was thankful for his military connections.

"Come on. One rocket left. Might as well, right?"

Victor took the launcher from Dwight, secured another rocket in the rear, secured the wire in the back, then looked up at Dwight. "What should I shoot at?"

"How about that stump over there," Dwight said, pointing at it. "I tried digging it out once, but gave up. See if you can blow it out for me."

Victor positioned himself on one knee, raised the launcher on his shoulder, positioning his left elbow on his other knee to steady the bazooka. Then by hooking his left hand around his right hand on the trigger grip, he turned his shoulders, twisting them slightly, to test his arm. It was uncomfortable, but he knew it was good to stretch the injured muscles.

"You okay there?" Dwight asked, having noticed his grimace.

"Yeah. I'm fine."

Victor checked to make sure Dwight was to the side. He lined up the site, checked to see that the safety was off. Then taking the same breath in and letting out half, he pulled the trigger. 'WHOOSH'. The rocket blew the stump to tiny pieces in a fireball of flying wood chips.

"YEAH, BABY! TOOTHPICKS FOREVER!" Dwight said, putting his palms up to catch them. Then he stopped to look at Victor pumping his right arm.

Victor looked at him, smiling still on one knee. "I don't think anyone's going to bother us. Do you?"

"No way," Dwight said, still pumped and happy.

***

Dwight dug holes about the size of a grave among the hills where more rifles, guns, and ammo packed in military trunks were buried as a backup to be used in case of a semi-retreat. They were hauled to the place using the Ford Ranger. Caches of bottled water along with an endless supply of MREs were put in place, so that when the time came, they could all live and fight, regardless of the outcome. Victor didn't want that, but he believed in being prepared. He knew it could be overkill, but the area would serve as a last stand where they could dig in and fight, if needed.

His thinking was, "This is my home. And I'm not moving for anyone." Dwight told Victor that he would never go back to prison or let anyone beat him again like the Sheriff's men had done. Victor agreed to fight along with him, if needed.

A surge of happiness overtook him. A feeling of home, a place to defend, to come back to when the forces that sought to take him down encroached upon his space. He would be happy to die here, if he had to. He felt renewed, because his life had a new purpose.

What they didn't realize was that Deputy Dave Beisley was lying flat on his stomach up on a hill camouflaged by the trees, watching them through binoculars. He tried to take pictures using his phone but they did not come out clear enough to see what was going on. He laid eyes on the destructive power of the bazooka, and the delivery of the military cases, which he assumed held rifles, and supplies. He crawled backwards until he could stand unseen. He was wearing coveralls over his uniform. It was hot wearing them, so he took them off and tossed them over his arm for the walk back to the car. When he reached it, he tossed them into the trunk, got in, and called Sheriff King.

CHAPTER 27

Sheriff Floyd King had finished talking to Deputy Beisley about what he saw and decided to pay another visit to the Taylor Farm. He didn't say anything to his deputies and went about his work in the normal course of the day's activities. Then quietly and nonchalantly, he told them that he would be back later.

He drove around town thinking about the possibility of some heavy fire power being out at the Taylor Farm. His concern was that it could be unleashed at the wrong time and at the wrong people, regardless of the cause it was intended for. He didn't like it one bit. It was potentially dangerous to those involved directly or indirectly. And he wanted to get to the bottom of it.

He went through the drive up at Sonic to get one of their Mint flavored shakes to calm his stomach. Then he continued out of town to turn off onto the gravel road that led to the farm. Pulling up to the barn and getting out, he found both Victor and Dwight inside working on the Grand Am, trying to connect the engine to the ignition system. They were making progress but had run into some power difficulties, which they originally thought came from the battery, but after replacing it with a new one, the problem still remained. Like two physicians examining x-rays, they were trying to diagnose the source from where it came.

Sheriff King was his usual arrogant, stern faced, cigar smoking self, and wasted no time in approaching them inside the barn. He was strapped with a side arm that Victor noticed right off, as he stood up from the engine wiping his hands with a rag.

"Good afternoon, fellows."

Dwight raised up, knowing who it was just from the sound of the voice. He nodded while wiping his hands with a grease rag. "What brings you out again, Sheriff?" he asked.

"Oh, thought I'd drop by and talk to you boys about a complaint I had. One of your neighbors heard an explosion out here...a couple of them, actually. The complaint said there was smoke and fire. You boys have been burning brush out back? Shooting a few rounds?'

Victor eyed him carefully, not sure where he was going.

"Yeah, there's a big ass stump out there. It's been a pain in my side for a long time. So we blew it out," Dwight said.

"Did that work for you?"

"Yeah, I was thinking about making some toothpicks from the mess. If you ever need some, drop back by."

The Sheriff smiled. "Yeah, you probably could. What did you use? Dynamite?"

"Ah, yeah," Dwight said, glancing at Victor, then back again. "Used some that dad had left over."

"I'm surprised it was still good. Those sticks sweat, you know. Then they're not worth a shit."

"Oh, these were good. Used the rest of it to blow up a rusty old truck out there, too. I guess the neighbors complained about that, huh?"

"Well, they said it was a couple of explosions. But you know how it is, people complain, then when I investigate, it doesn't turn out to be anything in the first place." He paused looking around inside the barn. He noticed the Boss Mustang, while chewing his cigar.

"How's that baby runnin for ya?"

"Like a swiss watch. With all the work I've had to do on it, taking it apart, then reassembling it. "

The Sheriff slipped around the car, then said, "Yessir, you've done some work on 'er. Yer one helluva mechanic, Dwight. You should put a sign out by the highway to help draw some business.

And get yourself a real hoist. That monkey ass one ya got over there ain't worth a shit."

"Well, it serves the purpose. Used it to put that engine in the Grand Am."

"Well, how about that? Who's going to use that car?" He looked at Victor and pointed at him. "You?" Victor didn't say anything. "What's the matter? Cat got your tongue?"

Victor paused, wondering if he should answer, then said, "I'll be using it."

"Well, hey!" The Sheriff stuck out his hand. "Put 'er there, partner! You can speak after all."

Victor didn't shake his hand, but just looked at him. "What is it that you want, Sheriff?"

The Sheriff looked at him. "Right now, I'd like to shake your hand."

"Why?"

"Because you're talking to me. Now, tell me the truth, I'm rubbing off on you, right?" Victor laughed, then said, "Would that be in a good way or a bad way?"

The Sheriff raised his arms in a jovial way, looking at Dwight, then back at Victor. "Well, a good way, of course! I'm really a nice guy, fellows. Don't believe everything you've heard from the past." Then he turned to point at Dwight. "And Dwight, what's happened in the past, is past. From this point we start all over. I hold no malice toward you. Period!" he said, pointing at him. Then with a sign of false sincerity, he said, "I want you to know that."

Dwight was stunned. Victor was suspicious. It was Dwight's nature to forgive and forget. But the dark cloud inside him, caused by the unbelievable pain and rehabilitation he went through spearheaded by Sheriff King, was just too big of a jump to make any gesture to get on his good side.

Taking a deep breath, he said, "That took a lot of guts for you to say that, Sheriff, considering what went down here. And you still control the cards in this game. But I want you to know that I will cooperate, as I always have. Nothing has changed about that."

"Fair enough." The Sheriff stuck out his hand. "Will you shake on it? Just go easy because you've got a damn good grip there."

Dwight shook his hand without his usual strength. He was wondering what the Sheriff had up his sleeve.

"Good. I've been wanting to get that off my chest for quite awhile." He took a step toward the door, then turned back. "One final thing. Do you think you could show me the place where you used the dynamite?"

Dwight glanced at Victor, then back to the Sheriff. "Ah...yes. It's just out back in the hills."

"Can we walk there?"

"We could, but it might be better to take the Ranger. There's some ruts and things like that out there. And there's a partial path to follow."

"Good. I'd like to see where you blew out the stump and truck. You know, for the report. Just to make it official."

Dwight looked at Victor with a sense of dread. Victor returned the look with his own that read Don't worry about it. They walked outside the barn to where the Ranger was parked. Victor offered to ride in the back with his feet hanging off the tailgate, so the Sheriff could be more comfortable, as Dwight backed up the truck and drove it around the barn to the side and through a field of high grass. He followed the wheel marks where the grass was worn from previous drives, until they came to the beginning of the hills that formed a pocket where they used the Super Bazooka. Dwight pulled up close to where the rusty truck was blasted. There were roots sticking up and parts of saplings that were blown off from the force of the blast.

Victor hopped out first, then was joined by Dwight and Sheriff King. They walked to the blast site where Dwight pointed to the burn marks with remaining pieces of metal frame.

"This is where the old truck used to be," Dwight said, kicking some of the metal with the toe of his boot.

"Goodbye rusty truck, huh?" the Sheriff said, looking around at the ground.

"Yeah. The stump is a little farther down, but you won't see much there, either. Just a lot of wood pieces and a hole."

"Toothpicks you said."

"Right," Dwight said with a smile.

The Sheriff nodded. Victor stayed back by the truck. They walked down to the hole where the stump used to be. The Sheriff paused, inspecting the ground.

"So you say you used dynamite here?"

"That's right."

"And also for the truck back there?"

"Yes," Dwight said.

The Sheriff scratched his head and rubbed the back of his neck.

"You know, I'm having a problem believing that you used dynamite. The blast wave would have disturbed the ground more here. And it looks like everything just disintegrated, dynamite would have left a bigger hole in the ground. Same thing back there."

The Sheriff King paused, looking at the ground, kicking it with his toe. Then he came back with a question that startled Dwight. "So why did you lie to me?"

Sheriff King positioned himself so that Victor was in view also.

Lowering his head, Dwight said, "I don't know, Sheriff. I guess, because of what happened before, when you came with your men."

"The past is past, Dwight. I told you that. We start fresh from here, and then you lie to me like this? Makes me think you're trying to cover something up." He stepped closer. "Is that what this is? A cover up?"

Victor stepped forward and said, "Sheriff, I don't think you under---"

Sheriff King interrupted Victor, pointing at him with his outstretched arm. "You shut up and stay where you are! Keep your hands where I can see them!" He unclasped the fastener for his handgun. Victor stopped and knew that trouble was brewing. He was thankful for the secluded area.

"Now I'm trying to help you, Dwight. I don't want a replay of what happened back then. I don't want to see you go back to jail. You've done enough time. You've worked hard here trying to keep the farm going. I don't want to take you in, but if I'm going to help you, you have to help me. Now, why did you lie to me? What did you use to blow up that stump and the truck?"

Dwight squinted his eyes in a frown. "You're going to help me?"

"Yes, that's what I'm trying to do."

"No you're not. You're just trying to hook me up like you did before. That's it, isn't it Sheriff? You're not my friend. You never were. You just want to keep me down so you can check on me like a good ol' boy. I'm not your boy, Sheriff! And we didn't do anything wrong taking out that stump or the truck. You just want to hook us into something to make it look like you're doing your job. Well, you ain't doing your job! Your job is to get in your car and go figure out who you can bother besides me, because I won't take it! Not anymore! Not from you!"

Sheriff King took a deep breath. He looked at Victor, then back at Dwight.

"It saddens me to do this, but Dwight. Put your hands behind your back," he said, taking out his handcuffs.

"No," Victor said, stepping forward, but Sheriff King stopped him drawing his gun. "You hold it right there smartass! I don't know what you guys are pulling here, but we're sure as shit going to find out." He looked where the stump used to be. Then after a minute, he said, "Looks to me like you blew it out with a rocket launcher. Is that what you used? A rocket launcher?"

Dwight smiled. "Yeah. How could you tell?"

"I was in the military, dumbass! I know a few things about them."

"Actually, it's called a Super Bazooka. Military surplus. World War II. I got a good deal on it," Victor said.

"Well, there you go. That says it right there. It's illegal to have one in New York State. You boys broke the law. And you're going in. Both of you. Dwight, put your hands behind your back. And you Mr. Smartass, you stay where I can see you."

Dwight shook his head. "Sorry, Sheriff. 'No can do'."

Sheriff King came toward him, trying to knock him on the side of the head with his gun.

"I said put your hands behind your back, you big idiot!"

Dwight blocked the gun with his left hand on the Sheriff's hand, causing it to go off. Victor bent his knees ready to pounce, but paused, because Dwight seemed to have him under control. He watched them struggle, until Dwight turned him around in a choke hold from behind, his arm around the Sheriff's throat caused him to drop the gun. Victor moved quickly to pick it up, but Dwight did not let up with the pressure on the Sheriff's throat. He could see that he was choking him to death.

"Dwight, let him go! If you kill him you'll go back to prison! You'll lose everything, the farm and your life!"

"HE'S TAKING MY LIFE! I WON"T LET HIM DO THAT!"

The Sheriff was squirming and wiggling to break loose, his hands clutching at Dwight's arm that was just too strong. Victor picked up the gun and put it in his belt. Then he tried to break Dwight's arm away from the Sheriff's throat, but it was impossible.

He pulled the gun, holding it by the barrel and clocked Dwight on the head. Nothing happened. He kept on choking, as the Sheriff's face turned blue. Victor hit Dwight harder, twice, and this time he released the Sheriff who fell limp to the ground.

Kneeling on the ground and rubbing his head, Dwight said, "Why the hell did you hit me?"

"Because you were killing the Sheriff."

"That's the point! Eliminate the problem!"

Victor spoke softly and shook his head. "No Dwight. No." Victor was upset and felt his nostrils, but he felt no air. Victor was thankful that Dwight had not killed him. It was an accident, because the Sheriff was still alive when his limp body fell on the exposed root.

Getting up, he saw Dwight pacing back and forth. He said to him, "You didn't kill him, Dwight. Get that out of your head. He fell on that root sticking up like a thumb." He indicated it by using his own.

Dwight could see it. Victor reached down to pick up the cuffs the Sheriff dropped. Dwight still rubbed his head where Victor clocked him.

"You didn't have to hit me so hard. It's going to leave a welt," Dwight said. Victor noticed something about the Sheriff. He stood frozen looking down at him. "We have a bigger problem."

Dwight stood up thinking it would calm his throbbing head, but it only increased it. So, he bent over with one hand on his knee, and still rubbed his head with the other.

"What bigger problem…are you talking about?" Dwight asked.

There was a pause. The only sounds heard were chirping birds and distant, industrial sounds from Manorville.

"He's not breathing," Victor said, with a hurtful sound in his voice.

Dwight looked down. Took another step forward. "He's not even moving." He looked up at Victor and asked, "Did I kill him?"

"Looks like." Victor was kneeled down by the Sheriff's head.

He tried to turn it, but felt something wet. Looking at his fingers he saw blood. He tried moving the head with both his hands, but it wouldn't budge. Then lifting it, there was a sucking sound, as he saw that when Sheriff King landed on the ground his head was impaled on a sharp root sticking up that went right into the base of the skull. Dwight looked remorseful, but calmed down some after hearing what Victor said.

Putting his hand on Dwight's shoulder, Victor continued.

"It was an accident. You're not guilty of anything."

Dwight looked confused. "So no one's to blame?"

"No, not really," Victor said, looking at the Sheriff's body, then up at the surrounding hills. "But it doesn't look good for us...especially back here. And what's the Sheriff doing here anyway? That's the real question. You follow?"

There was a pause. Dwight felt the impact of what he was saying. "What do we do?"

Victor had been trained to keep his cool in situations like this. His ability to control his emotions, to reason and to problem solve was what kept him alive. Then arriving at a solution he said, "I was thinking, is there a remote place reasonably close where we could ditch his car. You know, shoot it with the bazooka?"

Dwight thought for a moment. "There's the landfill at Brookhaven. That's pretty remote. And there's some dugout cliffs to the side of it."

"Can we drive down there?"

"Yes, why?"

"I want to get rid of all the evidence. Fingerprints, everything. The badge and gun we'll dispose of later."

"And trash the car." Dwight nodded, waiting for approval. "Blow it up and burn it. I mean incinerate it."

Dwight nodded. "We can do that. I have a gas can."

"And Dwight, this is not your fault. I know you feel bad about it, but you're going to be Ok. It will take a little time, but you'll get over it. You know that, right?"

Dwight nodded.

"He was just going to interfere anyway," Victor said, looking down at the body. "This place at Brookhaven. Are they open at night?"

"No. But it's lit up somewhat. We can still drive down it."

"Are their surveillance cameras?"

"Not where we're going."

"Good. We should get ready to leave. It'll be getting dark soon."

CHAPTER 28

When they got back to the barn, the first thing they did was to remove Sheriff King's uniform and badge, his wallet with identification, and anything from the car that would identify him. Victor remembered to remove the keys to his Police Cruiser and put them in his pocket. He also remembered to remove the Vin number on the dash of the car, taking a flat end screwdriver to pry it loose. They used the Sheriff's undershirt to wrap the head, and then loaded the body in the back of the Ranger. They drove slowly to the garage. Victor got out first, started the Police Cruiser and drove it straight into the barn. Then he signaled for Dwight to back up the Ranger to the cruiser's trunk, so they could transfer the body.

When that was done, Dwight proceeded to remove the bubble lights on top. It wasn't difficult for someone who knew what they were doing. Victor assisted him by resting it on his good shoulder and then to the ground. Dwight took a sledgehammer and pounded them into many pieces that he put in a garbage bag and then placed it in the trunk. Dwight spray painted the Manorville Police emblems on both sides of the vehicle. The Sheriff's uniform was placed in another garbage sack and placed there also. The ID papers from the glove compartment were removed and placed in a barrel along with the Sheriff's wallet. Dwight lit a match to it and watched it burn. Victor took the gun and badge, placed them under the seat of the Ranger to dispose of separately. The inside of the Ranger was wiped clean of the Sheriff's prints, also the back where the body lay. The Super Bazooka was loaded in the back seat of the cruiser, covered with a blanket, along with a few rockets in case they missed.

Victor needed a shot of morphine. He was supposed to be resting it, but the present situation left no room for it. When he returned, he took an inventory of what needed to be done. When they were satisfied they had covered everything, they took off for the Brookhaven Landfill. It was close to an area that looked like a rock quarry where a bulldozer pushed the refuse where needed. Dwight drove first, taking the less populated roads followed by Victor in the camouflaged cruiser.

By the time they got there, it was dusk. Dwight pulled over on the main approach to the landfill which was in a seemingly remote area. Victor pulled up alongside him. They lowered their windows to talk.

Victor brought out a cigarette and lit it. Dwight saw it and said, "Can I get one of those?"

Extracting one from the pack, Victor sailed it like a dart through the lowered window. Dwight picked it up and lit it from the truck lighter. They smoked for a minute. The office area ahead had a couple of floodlights that lit up the immediate grounds.

"I want to make sure that no one's in the office, so if we wait a few minutes, we can drive around to the side. There's a road there that will take us down."

"I didn't know you smoked," Victor said. "I don't, but...you know."

"Yeah, I do," he said, enjoying his own. "Why don't we go on up there. If we see anyone we can turn around."

"Ok. If I keep going, just follow."

Victor nodded. Dwight tossed his cigarette. Victor did the same.

As they approached the main office area, there were no signs of anyone present. No cars or trucks. So Dwight continued around the facility and down the road that led to the excavated area for dumping. They drove down until they were completely out of sight on a level area where they could begin their cover up. The area was as big as a football field sunken into the ground with semi smooth walls all around. It gave them the appearance of a giant graveyard.

Victor drove the cruiser to the bottom of the northern dirt wall, where he thought the next mound of refuse would be pushed over to collect at the bottom. When he got out he walked to the back of the car and opened the trunk. He took out a pair of pliers from his pocket and a mini flashlight. He put on a pair of surgical gloves and positioned the head of Sheriff King to open his mouth. Then using the pliers he extracted all the teeth to place them in a small plastic bag. He kept moving his head in various positions to get the right angle of light. He struggled to get them out, getting blood on his hands. Finally, he went to his bag in the cab of the truck and brought back a roll of duct tape. He taped the flashlight on the lid of the trunk so he could tilt it to get the light he needed to perform the dental extractions. It was a bloody mess at first, but then the blood flow lessened because the heart was no longer pumping.

Dwight had followed him and stopped several feet away at a safe distance. He noticed what Victor was doing and grimaced at the thought of it. He brought out a 5 gallon can of gasoline and brought it over.

Victor finished pulling the teeth and walked to the cab of the truck and replaced the bag under the seat on the passenger side. Then he removed the Super Bazooka with the rockets and laid them a few feet away. Dwight soaked the body and contents thoroughly, then moved inside the car to empty the rest of the gasoline. He put the gas can back on the truck, securing it with a stretch tie with hooks on each end to the rail of the truck.

Dwight helped Victor connect the Bazooka and raise it to his shoulder. Victor had trouble raising his left arm that high. So he switched places with Dwight. He told him to shoot directly in the middle of the car. Victor loaded a rocket in the back end, then connected the wire to the ignition system. He backed away to the side and indicated to Dwight that he was ready.

Dwight lined up the sight, turned the safety off, took a breath in, let out half of it, held, and squeezed the trigger. The rocket sizzled with a loud WHOOSH leaving a trail of smoke like a clothesline. On impact, the car exploded in a dazzling fireball that lit up the area like a breathing evocation of spirit in the pronunciation of its mystery. Dwight was awestruck and felt humbled. They watched until the fire died down.

Victor brought out his portable ashtray that he carried in his pack. He set it on the hood of the truck. He pulled out another cigarette, offered one to Dwight, who took it. Then lighting both cigarettes from a disposable lighter, they smoked while watching the flames.

"When you're done don't throw the butt on the ground. Use the ashtray," Victor said.

"You are careful, aren't you?"

"It's what keeps me alive, Dwight. Think before you do something, analyze, wait to make your move. Like these cigarette butts. The police can extract DNA from the filter. Did you know that?"

"No. I don't stay up on that stuff."

"I always carry my own ashtray, so no one knows I've been there. If I was really careful I'd quit smoking. But...you know."

Dwight nodded, looking at the fire. "How long do you think it'll burn?"

"Long enough. I was waiting to see if the gas tank would explode, but I guess the rocket took care of that." They waited a little longer. Victor looked up at the stars. He pointed to the sky. "Cassiopeia. See it?'

"No. Where are you looking?" Dwight asked, turning several ways. "To the north. It forms a 'W'." He looked over at him. "See it?"

He pointed again, waiting for Dwight to connect the lines to form the 'W". Then Dwight said, "Yeah, Ok. I see it now."

"It's really bright tonight. Very distinctive."

"Who makes up those names? Cassiopeia?"

"The Greeks, I guess."

"What's it mean?"

"Cassiopeia was a queen in their mythology. Very vain, because she boasted that no one could match her beauty."

"So, she thought her shit didn't stink, huh?'

"Something like that," he said, smiling. "The Greek term for it is hubris."

"What's that mean?"

"Excessive pride. The Greeks considered it damnable, because it defied the Gods."

"How come you know so much about them?"

"I've spent a lot of time alone. So I began reading whatever I could get my hands on. And usually there's a library most anywhere you go. And you're always welcome there. Just think, what would a library be, if no one ever came?"

"Like a ghost town. Too bad the world isn't like that."

"You mean like a library?"

"Yeah, where you're always welcome. The only other place like that would be a car dealership."

Victor laughed. "Oh my God! What a tragedy! Don't go there!"

They laughed and smoked some more, until Victor finally said, "Let's have a look, huh?"

Extinguishing the butts in the portable ashtray, then putting it away in his pack inside the truck cab, they walked to the burning remnants of the vehicle. There was a low glow to the remaining pieces that were non distinguishable from what Victor could see. The heat was enormous and almost burned their faces, causing them to look away every few seconds. Looking toward the back where the body had been, they saw the outlines of the skeletal frame.

"Do you have anything in the truck to stir that around some?" Victor asked. "I got a flat end rake in the back. Is that what you're thinking?"

"That will work, I think."

Dwight nodded, then walked back to get the rake from the back of the truck and then returned with it. Victor took it, but before he did anything, he removed a handkerchief from his back pocket and tied it around his face to cover the lower part of it to guard against the heat. Then moving around to the back of the burn area where the trunk had been, he started raking the bones, until they dislodged at the joints to form a more level surface. Some of the bones disintegrated into dust as in a crematorium. The only thing left was the skull that stared back at them. Victor raked it closer, and using the flat end of the rake began pounding until it broke into pieces. Then using his foot stomped it until it was unrecognizable.

When he was finished, he looked up at the dirt wall behind it and got another idea.

He backed up to the bazooka, gave Dwight the rake and asked, "Go get another rocket, will you?"

Dwight didn't say anything. He put the rake in the back of the Ranger, then picked another rocket to lay on the ground when he brought it back.

"One more for kicks, huh?" Dwight said, smiling. "Something like that. Load me up will ya?" Victor asked. "Are you sure?"

"Yeah, just help me with my left arm.

When the bazooka was loaded and ready. Dwight raised it to Victor's right shoulder, then helped lift his left arm to steady the aim by hooking his fingers around the trigger grip. Victor nodded. Dwight attached the wire to the firing mechanism and stood back.

Victor aimed several feet above the fire to hit the wall, causing an avalanche of dirt to fall on the burning remains in a series of cascading thumps. A cloud of dust was released into the air that the wind above the rim quickly whisked away.

"Good shot," Dwight said. He watched as Victor lowered the bazooka. He helped him dismantle it and carry it back to the truck.

"Just curious...why did you do that?"

Victor stopped and turned to him and said, "Insurance."

CHAPTER 29

Before they left, Victor looked in the back of the Ranger and found another rake with teeth. He used it to smooth out any boot or shoe prints, and as Dwight drove the Ranger out of the landfill he also used it to remove the tire tracks. It took a little longer, but he convinced Dwight it was worth the time.

Driving back to the farm, they rolled down the windows to enjoy the fresh night air. Victor stuck his arm out the window on the passenger side letting his hand drift against the gentle wind current, feeling it with his fingers as if playing a tune. They didn't talk for a while, then Victor turned to Dwight and said, "I think it's best that Trina and I leave for a few days. There's some loose ends I need to tie up."

Dwight glanced at him. "Because of what happened?"

"It's a lot of things really. I'll let you know before we take off." Then looking over at him. "Ok?"

"Sure. Whatever you say." Then Dwight glanced over at him. "Is it something I can help you with?"

"No. God, no. You just keep doing what you're doing. You've also got the Mustang to fix up and the Grand Am to get running."

"Yeah, I'll get them."

"And now, your conscience should be free."

"How do you figure?"

"Your arch nemesis the Sheriff is no longer here." Pause. The cab was thick with silence.

"What is it? What's bothering you?" Victor asked.

"How long does it take to go away? well, it never does, to be honest. What you must do is change your attitude toward it. That takes time." Then, looking out the window, he continued, "It's like a divorce. Someone you love says they don't love you anymore and wants to move on with their life. You figure, *How am I going to get along without her?* You will miss her physical presence, but once she's gone, once you set up your life alone and get yourself organized, there is peace in the valley again."

There was a slight pause.

"You sound like you've been there."

"You mean divorced?" Victor asked. Dwight nodded.

"No, hell no! I couldn't imagine having a wife."

"What about Trina?"

He smiled. "We aren't anywhere near that."

"Ok. So where'd you get that divorce speech?"

"A wise friend of mine passed it onto me."

"Where's he at now?"

"Dead."

Surprised, Dwight asked, "Dead? How'd he die?"

Victor laughed. "Too many wives."

As they traveled down the highway, they came to a tributary of the Peconic River with a metal bridge crossing it. Victor told Dwight to stop half way across it. Then looking both ways to make sure no traffic was coming, he grabbed the gun and the badge and the bag of teeth. He got out, walked to the rail, and tossed the gun and the badge into the river. But he shook the bag of teeth until it was empty. Then he crumpled the bag and tossed it also. Getting back in the truck, he nodded for Dwight to continue driving. Nothing was said the rest of the way back to the farm.

When the truck was parked, they said good night. Dwight went to bed, but Victor checked the barn for any details of the Sheriff that they may have forgotten. Finding none, he went outside and sat in a lawn chair to gaze at the stars. After sweeping the sky, his vision fell upon Orion, the hunter, with his drawn bow and hunting dogs---Canis Major and Canis Minor---trailing behind him to the southwest just above the celestial equator. He focused on the constellation for several minutes. The longer he looked, the more it stood out to him. I am now the hunter, he thought.

CHAPTER 30

Several days went by as Victor and Dwight were working in the barn. The Buick engine was now in the Pontiac and Dwight was working out a few bugs in the electrical system that controlled the blinkers, the backup lights and also the brake lights.

Carrie had secured a job for Trina at the family restaurant where she worked. It had a steady turnover and, although Trina had no experience, Carrie was there to help her so that she picked it up quickly. They worked the day shift and filled in at night when needed, which allowed them to bring home leftovers, such as fried chicken, lots of ziti, sometimes pizza, portions of steak, and an Italian chili-like, spaghetti soup called Pasta Fazool, which kept down their grocery bill considerably.

Then one day, as Dwight was working on the body of his car, Deputy Jim Beisley from the Sheriff's Department dropped by to talk to them. They didn't hear him drive up in the cruiser, but they did hear the door to the car close. And when he walked up to speak to them, they were a little surprised.

"Hello. May I speak to Dwight Taylor?"

Dwight was under the hood with his hand on a wire when the deputy came into the barn. Victor was in the back looking for another ingenious way to strengthen his arm by the use of resistance. Dwight raised up and said, "What can I do for you, Deputy?"

"Hi. I'm Jim Beisley," he said.

Victor started walking slowly to the front of the barn.

"Glad to meet you," Dwight said, sticking out his hand.

"Same here," the Deputy said, shaking his hand in return. Then his eyes started feasting on the car. "That's a beautiful car. What kind is it?"

"A Boss 351 Mustang," he said, enunciating his words. "Is that classified as a muscle car? The end of the line for Ford," he said, nodding.

"She sure is beautiful."

"She's my lady," Dwight said, running his hand along the fender. "I named her 'Matilda'."

Beisley paused, nodding. "I'm sure there's a memory involved there. I hope it's good." They paused, looking at each other. Then Dwight asked, "What brings you here?" The Deputy tilted his hat back and said, "Well, we can't seem to locate Sheriff King.

I was wondering if he had stopped out this way the last few days." Dwight shook his head.

"Not here."

Hearing them, Victor walked over.

Dwight asked him, "What about you, Frank? Have you seen the sheriff?"

"Not at all," he said, shaking his head.

"What is your name, sir?" Beisley asked. "Frank Greene."

The Deputy smiled, looked around, then got right to it. "I was out here about a week ago, back in the woods," he said, pointing, "and I saw you guys shooting a bazooka back there in the hills.

"What were you doing back there?"

"Sheriff King told me to go back there to look around to see what I could see behind the barn." Then he looked at them both. "Of all things, why do you guys have a bazooka?"

Victor spoke up. "It's mine, Deputy. I ordered it online, got a great deal, and we were just trying it out."

"Are you guys planning on going hunting with that?"

"No. No, at all," Victor said, laughing. "It's just a collector piece. Nothing more than that."

"And you haven't seen Sheriff King, after his initial visit?"

"No sir," Victor said.

The Deputy looked over at Dwight who shook his head.

"It just seems strange that he wouldn't follow up on what I saw. He didn't like it one bit."

No one said anything. A sparrow was flying in the rafters confused on how to get out the barn.

Looking up, Deputy Beisley saw the trapped bird. "I guess he'll find his way out eventually." Then turning to go, he said, "Let me know if you see anything."

"Sure thing, Deputy," Dwight said. Victor acknowledged with a wave of his hand.

As the Deputy drove away, Dwight turned to Victor and asked, "What do you make of that?"

"He's just doing his job. Don't get nervous about it. Just stick to your story. You don't know anything."

"But I killed him!"

"No, you didn't! It was an accident! Get that through your head!"

"They won't see it that way!"

"All you have to do is just stick to your story. Stop worrying."

"That's easy for you to say. You've done it before."

Victor paused, looking at him. "Do you want to go back to prison?"

"No."

"Then get over it."

CHAPTER 31

A few calls had come into the Suffolk County Sheriff's Office that were passed on to Deputy Beisley, now the acting sheriff, concerning a fireball seen in the area of the landfill on Horses Back Road. Beisley notified the Missing Person's Squad, headed by Detective John Velasco, and brought him up to speed on the disappearance of Sheriff King. Detective Velasco brought Detective Ken Dorman with him to investigate the fireball seen at the landfill.

On the way there, they got the sense of being far removed from the city. They drove through open fields of undeveloped land on both sides of a road that were paved with no center dividing line. Pulling into the parking lot, it was empty except for a few cars of the employees. They parked close to the door. They got out, looked around with suspicion, and smelled the foul odors rising from the landfill. So they quickly entered through the front door covering their noses.

The office was stark with an economy of furniture. Few pictures were on the wall. The counter was a dull white and marked from use. A black telephone sat to the right. There was a door to the left behind the counter that said employees only. The woman at the front counter was plain, overweight and wore her graying hair in curls and waves, just enough to cover her ears. She wore a plain work shirt with snap closures and a purple bandana tied around her neck that she could pull over her nose if the stench was too much.

She looked up and said, "Can I help you fellows?"

Velasco stepped forward and said, "I'm Detective Velasco, my friend here is Detective Dorman," he said, showing his badge and ID. "We're from the Missing Person's Squad of Suffolk County. It seems that our Sheriff King has been missing for a few days. At this point, we suspect foul play. And we are here to enquire about a fireball that was seen either here or close to here. Are you aware of anything like that occurring?"

"Are you kidding me? My phone was ringing constantly a couple days ago. People wanted to know what exploded. I said, "Well, nothin' that I know of."

Velasco smiled. "Have you looked around the grounds to see if anything looks different?"

"No, I haven't. People are out on vacation. We run a staggered shift. Plus, sometimes people just don't show up or come back to work. It's hard to get the smell off your clothes. I could take you around, if you like. I have an old Bronco outside. It's comfortable."

"Well, that's nice of you. I don't want to trouble you though."

"No trouble," she said, putting up a sign that said BE BACK IN A BIT, as she came around the counter and opened the door.

They got in her Bronco. Velasco sat in front, Dorman in the back. She started the Bronco then turned to Velasco. "I can take you down into the pit if you want."

"What's the pit?" Velasco asked.

"Just a big hole in the ground. When the garbage piles high enough, the dozers come in and push it down there."

Velasco said, "Ok."

"It's really exciting," she said. Then she burst out laughing and backed up the Bronco and drove around the building. They continued down the road that took them to the pit. A huge hole squared off that was a little bigger than a football field. The sides looked scraped and perpendicular to the floor which was flat and graveled.

"Any special area you want to look at? It's all pretty much the same."

"Drive down to the far end," Velasco said, pointing at it.

She drove over to the area that he indicated where a lot of fallen dirt stood out from the rest of the walls that were smoother. Velasco and Dorman got out of the vehicle gesturing to the woman that they would only be a minute. They both looked around at the rectangular walls, some a little rougher than the others, then back to the mound of dirt that had collapsed the wall.

Velasco looked at Dorman and said, "Are you thinking what I'm thinking?"

"Yep," Dorman said.

Velasco nodded, then walked around the Bronco to the driver's side. She rolled down the window. "If it's not too much trouble could you get someone with a piece of machinery to stir that dirt pile around? We want to see what's under it."

"Why sure. Hold on," she said, picking up the mic from the radio attached under the dash. "Hello, garage! This is Nancy. Somebody pickup!"

There was a pause, then, "Go ahead, Nancy. This is Jim."

"Jim, can you get an endloader and come down to the pit? I got two detectives here with me and they want you to move some dirt."

Pause. "Yeah...I guess so. Just an endloader? That's all you want?"

"Better grab a couple of rakes too."

"Ok. Got it. See you in a few."

She replaced the radio mic and looked at Velasco. "So you think the Sheriff's underneath all that dirt?"

"I hope not, but that's what I'm thinking."

"What happens if you find him there?"

"That would mean a whole lot of people would come down here. We'd seal off the road, and this would be a crime scene."

"Oh, Lord have mercy."

***

When Jim arrived with the endloader per Velasco's instructions, he started to level out the top of the mound of dirt by turning the bucket down, so he could rake the dirt from the center to the outward edge, flattening the ground. He consistently worked the mound until it became smaller, then he hit something hard like metal. Getting down from the cab, he grabbed a rake and began working it around the bucket. Then, he waved for the detectives to come over.

He had uncovered what looked like the frame of a car burnt to a crisp. Jim kept working until the outline of the frame could be seen and in the back end some crispy bones were visible.

"Ok," Velasco said. "Don't touch anything else. We'll have to get a forensic crew out here to dig the rest. This is now an official crime scene," he said, talking to Nancy who had got out of the Bronco, curious to see what they found.

"You want me to move some more dirt?"

"Why don't you leave it here until the rest of the guys come. Unless you got something else to do."

"No. This is it."

Velesco looked at Nancy. "Why don't you go back to the office and post a sign that there is to be no dumping down here until further notice. Ken, you go with her. See if you can come up with some way to block the road. We don't want any unnecessary traffic down here."

Detective Velasco called for more officers to come prepared with shovels and rakes to help unearth what was beneath the mound of earth. The Coroner was called from Hauppauge, a town west of them off of 495. So they had to wait for his arrival. His name was Sidney Collier, a short man very prim and proper, a neatly trimmed mustache that covered his upper lip and then curved down framing his mouth as a fallen crescent moon. By the time he arrived, along with a County Coroner's Van with technicians, the police had blocked off the road and checked his identification before he drove down into the pit. A cluster of cars began to congregate by the dirt mound.

He drove an unmarked Cadillac SUV. He got out and was met by Detectives Velasco and Dorman.

"Dr. Collier. Thank you for coming."

"It's my job. No thanks necessary. What do we have here?"

"Detective Dorman and I are from the Missing Person's Squad investigating the disappearance of Sheriff Floyd King. That's why we're here. This area is referred to as the pit---"

"Just roll it forward, detective. What did you uncover?"

Surprised by the interruption, Velasco continued. "It looks like the frame of a car and some smaller bones, severely burned."

"Alright. Show me."

They walked to the end of the mound where the car frame and bones were found. Dr. Collier knelt down and with a pocket flashlight searched the area where the bones were showing through. Then he looked up and saw it was overcast. Some thunder was rumbling in the distance. Then he stood up and looked at Velasco.

"Did you bring portable tents?"

"No, we did not."

"Better call for some. We don't want to get caught in the rain."

"How many?"

"Two...three if you guys want to stay dry." A loud thunderclap was heard. Velasco pulled his phone. "I'll get on it."

"Better hurry."

***

The rain held off until the portable tents arrived. They were raised on poles with side flaps that could be lowered to block out the wind and rain. The thunder cracked and sizzled, sounding like cannons firing from behind the clouds, some with lesser power, then a tremendous boom rumbled the earth.

The tents arrived in time. The officers dressed in rain gear worked feverishly to get them up. Then rain came in torrents, at first causing the policemen and workers to hold the tents in place. The torrents continued until all present wondered if it would stop. Then, it lessened to a more bearable drizzle that extended throughout the night. Flood lights were put up on poles to shine in the area where the technicians worked with shovels to remove the major portion of the earth to reveal the burnt car frame.

What looked like tiny bone fragments were treated with exceptional care using brushes to whisk away dirt and ash. Gloved technicians placed them separately in a box. The crew recovered what they believed were all the salvageable fragments and put them in evidence bags. The car was burnt almost beyond recognition. The steering column remained but was now laying on its side. The engine block was intact but out of place. The engine was scattered in burned black pieces.

Deputy Beasley was called to help identify the car. He said right away that it looked like the shape of one of their cruisers. As they conferred, Dr. Collier said dental records were useless, because all the teeth had been pulled. Everyone knew it was the Sheriff's car anyway, so no one worried about identifying it.

***

Dr. Collier took the bone fragments back to his autopsy suit. As he examined the bone joints and vertebras, he arranged them on the table to simulate a skeleton with missing parts. The scenario that went through his mind was that a murder had taken place. But it was impossible to determine because of the intense heat that resulted in the fireball. It was only a theory.

CHAPTER 32

Trina and Victor decided it was best to go to the beach house on Rockport Road to stay out of harm's way. It was easy to unload their few belongings and easier to make themselves at home.

At present they were sitting on lounge chairs in the back patio sunning themselves. Trina had changed to a two piece swimsuit and Victor had removed his shirt. They both had their backs facing the sun. Trina removed the top of her bathing suit to reveal her beautiful breasts, allowing them to soak up the sun as well.

Victor glanced at her through his sunglasses.

"You're going to burn those tits."

"I wish there was a chaise lounge so I could lay down. My back side needs it, too."

"Go inside and get a few cushions. Then lay on them."

"Good idea."

She got up and went inside to return in a few minutes with the cushions and a beach towel that read Yankees all across it with the logo in the center. Victor noticed the towel as she positioned it in the right place to catch the sun.

"Are you a Yankee fan?"

"I don't know. It was on the sale rack." She turned to him and asked, smiling, "Do you like it?" Victor just smiled.

Victor watched as she removed the bottom half of her swimsuit to reveal her beautiful pear-shaped hips and buttocks, full and plump as melons.

"I've never seen this side of you." Then he paused to say, "Correction. I've never seen you from this angle."

She took a deep breath. "Do you like what you see?"

"I believe I do."

"Well, that's good. Don't let me fall asleep."

After a few minutes of baking in the sun, Victor said. "Let's go down to the beach."

"Oh...it feels so good here."

Victor got up. "Come on. I'll get the rifle."

After Victor was inside the house, Trina rolled over and looked at the sky. It was high blue. No clouds to be seen. She looked out to the beach and remembered she had forgotten to put sunscreen on her front, so she grabbed the tube again and began rubbing it on her legs, then her arms and shoulders, her belly and breasts. Then took her swimsuit with her. Also an oversized yellow t-shirt and a pair of high cut off jean shorts she had brought with her that exposed the majority of her thighs. Walking down to meet him, she was 'au naturale'.

Victor brought out the rifle. An HK-416 assault rifle equipped with an infrared beam to light up targets. It had a sound/flash suppressor, an optic sight, and a 30 round magazine. It was a badass weapon in anyone's hands. He had his bag on his right shoulder ready to go.

Trina looked at the rifle then at him. "You expect me to shoot that?"

"It's easy once you get the hang of it."

She paused, looking at it. She put on the t-shirt, then quietly said, "Ok."

They walked down to the beach and when they found the proper dunes to Victor's liking, he demonstrated the rifle showing how easy it was to use.

"So the CIA uses this?" she asked, holding the rifle in different positions to get a good look at it.

"Standard issue. It's a lot like the AR-15. Try it."

Victor handed her the rifle and helped position her hands, and the stock in her shoulder pit. They were standing in front of a larger dune and no one was around. "You'll have to get used to the kick.

But it isn't bad. Make sure you place your left foot forward to balance your weight." Then moving away, he waved his hand, telling her to fire when ready.

Looking around at something to shoot at, she saw a rather ugly looking plant that stuck up from the verbena that crawled on the dune like fingers. So she raised and positioned the rifle as instructed, then remembering to turn off the safety, she let go a quick burst of bullets at the plant that destroyed any sign of it.

Then lowering the rifle and looking where she shot, she said, "Wow. This could tear someone apart."

"Yes, if you press the trigger long enough. Now, choose something else and fire only once. Remember, press and release to control the burst." She turned to look at him.

"I know, but it's more fun to shoot a bunch of them."

"It's also a waste of ammunition."

Victor smiled and pointed at what looked like a piece of paper farther down the dune. "See if you can hit that piece of paper."

She positioned herself, raised the rifle, zeroed in with the sight and squeezed the trigger but three shots were fired that missed the target causing sand to be scattered around the paper.

"You did not press and release. You pressed down causing two needless shots. Try it again. Remember. Press and release."

She raised the rifle, and using the sight, she took a breath and let half of it out, then squeezed off one round that caused the paper to jump."

"Excellent! Good job! Now, practice that, until it becomes natural."

She continued firing the rifle until she became very well acquainted with it. Victor had her put on her swimsuit covered by the t-shirt, then crawl up one of the dunes and fire on her belly, propping the rifle with her elbows until she became comfortable with that position as well. It took her a while to zero in on the targets she chose, adjusting the sight for the right distance and positioning herself with the sun to her back so as not to give off a reflection to indicate her presence.

Standing at the top of a dune, she looked west and noticed a radar antenna that looked like two giant ears above the treeline.

"What's that?" she said, pointing.

Victor turned to look, then said, "That's the radar tower at Camp Hero."

"What's Camp Hero?"

"It's an old military installation from World War II. Once called the Montauk Air Force Station."

"Can we walk down there?"

Victor looked at the distance. He knew there would be cliffs to climb. "Maybe another day. I need to rest my shoulder."

"I like exploring," she said, pressing against him.

CHAPTER 33

When they reached the beach house, Trina decided to browse websites that aroused her curiosity about Camp Hero to learn its history. To her disbelief she read that early experiments in mind control using small children were conducted there. Later, the experiments were called Mk-Ultra. The giant radar antenna played a major factor in the experiments. Also time travel was mentioned to her astonishment.

Their routines went on like that for a few days, as Trina kept her eye on Victor while still sunning herself to take on a Mediterranean look. She noticed his energy increasing each day and the wound on his shoulder looked better to the point that he didn't need a bandage anymore. She coaxed him into the waves and splashed water on his shoulder, which didn't seem to bother it. Frankly, it felt good, so Victor submerged himself and came back up spitting water in her face. Whereupon she jumped him, being careful of his left side, to submerge him again. He tried floating on his back, then stroking the water in a simulated swimming motion. He felt the ligaments pop, to loosen and take away the stiffness.

"I think we've found the right therapy for your shoulder," she said. "Now, can we go to the radar tower? I've been very patient."

They were already dressed for the hike. So grabbing their jacket they walked along the smooth beach the next morning washed clean by the tide, the sun glistened on the water to make it look silver. The morning wrapped them in a cool affection, invigorating and refreshing. They breathed deep into the morning air, and felt comfortable holding each other as they walked, rejoicing in the fact that they had found each other despite the confusion and mental torment that lay all around them.

They walked arm in arm until the beach changed to a more rocky landscape, which made for an unstable walk. Using the rocks as stepping stones, they came to a road that looked like a truck path because of the impressions in the sandy soil. There was also a walking path that stretched on a gradual rise to the top of the cliff. They took the walking path that veered away from the road.

At the top there was a wire fence that stretched into a wooded area as far as they could see with a sign on it that read NO TRESPASSING. There was also a place where the fence was curled back so that people could enter.

Trina looked up and down the fence, then back at Victor. "Should we go in?"

"If you want to see the radar tower." Then he gestured with his arm for her to enter.

Trina smiled and crawled through the opening. Victor passed his pack to her and crawled through awkwardly using only his right arm and knees to support him. They saw another path through the brush and trees and they followed it until the treeline opened into a small abandoned village. The grass was maintained and the roads and walking paths, but the buildings had fallen into disrepair. Some were left open with junk scattered on the floor. Others were locked with warning signs that read OFF LIMITS.

They didn't say much on their carousing of the buildings. Trina stopped to take a picture with her phone. Victor saw her and grabbed it.

"Hey! What are you doing?" she asked.

He opened the back and took out the battery and sim card, then gave the phone back to her. "I told you to take out the battery and sim card. Why didn't you do it?"

"I did, but I wanted to take some pictures."

He paused, looking deep into her eyes for signs of lying. "How many times have you used it?"

She paused, looking around, then back to him. "I use it to look up things."

"What things?"

"Girl stuff. Ebay. Shoes. You know?" He paused.

"Who did you call?"

"No one."

He grabbed her wrist to get her full attention. Then with a look that frightened her, he asked, "Who did you call?"

She let out a gasp. "I didn't call anyone! I know you didn't want me to!" He put the battery and sim card in his pocket.

They stood there for a minute. Then she said, "I'm sorry. Ok?"

"Sorry can get us killed or arrested! You've got to take this seriously!"

"Alright. I won't do it again." She looked at him. "May I have the battery and card back please?"

He turned to look at the radar tower. "Come on," he said, pointing. "Let's see if we can climb it."

Trina shook her head, thinking to herself, "Men!"

CHAPTER 34

They walked through the village to the base of the radar tower that rose like a monolith. The AN/FPS-35 radar antenna at Montauk was an elongated oval, approximately 126 feet wide and 40 feet high. It weighed around 70 tons and was mounted on a concrete and steel pedestal. The metal door was open slightly and rusted badly. Victor put his shoulder against it, but it wouldn't move. Stepping back, he took two steps forward and using the force of his foot kicked it open wide enough for them to enter. He had taken out the flashlight from his pack and shined it around. Colored graffiti of different varieties decorated the walls with huge sweeping letters sized differently to spell out their messages. Trash was everywhere, splintered wood, pipes, scrap metal rusted to the point where you only wanted to touch it if you were wearing gloves.

Trina looked up the dark staircase and said, "You go first with the light."

She moved to the side allowing him to pass. "Just be careful where you step."

"I know. It's not like climbing inside the Statue of Liberty, is it?" They had gone to Liberty Island several days before where they encountered the two CIA operatives that he later had to kill on Mercer Street.

There were places where the steps had collapsed and all that remained was empty space. Previous explorers had placed wooden planks to step on. Trina paused to ask Victor how to proceed, not wanting to trust the wooden planks. Victor placed his feet along the bottom of the rail and pulled himself up. Then Trina repeated his steps as he reached out to pull her up as well, shining the light where she stepped. They did this a few times until they reached the top, where they walked out and circled each other looking in all directions admiring the view.

"Wow! What a spectacular view! You can see the end of the island."

"That's Connecticut over there," Victor said, pointing to the left.

"Everything looks so different up here. I'm...," she opened her hands to speak but nothing came out. Then she said, "...speechless."

They walked around the radar antenna observing the area trying to identify what they saw from this different angle. She came up to

Victor and hugged his arm to ask, "Where are we staying? Can you see it?"

Victor looked for a moment, then said, "You can see the house on Oceanside, but not the one on Rockport. There's a cliff in the way," he said, pointing. "Find the one on Oceanside, then look up a little to the cliff. See it?"

She put her face against his hand with the pointed finger. "Yes, I see it." Victor lowered his arm. "We're staying on the other side of it."

Trina thought for a minute. "That hill must be the one where I first saw the tower."

"Could be."

The wind was whipping and blowing Trina's hair. She turned to face it and tied her hair back to keep it out of her face. They could see Connecticut, Rhode Island, and the smaller islands in the Bay. Gardiner's Island caught their attention, curved like a hook. It looked deserted, untouched by human hands.

It was solid forest from where they could see, except for a few roads cutting through to connect to others disappearing in the trees. To the right they looked at more cliffs.

The weather was semi overcast. The sun pierced through occasionally to warm the chill from the ocean breeze.

They continued looking up at the antenna as they walked around it, like strolling in the park, not holding each other but separate, trying to recognize what they were looking at. Victor discovered a place to sit under it. Trina joined but sat a little away from him. They didn't say anything. They just listened to the wind whistling through and around the massive structure.

At times, depending on the strength of the wind, it gave an extended hum that seemed eerie.

Victor brought out a cigarette and lit it. The smoke was swept away by the wind causing Trina to catch a whiff.

"That smells pretty good. What kind are they?"

"Rothmans. It's an English cigarette. They're about ten bucks a pack."

"My God. Why is it so expensive?"

"Better quality, I guess. The cost of importing them."

"Let me try one."

Victor hesitated. "No. You don't want to."

"Yes, I do. That's why I asked."

He gave her the cigarette. She took a puff. Then gave it back. "What do you think?"

"About what?"

Victor smiled. "The cigarette. Did you like it?"

She shrugged her shoulders, smiling. "I guess. I'm really not a smoker."

"No shit," he said, smiling back at her.

They just looked at the view for a while.

"You can see ships coming in." She pointed. "Way out there."

Victor made no comment. Their pause was extended. Then she looked at him, and said, "Are we going to make it?"

Victor paused. He had been expecting the question. "I told you before you could leave at any time. But don't forget. You're an accomplice now. If you turn yourself in they'll try and play you against me. That's how they work." He paused again. "Is that what you want to do? Are you ready to leave?"

She paused, then said, "I don't know. Give me one of those."

Victor gave her a Rothman and using his lighter cupped his hand against the wind to light it. She inhaled the smoke, then took another drag to exhale it fully.

"I do like these," she said, holding the cigarette out looking at it. Then she turned to him. "So you're saying it's too late? We've gone past the point of no return?"

Victor took a deep breath and exhaled. He didn't want to answer her question, but it wouldn't be fair to ignore it. "If you really want to leave, I'll talk to Boyle. Try to make a deal for you. But more than likely it will involve me. Yes. It will be very difficult for you to go back now. The way it was. You've changed. I've changed."

"So you mean they will reduce my charge or maybe let me go if I help them get you." Looking away, he said, "Now you're thinking smart."

She took another puff of the cigarette. Victor sensed she was beginning to feel the reality of it all. It wasn't her fault. It was all new to her. She was so young and innocent to his way of life and its repercussions. She put her head on his shoulder. The good one, and said, "Why does it have to be so hard?"

Victor thought for a minute, then said, "Because we're pursuing the truth."

She raised her head and looked at him. "Really?" It was both a question and a statement, but more a question.

Victor nodded. "That's the way it is. You can lose your life pursuing it." He looked at her thinking of what to say. And then it just came out. "I love you no matter what you decide. I just want you to be safe. I care about that more than anything. We may get caught. I don't know. The odds are certainly against us. I can use the trickery I've learned, but sooner or later it will happen, if I don't get Boyle on my side. That's what this is all about. Getting him to agree with me. Then maybe we can add more people from there."

"My daddy would help both of us, but I'd have to talk to him first."

Victor nodded, knowing the answer ahead of time. "I'm afraid this is beyond his reach, honey."

"My daddy is a very influential man. He knows people in high places."

"What places?"

"Washington."

Victor chuckled. "That's who I'm fighting against." Victor took a drag from his cigarette. "One way or another."

"But not all of them," she said, grabbing his arm. "Not everyone is bad. You just have to find the right ones...don't you?"

Victor took a deep breath, smacked his hands on his thighs and stood up.

"Well, you'd better think about it. If you decide to call him just relay circumstantial facts. No names. If he's as big as you say he is, he could trace the call, record it probably. All the stuff police agencies do."

"I haven't decided yet," she said, looking away

Then he turned to her with a hard expression. "And if you decide to turn me in, I will disappear. Understood?"

"Yes," she said, sadly.

Searching her eyes, he said, "Good. You've come that far."

CHAPTER 35

After smoking another cigarette each, Trina said, "We could explore some other buildings down there. I read that those early experiments with mind control happened over there," she said, pointing.

"Where?"

"In those buildings. See?" She continued pointing.

"Alright. Let's have a look."

Knowing what to expect made the descent of the stairway easier. Victor used his flashlight again to illuminate shadowed corners. The sun was now hidden behind a gray cloud mass moving in. Upon reaching the front door, they were happy to see that it was still open. They squeezed through sideways and hugged each other having successively completed their efforts.

Camp Hero was originally a coastal defense station disguised as a fishing village. Its location was chosen to prevent a potential invasion of New York from the sea during World War II. Three gun batteries were built, two with and another one with two were built. All three consisted mainly of a large concrete bunker covered with earth. Everything was still there except the guns and the bunkers had been sealed up with concrete.

Walking to the central area of the village, highlighted by a circular road with buildings all around it, the place looked like a ghost town. They explored some buildings off the circle that allowed them entry. Once inside they saw most of the electronic equipment had been removed and in some cases ripped out by whoever had need of them. What they found were remnants of a time gone by.

In a back corner of the area, Trina noticed a manhole cover slightly ajar. She remembered seeing others they had passed that were cemented closed, but this one looked open. She called Victor over.

"Victor. Come here." She stood there beckoning with her hand.

He walked over to her and asked, "What can I do for you, my dear?" he asked, imitating a grand gentleman.

Pointing down, she said, "Look what I found."

Victor looked where she was pointing, then back at her. "What about it?"

"Don't you want to go down there and have a look?"

"Not particularly. Do you?"

"Yes, but I don't want to go alone. Come with me." she pleaded. He paused. "If I don't, you'll make me regret it, won't you?"

She smiled at him playfully. He paused, looking into her eyes. Then he walked over behind a building and after searching a bit, picked up a piece of metal. He brought it back to help move the heavy cover, sliding it to the side.

"Does your flashlight still work?" she asked.

"Yeah."

"After you," she said smiling.

Victor shined the light down the hole. There was a ladder to lower him to the floor of the underground place. The bottom looked dry, which was good. He stuck the end of the flashlight in his mouth to enable him to descend the ladder. When his feet were on solid ground, he looked around and saw tunnels leading in both directions. One to the left, another to the right.

"Are you ready? I'm coming down," she said. Victor eyed the bulbous symmetry of her perfect backside on her descent of the ladder. One side rising as the other lowered in a slow, piston-like journey to balance at the end. He shined the light both ways to show her a trail of water trickling to lower ground that they followed to the right, and then left to enter a larger room that looked like a centralized area for laboratory experiments and operations perhaps.

"I didn't expect to see this here," she said. "What do you think it is...or was?"

"I'm not sure," Victor said, inspecting the walls and ceiling braced by some kind of steel support.

There was a light switch that he turned on that lit fluorescents in the room flooding it with light. After a minute Victor heard the sound of talking. Then a sound like the door to a truck shutting. An engine starting. He sensed it moving toward them. He grabbed Trina's arm and they ducked down a side tunnel where they hid in the shadows. The truck entered the room and with the guidance of another man maneuvered the close right turn. Then he pointed to the driver to take that tunnel. The driver stopped and got out to stretch his legs while talking to the other man.

"Ok, Norm. I'll probably be back tomorrow," the driver said, looking around listening to his voice echo in the tunnel.

"Alright, just give me a call. Ok?"

"Got it. Say listen, why am I hauling all this stuff out of here? Do you have any idea?

I'm sorry," Norm said, shaking his head. "They should have explained that to you. But it's just like those damned government bureaucrats. Always too busy to give you the straight facts." He stopped to light a cigarette and looked up. "I'm surprised these lights still work. I thought I'd turned them off. Anyway, maybe I can fill in the blanks for you.

"When this place was called the Montauk Air Force Station, they donated the above ground area to New York State to be turned into a park. Now get this, in the deed that's on file at the Suffolk county courthouse, it states that the underground part is still government property. So they can do whatever they want to with it. And that's the reason you see all this, and that's why you're hauling all that stuff out of here. Someone else is taking over. And unless things change, because you never know when you deal with the government, state or federal---this is where they'll do the experiments."

"Who? What kind of experiments?"

"I don't ask, and I don't want to know. It's just better that way. I have a family to support. This job pays too much for me to go asking a bunch of questions that could ruffle someone's feathers. I know how to keep my mouth shut, you know what I mean?"

"I hear that," the driver said, tossing his cigarette. "I'll see you."

"Hey. Don't go giving out my number. Most people don't know I'm here, and that's fine with me."

The driver waved his hand and the truck roared down the tunnel with loud echoes. The man stood there and watched the truck. Then looking up, he walked over to the light switch and flipped it off. Using his flashlight, he walked back the way he came.

CHAPTER 36

"What was that all about?" Trina asked, turning to Victor.

"I'm not sure," he said, turning on the flashlight. Then he pointed at the truck. "Let's follow it."

They walked down a tunnel with the flashlight off so the driver wouldn't glance in his mirror and see the light. The tunnel widened as they walked into a concrete passageway. The outside light gradually grew brighter and was enough to see. They walked until they reached a road that looked out to the beach. The truck had pulled onto the road that connected to highway 27. They were standing at the opening to a concrete bunker built into the bluff.

Victor looked back at the road, then looked at the bunker again.

"Looks like they have access to deliver whatever they need. If they don't want to drive inside, they could just unload here, then put it on wheeled carts to push inside."

"I heard that man say someone else is taking over. And then he mentioned the government. Does that mean anything to you?" Trina asked.

"Maybe." Victor thought for a minute, then said, "Let's walk back a ways."

Turning on the flashlight, they walked back to the huge room. Along the way Victor shined the light on a ventilator system in a place where generators used to be. There were air conditioning ducts and vacuum tube computers still in place. Reading the labels on another piece of equipment, he read 'Amplitron', which he assumed was a kind of amplifier for the signal piped in from the 'Sage' radar dish, where they had climbed to stand at its base.

Moving on, they came to rooms that looked like apartments, some with old furniture, tables that looked like counters, and cages lined up along a wall.

"What were the cages used for?" Trina asked.

Victor paused, not wanting to answer. Then he said, "I don't think I want to know."

"Animals, do you think?" she asked. Victor looked at her and said nothing. Trina stopped. "You don't mean…?"

Victor had walked a few paces in front of her, stopped, then looked back.

"We don't know anything," he said, taking her hand. "And keep your voice down. There may be others."

"Give me the battery and sim card. I want to take some pictures."

Victor hesitated. "Alright. Just a few. He gave back the battery and sim card and shined the light so she could put them in.

"Does your camera have a flash?"

"Yes."

He looked up the tunnel, then back. "I guess it's alright. Go ahead."

She commenced taking pictures of everything she thought was important. He pointed at two upright electronic receivers that she missed. She lined up the shots then snapped the pictures.

They explored other tunnels branching off from the centralized room. And there were more rooms similar to the one they had seen, but some were more business oriented with roll chairs and desks and lamps on top of the desks. Filing cabinets and metal storage units lined the walls. Additional rooms with electronic equipment were seen. Trina took more pictures. On her way out of the room, she saw something that looked like a barber's chair, but with wires coming out of it.

When they were back at the beach house, Trina used her laptop to look up the information again. She turned to him and said, "Didn't you tell me that the government conducted experiments on children after the War?"

"Yes."

"When I looked up that information on the internet, Camp Hero came up." He turned quickly to her. "It did?"

"It was one of those places. Maybe that's where some of the experiments took place. When they operated on your head. Was it there, do you think?"

"No, no. That was…somewhere else," he said, rubbing the scar on his head. "Do you think they brainwashed you?"

He turned to look at her. "You watch too many movies."

Trina could tell he wasn't in the mood to talk. Their conversation about it stopped for a while. Trina made some sandwiches, but Victor wasn't hungry. He was tired and went upstairs to lay down. Renegade thoughts entered his mind and fought to take hold, but he refused to give them space. He fell into a broken sleep.

***

After eating the sandwiches Trina made, she went outside to sit on the porch and look up at the sky. A shooting star shot across it to quickly disappear. The heavens felt alive to her. She believed there was some kind of intelligence out there. Thinking back to her conversation with Victor on the radar tower, there was no way she could leave now. He was a good man regardless of what had happened and she believed he was innocent, as far as that went. She reaffirmed to herself that she was in it to the end, no matter what.

CHAPTER 37

It was a long drive for Henry coming back on the Long Island Expressway. The Manhattan skyline held a magnificent view, and he never grew tired of approaching it. As it grew in the distance, a sense of pride ran through him to be able to say he was a New Yorker, living in the greatest city in the world.

It seemed like only a few minutes until he had come through the Tunnel and was cruising through midtown to the precinct. Coming through the front door, the desk sergeant was busy. He had seen him before but didn't know his name. So he went up the stairs without acknowledging him.

It was well into the second shift and the officers still there were antsy to clock out and get a drink or go home to hit the rack for some much deserved sleep. The squadroom was practically empty with the exception of a few die hard rookies trying to focus on a difficult aspect of a case, others just catching up on stacks of paperwork that no one really wanted to do.

He saw Judith Kramer in the back by the breakroom, busy with her head down typing away on her keyboard. He had never worked with her, but heard that she was conscientious and accurate with her work, but like all women, who were worth their weight, the department was slow in giving her a chance to prove herself in the field. She was attractive but didn't flaunt it or try to use it to her advantage. Word had it that she was a walking time bomb for sexual harassment, but Henry never looked at her that way. She was kind, pleasant and that was good enough for him. He had to pass her on his way to get coffee.

So when he got close, she looked up and leaned back in her chair.

"Hello, Henry."

"Judith. Working late, huh?"

"It's the only time I can get caught up. How's things with you?"

"In general, or...how do you mean?"

She smiled. "Whatever way you want to spill it. How's the Grand Central case going?"

"It's going...got some leads, and a...you know," Henry said, rolling his hand as if unwinding something.

"You look tired. Long day?"

"It never ends."

She studied him the way cops do to each other. "What are you doing back here?"

Henry took a deep breath. "It could've waited until tomorrow. Just a force of habit, I guess."

She paused again. "Are you making any headway, Henry?"

"Slow, but we're getting there."

"Good," she said smiling. Then turning back to her work, expounding on what she knew to be true, "You always get your man!"

Henry laughed. "I don't know about that, but thanks for saying it."

"Anytime." She gave him a big smile.

Henry walked into the breakroom and saw the coffee pot was almost empty, so he made a fresh one. He sat down at the table to check his phone and saw that Dan Kearney had called him, so he called back. Dan answered on the second ring.

"What's up, Henry? How did it go?"

"I admit he's hard to take," Dan said, laughing. "But like anyone who kisses ass, the brass promotes him. So, what're you going to do with him?"

"Put him down in the subway walking the tracks. That would be a good job for him." Dan spoke while laughing. "You mean as a repairman?"

"No, that's too difficult. The trains would derail."

"If he got pushed in front of an express train, I wouldn't cry at his funeral."

"You mean you'd go?" Boyle asked.

Slight pause.

"How did we get off on him anyway?" Boyle asked.

"I don't know. Guys like him rub off on you like a wart. He stays with you." He took a breath, then continued. "What's the latest and greatest with you?"

Boyle paused.

"Are you ready for this?"

"Go ahead."

"Are you sitting down?" Henry got up to shut the break room door, checking to see if anyone was close.

"Just say it!"

"I met Victor Enmerkar. He came out of the woods by the motel. He was just waiting for me. Made quite an entrance."

Dan paused. "Dan…you still there?"

"I'm here."

"Kind of leaves you speechless, doesn't it?

Dan paused again.

"So did you guys talk, or has he been killing someone else?"

Boyle paused, then said, "He wants to set up a meeting with you and me."

"Get the fuck out of here!"

"I'm serious!"

"I don't think so! Some other time! Why can't you just shoot the son-of-a-bitch and be done with it?"

"What do you mean?"

"I mean, you must be losing it! Get some sleep, Henry."

"Hey! I am serious! He met me at the Beachfront Motel and spilled his whole story. I believe him, Dan. I'm going to try and help him, and I asked that you be included."

"Have you ever gone off the deep end?"

"He wants to meet you!"

Dan paused, then repeated, "He asked to meet me?"

"Yes! Are you coming?"

Another pause from Dan. He knew his friend was not a liar and didn't joke about such things. "I don't know about this, Henry. I get this sense that he's just playing you."

"Dan, I believe him. Trust me on this. Ok?"

Boyle could feel Dan squirming on the other end. "You're really going to have this meeting?"

"I was thinking about Mercer Street. My place is too visible and yours...well, you know your wife."

Dan quickly jumped in. "Keep it at Mercer. That's where you guys had the stakeout, right?"

"Yeah. Where the two CIA guys got whacked. But that's history. It's no longer a crime scene. I can meet you out front."

"When?"

"Tomorrow evening...about 7:30?"

"Give me the address."

"169 Mercer Street. This is all tentative, you understand. I've got to Ok it with Victor."

"Oh, you guys are friends now? First names, I see!"

"What can I say? He loves me," Boyle said, with a rare, mischievous grin.

***

CHAPTER 38

When Victor returned to the Taylor farm, Dwight was in the barn sanding the sides of the Mustang prior to painting it. It was late and Dwight had the barn light on. Victor parked the Ranger by the fence and walked to where Dwight was working on the car. Dwight was wearing goggles and looked up when he saw him.

"Hey. How'd it go?" Dwight asked, while raising the goggles to the top of his head.

"Good. I talked to Detective Boyle. It was productive."

"So he's going to help you?"

"He said he would if he could. There's another person he wants to bring into this. And we have a meeting scheduled for tomorrow night on Mercer Street in Manhattan."

Dwight wrinkled his brow and asked, "Who's this other guy?"

"He's FBI, a retired profiler. He works alot with Detective Boyle."

"So you and Trina are leaving tomorrow night?"

"I was wanting to talk to you about that." Victor walked a little closer. "This is kind of hard to say. But in case something goes down and I'm not able to return, someone will be in touch with you." Dwight looked confused. "In other words, if something happens to me, in case these men try to arrest me, I want you to be taken care of. If that happens, which I don't anticipate, a representative from a law firm will contact you. And then he'll take it from there."

"But you've done enough for me, Victor. I don't need to be included in your will."

"Oh, yes you will. I don't have anyone else to leave it to, and I'm sure as hell not going to leave it to the government. I want it to go to someone who can use it and appreciate it."

"What about Trina?"

"She's got money, but I'll take care of her, too."

"It sounds like the odds are against you."

"And they'll be greater if I don't go. This is a step in the right direction."

"You want me to go with you? Just in case."

"No. You can't lose your temper around these guys. I'll be talking to the NYPD and the FBI. So that's out of the question."

Dwight turned back to the car. "Alright, then. When will you be leaving?"

"Probably tonight. We'll grab a few things and then take off. I'm sure we'll have to clean up after the crime scene people."

Dwight turned back to him. "When will you think you'll be back?"

"The next day, if everything turns out alright."

Dwight nodded and turned back to the car. Victor didn't know what else to say so he went inside to tell Trina. They packed the few things they needed for the trip then came out to say goodbye to Dwight.

Victor stuck out his hand. "Remember what I said, It'll just be a couple of days. If it's any longer I'll call you."

Dwight looked at them both, then put his arms around each of them pulling them into a bear hug. Trina felt smothered and had to turn her head to get some air, until he released them.

"You guys be safe. And make sure you come back."

They got in the Ranger and drove away. They didn't say anything as they pulled onto 27. As they pulled onto the LIE, Trina said, "Dwight looked like he was going to miss us."

Victor nodded, then once they were on the LIE, he said, "We'll probably have to clean up after the crime scene."

"Oh, I can't wait," he said, raising her hands to cheer.

"It won't be that bad." She leaned to him and put her arm through his.

***

Deputy Beisley received the update from Dr. Collier, and was frustrated by the lack of a positive identification on the salvaged bones from the landfill. Everyone knew they belonged to Sheriff King, but without positive identification no charges could be placed on anyone. Beisley took solace in the fact that the frame of the unearthed car belonged to one of the cars used by the department— the dash, the radio, the side spotlight, and the cage dividing the front seat from the back further upheld his notion. So he used that to interrogate on his return visit to the Taylor farm.

He parked in the usual place and getting out, he walked up to the garage and looked in. He saw Dwight working on the Mustang, pulling dents out with a suction tool that had various sized suction discs that could be attached to the bottom, screwed down from the top and then squeezed with the two handled grip to pull out the dent. Looking behind him he saw no dents, so it looked like it was working pretty good, as Dwight worked toward him.

In between popping out dents, Dwight said, "You're back. What's up, Beisley?"

"Just out driving around. Thought I'd drop in."

Dwight was on one knee. He stopped and looked up. "Nothing in town to keep you busy?"

Beisley looked around. "I was wanting to tell you that I turned Sheriff King's disappearance over to our Missing Person's Squad."

"Is that still Suffolk County?"

"Yes. And they went by the landfill because they got several calls about that fireball. They went down in the pit. And guess what they found?"

"Well, it must be bad news, because you're here."

"Under a pile of dirt, they found the frame of a car burnt to a crisp. It looks like one of ours. Then a bunch of metal fragments. Anyway, all of that points to the fact that it was a cop car. The detectives in charge are taking some of those fragments to be tested to see what they come up with."

"What do you mean tested?"

"I mean, since it was burned so badly and something obviously blew it apart, experts have to determine what actually happened. It's the procedure we follow in a case like this."

"What do you think, did it?" Dwight tried to act surprised.

"Well, that's just it. I don't know. No one does." The deputy paused, remembering when he saw him firing the bazooka.. "Is there anything you need to tell me?"

"Like what?"

"They found some bones out there, too. Not many. The heat incinerated most of them, but they recovered a few."

"My God! Who would want to do that?"

"Do you know of anyone who would want to harm Sheriff King?"

"If I did, I'd tell you."

"I don't need to remind you that you and the Sheriff had problems. You know what I'm talking about. And just so you know, Dwight, when a suspicious death like this happens, we look first at the people who would stand to gain from it. And that points to you. I'm not saying you did it, but you're now a suspect."

"Beisley, I didn't kill anybody!"

He nodded. "I can help you get through this."

"Get through what? What are you talking about?"

"You don't want to go back to prison, do you? Everything is pointing to you."

Pause. "Am I under arrest?"

"Not yet. But you know what happened."

Dwight took a deep breath and exhaled. "I don't know anything. You're wasting your time here."

Deputy Beisley nodded. Then he started looking around the barn over to the car, trying to change the subject. "Your Mustang's lookin better. What color are you gonna paint it?"

Dwight spoke without smiling. "I was thinking of Acapulco Blue. Tan stripes down each side."

"That'll look really nice." They eyed each other. "You take care, Dwight."

The Deputy turned to leave and Dwight walked to the door to watch him drive away.

He wished for a few seconds that he had the bazooka loaded to blow up the cruiser. He shook his head and walked back into the barn. Before picking up the sander again, he stopped and walked over to his work bench. He reached underneath it to remove a box that he placed on the counter. He opened it and removed a .357 Magnum revolver, one of several varieties that Victor had shipped to the farm. He checked it to make sure it was loaded. Then, he placed it on a shelf above the counter and covered it with a garage rag, so he could grab it easily.

CHAPTER 39

When Victor and Trina arrived at Mercer Street, they had to park on the next block and walk to the building. She unlocked the heavy door, and they took the elevator up to the sixth floor. When the door opened, they walked down the hall and noticed a few bullet holes in the hallway by the door. Trina ran her fingers over them. She stuck her finger in one of the holes and thought she felt the bullet. She decided that later it might be fun to try and dig it out.

They had not been back since the shooting, so the door was unlocked because the police had no key to lock it. They looked around the apartment and nothing seemed to be missing. Drawers were gone through and the contents scattered on the floor. The place looked searched, as if someone was looking for drugs. They went about the work of putting everything back the way thru thought it was, except for the blood stains on the floor.

Biocleaners had been in to remove the stains. All that remained to be done was to re-varnish the spots. For now, Trina moved an area rug to cover them. After that they began planning for the meeting the following night.

And when the following night arrived, Boyle met Kearney at the front door. Kearney looked at him with an eye of trepidation and Boyle tried to shake hands, but Dan shook him off. Realizing Dan was in a real mood, he pressed the call button and waited a few moments.

Turning to him, he said, "You need to lighten up, man. This attitude isn't going to get you anywhere with him."

When they were buzzed in and rode the elevator up,the door opened to a pleasant greeting from Trina. Her beauty was appreciated by Kearney who looked at Victor with an encouraging grin.

They nodded to each other, and before sitting Victor asked if they could all remove their weapons and place them in the microwave. Dan looked at Boyle who nodded. Then everyone slowly withdrew their handguns including the ones strapped to the ankles. Trina collected them and placed them in the microwave.

"Just a precaution," Victor said.

Sitting at the table Dan inquired about Eddie to see if he would be joining them. Boyle explained that he was being used as cover at the precinct, which was fine with Eddie, who did not want to risk his career in such an unpredictable situation. He would still contact them by phone to give updates and receive information, but he would not participate in any field operations.

Victor gestured to the table where they all sat. Trina had displayed a wide assortment of Chinese takeout for all to devour while devising the plan. Tsingtao beer was placed around the table. They ate sparingly, except for Victor who did not get the opportunity to eat at such a plentiful Chinese display that often. Henry and Dan ate a few egg rolls making use of the duck sauce packets that they tore open with their teeth and squeezed, licking their fingers when finished.

Boyle started by looking at Dan saying, "Are there any aspects of this that you're unclear about? I thought I explained it well, but I might have missed something."

"No, you did fine. But I have a question for Mr. Enmerkar," Dan said.

"Can we address each other by first name from now on? This Mr. stuff... it makes me uncomfortable," Victor confessed.

"Well, we certainly don't want to do that, now, do we?" Dan leaned forward. "But let me explain something to you. I don't know you. I've heard of you, but I don't know you," Then turning to

Boyle, he put his hand on his shoulder. "I know this guy, and I trust him.

And I'm here, because he asked me to come, not because you requested it. So what makes you think I should believe anything you've said about what happened to you?"

Victor eyeballed him, taking his time, then spoke softly in a matter of fact tone. "Because you trust your friend. And I didn't ask you to come. It was his request, and because I have the highest regard for Detective Boyle, I agreed to have you join us under the condition that I meet you first. Your suspicion is good, natural and expected. But frankly, Mr. Kearney, with all due respect, if you don't want to stay," then he pointed to the elevator door, "you know the way out." Victor took an egg roll and ate part of it.

Dan leaned back in his chair. He looked at Boyle and nodded. Trina got up and started to clear the plates and food, sensing the tension starting to rise.

"So what's the goal here," Dan said, looking at Victor. "We have to define what that is before we can come up with a plan."

Boyle cleared his throat and said, "We want to apprehend the person or persons who are responsible for the murders at the Terminal. We're all clear on that, aren't we?"

"Responsible for what?" Dan asked. "Tell me again because I'm still in the dark here. What crime was committed?"

"They put an implant in his brain to control it," Boyle said, pointing at Victor.

Dan nodded, sucking his teeth, wishing he had a toothpick. "And, I assume, the purpose of that was used for the killings at Grand Central?"

"And on 10th Street. Vernon Fahey," Boyle added.

Dan nodded again, as if to say 'Oh, yes! Of course! Don't want to leave that out!' Then, he glared at Victor. "And you have no recollection of the murders you committed?"

"Not as it happened. My memory was erased, but it's returned now."

"So now you remember the killings?" Dan asked.

"I remember that it wasn't me who killed them. It was the thought processes that prompted me to commit them."

Dan was thinking a lot of obscenities, but kept control. "What do you mean?"

"I mean, something took over my thoughts, forcing me to do things that I never would have done. It was like I was a bystander looking on, as something controlled my actions, my arms, my hands to make me perform the way I was programmed to or whatever it was. I don't exactly know. And then when it was over, my mind was erased."

Laughing inside at the absurdity of the statement, Dan asked, "Erased?"

"Until now."

Dan nodded, saying, "Until now? That's convenient, isn't it? Why not in between each one?" He tapped his finger on the table. "You have to understand I'm not following you one bit."

Victor exhaled loudly. "If I were you, I wouldn't either. All I can surmise, if that's the right word to use, is that the implant has malfunctioned."

"Show him the scar," Boyle said to Victor.

Victor leaned over and said, "Feel behind my ear."

Dan inspected the area, saw the scar, and felt the bump. He was taken back a bit from the sight of it. "Do you have any headaches from that?" Dan asked.

"Sometimes."

"What do you take for them?"

Victor looked at him strangely. "Excedrin Migraine. Why? You think I'm on drugs?"

"I'm trying to make sense of this, Mr. Enmerkar."

"There is no sense to it! That's the point! That's why it's so bizarre!" Victor turned to Boyle with open hands as if asking for help.

Dan continued, unphased by the reaction to his questions. "Have you experienced any recurring episodes since then?"

"No. What they put in my brain, I don't believe it works anymore," Victor said, adamantly.

"But you don't know."

"Hell, yes, I know! When it happened before, I felt like something was taking over and I was watching it! Nothing like that has happened since." He went on to explain what he remembered from the operating room, the bright lights and people around him, while his head was secured in a metal ring to stabilize it. He still remembered the sound of the drill.

"They were experimenting on him to see if he could be turned into a controllable killing machine." Boyle said.

"For the government?" Dan asked.

"The CIA. Remember MK-ULTRA?" Boyle said.

"It's still going on but under different names. It happened at Brookhaven. It was funded through DARPA, and headed by Dr. Carl Emerson," Victor said.

"What's DARPA? I don't remember," Dan asked.

"If I'm right, it stands for Defense Advanced Research Projects Agency."

Dan paused. "The military." Victor nodded.

Slight pause. "Who's this Carl Emerson?" Dan asked. Victor took a deep breath and then continued.

"The real question is, what isn't he? But to give you an answer he's a microbiologist, a physician, a neuroscientist, a research analyst...kind of a jack of all trades with an IQ that goes through the roof. He's whoever you want him to be, and he goes where the money is high, fast and untraceable---which means he works, primarily, as a CIA contractor."

"And you're saying he put the implant in your head at Brookhaven?"

"Yes."

"Do you have any proof?"

"The scar on my head and my testimony," Victor said, rubbing it behind his ear.

Dan turned more toward him. "I mean like paperwork showing you were there with a date and time?"

"It was supposed to be a physical exam. If there was any paperwork on it, the CIA classified it or it's now destroyed!"

Boyle interjected, "You mentioned earlier that you would need to gain access to the classified files at Langley."

"Yes."

"Whatever we do, it has to be undercover," Boyle said to Dan. Then he looked at Victor. "Sorry. Clandestine, I believe is the word."

"What are you suggesting? Breaking into the CIA?" Dan asked. "Whatever needs to be done," Boyle said, with both hands open.

"That can't be done!" Dan said, voicing his opinion.

Victor's eyes opened wide. "I can do it, but it just takes time. A plan needs to be devised, then set into order," Victor said.

Dan looked from Boyle to Victor, "Are we talking about killing him, this Carl Emerson?"

"No, but we can certainly put the squeeze on him. Make him think we've got evidence against him. Then maybe he'll give up the rest of his crew for Project Takeover," Victor said.

Dan took a deep breath and exhaled loudly, raising his arms.. "Ok. I'm lost. What's Project Takeover?"

"Yeah," Boyle said. "What is it?"

Victor paused, then said, "Just what it says. It's classified like everything else. I'll let you fill in the blanks."

Dan looked at Boyle, then back at Victor. "How far up does it go?" Dan asked.

"A long way," Victor said.

Dan shook his head and grabbed it. "Jesus Christ!" Then he stretched his neck, rubbed it, and pointed his finger at Victor. "I want no part of killing, you understand! I don't care to spend my retirement years in prison!"

"Neither do I," Victor said.

"Then get that idea of killing out of your mind!" Dan leaned back in his chair and said nothing else. Boyle looked at Victor who returned his empty stare.

Then Boyle finally spoke. "So what do you think, Dan?"

Dan hiked his shoulders. "I think it's a hell of a lot easier to go after one guy, as opposed to a department or the whole damn CIA. Is it just me or am I missing something here?" Then he looked at Victor. "Is that what you were thinking?"

Victor nodded. "To start with."

Dan laughed. "Are you fucking kidding me?"

"We have to start small in order to go big. Let's take it one step at a time."

"Yeah, you're damn right!" Dan looked at Boyle, then back. "So there are others?

There has to be."

"Of course, but let's get Dr. Emerson first to send them a message. We can always come back to re-evaluate our actions to see what comes next."

Dan looked at Victor. "You're fucking crazy! You know that?" Then he turned to Boyle. "Why the hell did you ask me here? This is nuts! It's pure insanity!" Then he focused on Victor. "You seem to be a smart guy. You'd have to be to live this long doing what you do, and I'm sure you've got money! So disappear! Become someone else! Start a new life and stop killing people!"

"I'm trying to, don't you understand? But I'm tired of being chased everywhere I go."

Dan tried to calm him by saying, "I get that, but it's like the witness protection program. You just recreate your life and start fresh. It's done a lot."

Victor lowered his head. "I've done that to a degree. But if I go full tilt, I don't want to end up like Whitey Bulger, getting nabbed when I'm 80, because I let down my guard. "

Dan nodded. "Yeah. I read the transcript of his confession. He said the reason he got caught was because he was free for so long, he stopped thinking like a criminal."

"He got too comfortable. Lost his edge," Victor said.

"Otherwise, he never would have gone downstairs where they called him to check his storage closet," Boyle said

"But I'm not like him. I'm not a criminal, so that option's out," Victor said.

"Jesus! You sound like Nixon! If you think you're going to pull this off, you're crazy! It's too fuckin big!"

"If you were in my shoes you'd be crazy, too! You can leave at any time, Mr. Kearney. Detective Boyle and I can handle this on our own."

Dan looked over at Boyle with raised eyebrows. Boyle looked back as if to say, 'Hang in there. Just be cool.'

There was a period of prolonged silence, where only the sound of their breathing, the clearing of throats, and the muffled noise of traffic from Mercer Street rising up through the enormous windows was heard. Trina stood in the kitchen motionless, listening, as she felt her heart beating like a drum.

Then Dan asked quietly, "Where does this Dr. Emerson live?" Victor looked at him. "Long Island."

"Where, in Long Island?" Dan asked.

"Around Brookhaven," Victor said, smiling. Then he looked over at Boyle who smiled back.

Dan noticed their exchange of smiles and asked, "Do you mind filling me in on what you're smiling about?"

"It's on the Northern Peninsula. Close to where we were previously," Boyle said.

"You guys forget I live on Long Island. You're thinking of Brookhaven National Laboratory which is on the Northern Peninsula, but there is also a Brookhaven town on the Southern Peninsula. You see, the township consists of several villages and runs from the North Shore to the South Shore." Then turning to Victor, he asked, "Do you happen to know which village he resides in?"

Victor thought for a minute then answered, "Farther east...a place called Riverhead."

Dan paused, then picking up his bottle of Tsing-tao beer, he took a drink and leaned back in his chair.

"Well, that sounds better. And how convenient!" he said smiling. "Any address?"

"No, but that shouldn't be hard to find," Victor said. Dan took another sip from his beer. He smiled in Boyle's direction. Victor turned to Trina, and said, "Are you ready to move back to the beach house?"

Trina broke into a huge smile.

CHAPTER 40

It has long been noted through the help of satellite photography that the shape of Long Island resembles a great fish--the head pointing west to Manhattan. the two-pronged tail eastward to the ocean. The Atlantic tail splits into the North and the South peninsulas where the town of Riverhead rests in the notch of the split, which is actually the mouth of the Peconic River, thus making it the "crossroads" to the eastern end of Long Island.

Dr. Carl Emerson lived on the outskirts of the town in a secluded, densely wooded area with a wonderful view of the river, which emptied into the Great Peconic Bay.

Victor was given the responsibility of finding his unlisted address, as well as his phone number. Dr. Emerson had worked regularly for the CIA, NSA, on projects funded through DARPA, but mostly out of Brookhaven National Laboratory. Their policy on the releasing of employee information was one of non-disclosure, so they did not waste their time there. The plan was to scout around and ask different people in several different places, if they knew of him and where he lived. But he knew that the doctor's purpose was to remain hidden and unknown, something that Victor could identify with completely.

Dan Kearney offered his assistance knowing his FBI credentials would be an asset in gaining information, especially by those who had never seen them and didn't know they could refuse to talk to them. So he left early to make the trip from Hicksville to meet Victor at an IHOP restaurant. They both had breakfast and decided to start there at the restaurant asking about him, but they had no luck. From there they moved uptown stopping at eateries, various businesses along the way, and then up around the town square to ask at ladies dress shops, wine stores, a men's tailor shop, car dealerships, even the county tax collector who had no record of his name.

They had been riding around town in Dan's silver Jeep Cherokee, when they saw a neon sign that read 'Sam's Bar and Grill'.

Dan looked over at Victor and said, "I sure could use a beer. How about you?"

"My thoughts exactly," Victor said. "Maybe the bartender will know something."

Dan parked in front of the place. When he got out and locked the vehicle, they entered the bar to see it was a narrow establishment with one row of tables against the wall to the right. There was a long mahogany bar to the left with a huge mirror, mindful of frontier saloons. A wide variety of bottles stacked in three tiers in between ornate wooden frames on each side of the mirror suggested a finer time now gone by.

The bar looked freshly varnished. The floor was wooden and the walls were decorated with mirrors advertising various kinds of beer and whisky in a random, chaotic manner that seemed to fit. Jameson's, Crown Royal, Glenlivet, Millers, Budweiser, and Harp's among others. The mirrors were placed on the wall so that wherever one looked you could see yourself in a multilayered splash of reflection.

In the back was the kitchen and several tables for those who wished to dine in peace. An ancient Wurlitzer Jukebox was against one wall, the kind that played four 45's for a dollar.

Dan and Victor sat at the bar. The bartender was a middle aged man with a bald head, gray hair on the sides. He came over and asked what their pleasure would be.

"What do you have on tap?" Dan asked. "Harps, Guiness, Killian's Red, and Bud Light."

"Make it a Harp's for me," Dan said, then looking over at Victor who held up two fingers indicating the same choice.

The bartender grabbed two fresh steins, snapped the beer tap at the base to ease up on the foam, and poured the two beers without stopping for the second. He brought them over and placed them on coasters. Dan tossed out a twenty, the bartender took it, rang up the price, and gave back his change.

Dan looked at it and said, "Three dollars for a draft beer. It's cheaper to drink here than Hicksville."

"Hicksville. Is the town synonymous with the name?"

Dan looked at him. "If you mean do a bunch of 'Hicks' live there, I have no idea. I live a little out of town away from that."

"So you're a loner?"

"I prefer it that way. When people find out you work for the FBI, they suddenly become your new best friend, or they avoid you altogether."

"How did you and Boyle team up?"

"Through the job."

"I figured that. What was it that made you guys decide to go out on your own?"

Dan paused, sipping his beer. "We got tired of seeing suspects walk on technicalities. Usually by a flaw in the system, the limitations of the workforce, not enough manpower, jealousies between my agency and his."

"So, what was it, a special case that caused you to hook up?" Dan looked at him again. "Why do you care?"

"Just trying to make conversation."

"Well, thanks for asking, but I'm not talking about it. I just met you."

"I respect that."

They sipped in silence for a while, thinking that maybe their newly acquired relationship may be tarnished. But Dan came back with a good general question.

"What brands of beer did you drink in the Middle East?"

"Whatever I could get, usually. Almaza was good...Goldstar was very popular, Petra was another...even Cassablanca, but that was hard to get."

The bartender, who was pretending to read the paper at the end, had been listening to them talk and came over to greet them.

"So how are you fellows doing? Can I get you anything else?"

"Maybe some information," Dan said, taking out his ID and showing him.

The bartender looked at the ID then up at Dan's face to match the picture, then asked, "What kind of information?"

"Have you heard of Dr. Carl Emerson? And better yet, do you know where he lives?"

"Yes, to both questions."

Victor and Dan looked at each other surprised, then back at the bartender. "So you know him?" Dan asked.

"Yeah, he comes here every now and then. Sits over at one of those booths. Just drinks and doesn't talk to anyone," he said, leaning against the bar.

"Where does he live?"

"Can I ask why you're lookin for him?"

"We're running an investigation. His name popped up, so we need to ask him some questions."

"Ok," the bartender said, then stuck out his hand. "By the way, my name is Ralph Jacobs. I used to be with the Suffolk County Sheriff's Office."

"I thought your name would be Sam," Dan said, smiling.

"Nah, he's the guy I bought it from. Too much trouble to change the name."

"You retired?"

"Yeah, thank God! If I had it to do over I think I'd go to college. Become a lawyer or maybe a doctor. It's a thankless job being a cop."

"So you like this better?" Victor asked.

"Once I got used to it, yeah. I dropped most of my savings in this place. Bought the building for a song and a dance. The good thing is I live upstairs, no rent, just taxes, which are high enough. But hey! It's a living! Less stress that's for sure."

"So when does the doctor come in?" Dan asked. "No special time, really. Just...you know, whenever."

"Where does he live?"

Ralph leaned on his hands against the bar. "Let me explain something to you about Dr. Emerson. You won't find his name in the phone book or any city records. He's got some high-powered job with the government. He works over at the Lab a lot."

"What lab is that?"

"The one at Brookhaven. But he lives on...Riverside Drive, I think. It's this huge stone house. Looks like a fortress. I asked him one time, why did you buy a monster house like that? He said he got it real cheap in a foreclosure, and he likes a lot of space. Has a wall around it and everything. You can't miss it. It's the only one on the road and it has a big gate with one of those call boxes, you know. Like he's a big shot or something."

"So you say Riverside is the street?" Dan asked again.

"I think so. It has a view of the river. If you go out east and drive around on those roads you can't help but run into it."

Dan looked at Victor, then back at the bartender. "Ralph, thanks a lot. You've been very helpful."

"Any time fellows. Come on back if you get stuck...or thirsty."

CHAPTER 41

They drove east on Main Street until they reached Riverside Drive, where they turned left and continued, circling around until it dipped south toward the river. Following it to the end, they saw no sign of a gate or a stone house, so they turned left onto River Avenue that followed the river for a good distance. They decided to check all the streets up and down to see if they could locate the stone house. When they were finished checking the more populated streets, they decided to go back to Riverside Drive and follow it farther out to a more wooded area.

When they came to Riverview it made sense to them that perhaps this was the street that Ralph was referring to because the name was very close to Riverside. They stopped the car and looking down the road they saw that it was more secluded, so continuing through a densely populated area of trees, they finally came to a turnoff that was wide and guarded by a brick wall and iron gate with two letters emblazoned across it. So Dan maneuvered the Jeep closer to try and make out what they were. Finally, he saw the letters were CE, standing for Carl Emerson. Then he looked over to the left and saw the camera and call box.

Focusing his eyes on the gate, he looked over at Victor. "This must be the place."

"I believe you're right," Victor said, pointing through the gate. "There's the house up ahead."

They got out and walked up to the gate. "You think he's in there?" Dan asked.

"I don't know," Victor said. "Probably not. I don't see any cars, do you?"

"Nope."

"We should come later. After dark," Victor said. "I'll notify Boyle."

"Yeah. Tell him to come loaded," Victor said. Then he turned to Dan and pointed to his car. "What are you carrying in the Jeep?"

"A shotgun, Mini-14...some grenades and smoke bombs." Victor was impressed. "Did you forget the rocket launcher?"

Dan smiled. "Well, I wasn't sure. But we need to find out if he's even there. He could be out of town. We could call to see if he's at Brookhaven. Do you have any good phone routines? I'm a little rusty. You said he works where?"

"Mostly through DARPA, but at Brookhaven."

"So, we can call up wanting to speak with him. If they say no, we could…no, fuck that. That sounds like an amateur."

"Wait a minute. I know a hacker." Victor took out his phone and dialed a number. He let it ring a few times. He waited and was almost ready to leave a message when someone picked up.

"Who is it?" the voice asked. "Joe. It's me."

"How goes it, Victor? You keepin' low these days?"

"Well, as much as I can, you know. But I'm pressed for time here, Joe. Can you run a make on Dr. Carl Emerson? Works out of Brookhaven National Laboratory on Long Island. And he lives in Riverhead, also Long Island. I need to know if he lives on Riverview Drive."

"This guy sounds like a big shot."

"Yeah, he is. I need to get close to him."

"I hear you. How soon do you need this?"

"Just as soon as you can get it."

"Alright, it shouldn't take long. Can you hold on?"

"Yeah, sure."

"If we get cut off, I got your number. So hang tight for a minute."

"Ok," Victor said, then he looked over at Dan. "He's checking now."

"So where do you know this guy from?" Dan asked.

Victor smiled at him. "You don't want to know, but he's very reliable." Joe came back on the line.

"Ok, Victor. I got a hit right away. Man, this guy has a long list of credentials. Who the hell are you dealing with?"

"That's what I'm trying to find out. What does it say his present address is? Is there a listing for Riverview Drive?"

"There's a bunch of them, but I don't see—"

"Go to the bottom."

Slight pause, as Joe read the screen.

"You're in luck Victor. Address is 98 Riverview Drive in Riverhead, New York."

"Great. You got a phone number with that?"

"I don't know if it's still good, but try this, 212-862-4040."

"Got it," Victor said, writing it on his hand with a pen pulled from his pocket. "Now, just to be sure, does it say anything about Brookhaven or DARPA as places of employment?"

"Sure does. And a list of other places as well. You want me to mail this to you."

"No. I'm on the move."

"Ok, my man. I'll put it in a pdf on my website. Encrypted, but you know how to get there. You stay low and take it slow, my friend...if you can."

"I'll send you a wire when I land."

"It's on the account."

"Thanks, Joe."

When Victor ended the call, Dan started to say something when a voice from the call box squawked at them. "Do you guys want something there?"

The voice startled them both. Dan spoke up quickly.

"No, thank you!" Dan said, looking at the camera and waving with a smile. "We're just lost and noticed the house. Very interesting! Hope we didn't bother you!"

"This is private property! You are trespassing!" the voice blared again.

Dan looked at Victor as if to say 'Let's get out of here'. He waved at the camera, then they both got in their vehicle and used the wide expanse of asphalt at the entrance to turn around, then they drove back the way they came.

Victor noticed that no one could drive on without obtaining permission to have the gate opened. But walking from farther up the road, entry could be obtained from the wooded area. Anyone willing to get dirty and, perhaps, wet feet by slogging through the underbrush could make their way inside the grounds by scaling the short wall made easy by the protruding edges of the river stone. The surveillance cameras would have to be disabled, but he had the correct software on his laptop to hack into their system which did a search to find out the correct one. It was a product of Vault 7. One of the CIA's hacking programs for National Security. The set up from what he saw was a classic deficiency in security. All for show and not much else.

"Did you bring your boots?" Victor asked Dan. "I keep some in the back."

CHAPTER 42

Dan called Boyle, who said it would take him at least an hour. Dan told him they would meet at Sam's Bar and Grill on Main Street. Boyle agreed and told Eddie that he had to go to Riverhead and to try and cover for him. He checked to make sure that Eddie had Dan's number in case he couldn't get a hold of him, then he took off in his Charger, passing through the Midtown Tunnel, where he settled in for the hour drive to Riverhead. He thought about calling Delores again at the 911 call center to see if he could step on it uninterrupted, but he thought he'd better leave it alone, not wanting to face her wrath that he knew was sure to come. To soften his anxiety, he played a cd, Art Pepper's, 'A Taste of Pepper.' Great saxophone solos.

He pulled into the parking lot of Sam's Bar and Grill in record time, it seemed to him, his mind engulfed by the jazz music. He parked beside Dan's Cherokee, got out and surprised them both when he entered the bar.

They were sitting at a table having the evening special, which was some kind of fish with fried potatoes, cole slaw and iced tea with lemon served in tall plastic glasses.

"Hey. Sit down, Henry. You made good time," Dan said.

He shook hands with Victor and Dan, then sat down at the table.

"I've got to hold back that Charger of mine or the speedometer gets away from me," he said, smiling.

"Tell the truth. How fast did you drive?" Dan asked.

"Seventy-five, eighty...but then I'd look at the needle and it was ninety, ninety-five," he said, laughing as he looked away." Then back, he said, "So, you think you found where he lives?"

"Yes," Victor said. "I can guarantee that. We just need to find out when he's going to be there." He shifted his sitting position on the chair and spoke using his hands. "We thought we'd wait until after dark, go in from the woods on one side or both. I assume the house has some flood lights to help us see."

"You mean from the darkness of the trees?" Boyle asked. "Yes. Did you bring your boots?"

"Always. Got my coveralls, too." He looked over at Victor. "Do you have any infrared goggles?"

"No, but I don't think we'll need them."

***

Dan and Victor had checked into the Starlite Motel with a convenience store next door. It was a ranch style motel circa 1950's, which was fine because they wanted privacy where no one would be around to see them coming and going. Boyle thought it was perfect when he saw it because there was only one other car parked in front of the rooms. He wondered how his Dodge Charger was going to stand out in the midst of it all.

He didn't ask what the cost of the room was, figuring someone would tell him if they wanted him to contribute. Victor seemed to have an endless supply of cash anyway and from the looks of things, he decided the price of it wasn't going to break anybody.

After checking out the room, Victor told Boyle he would take the floor so go ahead and take the other bed. He was used to sleeping on the floor anyway so it really didn't matter to him, and besides, he was grateful that Boyle was there to help him. So Boyle took the bed and didn't feel that bad about it.

They waited until just after dark, about 8:30, then they packed up the back of Dan's SUV, taking inventory of what they had and what they thought was needed. Then they closed the back and took off for Riverview.

CHAPTER 43

After cruising by the gated entrance, Dan turned off the lights of the Jeep. There were no other cars on the road. He drove another two hundred yards to where the road curved slightly to the right, then turned around and pulled off onto the grassy shoulder of the opposite side. He had turned off the interior convenience light, so the car remained dark when he opened the door. Stepping out into the cool night air, he looked and listened. The night was silent with only an occasional chirp from a cricket or other unseen crawling creature.

Boyle got out and opened the back to get his boots and rifle, an AR-15 semi-automatic. Dan joined him to retrieve his boots also, as well as his knee brace. Victor was in the back seat checking signal strength on his laptop to see if it was strong enough so he could use the CIA software to disable the surveillance cameras. After checking the signal level, he decided it wasn't strong enough and even though he didn't want to lug his laptop with him, he knew he had to get closer to snag the wifi signal from the stone house.

Boyle was holding a mini flashlight so that Dan could strap on the knee brace and finish lacing his boots.

"Are you going to be alright out there? I'm not sure what we'll run into," Boyle asked.

"It won't be anything worse than what I've seen before."

"I was talking about the brace. You sure that'll work for you?"

"Yes."

Boyle removed his jacket and shirt to put on his Kevlar vest, then realized they were one short. He forgot to bring one for Victor. He thought for a minute, then realized he didn't want to take the chance that Victor would catch a bullet. So as he came around to get his AR-15, Boyle tossed his vest to him.

Victor caught it and said, "Where's yours?" Then, looking in the trunk, he said, "I don't see it."

"I'm good. You need it more than I do."

Victor smiled. "Ok, Superman." He took out the magazine, checked it, replaced it, then waited for the other two.

"What's with the shoulder pack?" Boyle asked Victor.

"I need to bring my laptop to check the wifi signal coming from the house. It's not strong enough here to disable the outside cameras."

Boyle nodded. All of them checked their equipment and extra magazines in their jacket pockets. Then Boyle asked, "You guys have a Mag-Lite?"

"I'm good," Dan said. "Me, too," Victor added.

"Ok. I guess I'll take the lead," Boyle said.

"We're just checking, right? To see if he's there?" Dan asked.

"But if he's there, we might as well be ready," Victor said, then checked them both with the light.

"Right," Boyle said. "Let's move out."

They started to move, then Dan said, "Oh, wait a minute." He reached into his pocket to pull out a piece of paper that he had written a note on earlier, then placed it under the windshield wiper on the driver's side. It read: GONE TO GET GAS—BE BACK SOON.

Stepping down a three foot embankment, they stepped softly into the dark solitude of the trees, being careful not to trip or stumble on a snag in the undergrowth of the forest floor. Looking up, they could see the stars peeking between scudding clouds through an occasional break in the tree canopy. Boyle made use of the Mag-Lite by keeping it pointed down to light the way, having to go around fallen trunks too big to crawl over in the dark. He encouraged Dan and Victor to do the same thing.

The plan was to move parallel to the road until they could see the floodlights of the house and reach the stone wall. There was water collected in patches only a few inches deep and the mud from it sucked at their boots to make walking slow. At one point they had to stop because the mud pulled at Dan's boot until he almost pulled his right foot out. They waited until he secured the laces tighter so they could continue their walk.

In some places the water patches reflected the stars and made them feel exposed. Every twenty yards or so they would move in under the trees for cover and to rest for a moment. The woods were deathly quiet, no insects were buzzing in the air. The only sound was an occasional rustling of the wind through the trees.

"I haven't seen any flood lights yet. Have you?" Dan asked Boyle. He was bent over with his hands on his knees catching his breath.

"No, but we're going the right way. We're just moving slow because of the mud."

"Yeah," Victor said. "I'll take the point now," he said, moving past them.

Boyle and Dan followed reluctantly, their boots feeling like concrete from the mud caked around them. After an hour, they made it to the entrance road. Stopping to find some sticks they managed to scrape off most of the mud from their boots. Then they proceeded parallel to the road just inside the trees until they reached the stone wall and the floodlights of the house could be seen through the branches.

Following the wall, they came to a place closest to the house when Victor said to stop. "What's going on?" Dan asked, trying to catch his breath again.

"I want to test the wifi to see if I can pick it up here." Dan nodded, then leaned down behind the wall. "You ok there, big guy?" Boyle asked Dan. "Yeah…just a little out of shape. That's all."

At the end of an asphalt drive they saw the house, a crude take on a French Chateau made of smooth river stones which, frankly, made it look more like a prison or fortress from the time of the Revolutionary War, than a residence. It had two stories with pitched roofs and turrets on the corners. The same river stone was used for a surrounding wall of the property, and the evidence of closed circuit surveillance cameras with black mounts on the outside of the house was seen. A few poles strategically placed on the grounds were used for surveillance cameras as well. The only outlet was the river in the back that also had a boat dock.

The house was lit with floodlights upturned from the ground. There was a large turnaround at the front and a smaller drive that wrapped around behind the structure. There was a large wrap around porch that continued to the side. A detached building in the back to the right, also made of the smooth river stone, served as a garage or at one time a carriage house. There was a raised section of cement farther to the right with a large E painted on it that looked like it served as a helicopter pad.

Boyle looked over the wall and saw the back of the house which had a parking area where he could see two cars. The garage door was closed, so he couldn't tell if a car was parked inside or not. But the floodlights did their job in lighting the house, and casting their decreasing light well out into the grounds that reached almost to the stone wall. He was sure that no one standing at the house could see them where they were. The surveillance posts could be taken out manually from their end but that could alert someone inside.

Looking at Dan who was obviously winded and favoring his knee that he and Boyle saw was hurting him, he spoke in a way to release Dan from any embarrassment.

"Ok. No problem. They run on a Windows System, so I should be able to disable the cameras," Victor said, coming over to share the news.

"That's a pretty handy tool you got there. Wish I had access to it," Boyle said. "You may someday. Who knows? Now, all we need to know is if the doctor is inside."

They gathered round and had a short discussion about if they should proceed. Boyle and Victor noticed that Dan's knee was bothering him which was a real detriment to their moving ahead. It was a straightforward approach. Climb over the wall and try to gain entry from the rear of the building, after deactivating the surveillance cameras. They both could see that Dan was not up to the task. So Victor spoke up with that in mind.

"I have a suggestion, fellows, let me come back on my own to do some further reconnaissance." Then he looked at them both. "Is that alright with you guys? It's not that I don't enjoy your company, but I'm used to working alone. Then we can regroup after."

Dan looked at Boyle who nodded his approval.

"Well, you don't need me for that," Dan said, thankful not to continue. "I'd just slow you down slugging through that mush."

"Are you sure you want to bow out of our great endeavor?" Boyle said, trying to make light of the situation.

"I'm worn out, guys. I didn't realize how much I would slow you down. I'm sorry."

"It's quite alright, Dan. I'll come back tomorrow and scout around some more."

They took an easier route back to the car just inside the tree line where the walking was easier. When they reached the car, they removed their boots, cleaning them the best they could by wiping them across the grass then placing them inside a box in the back of the Jeep. Dan decided he would drive back to Hicksville, so he dropped Boyle and Victor at the motel and told them to keep him in touch.

CHAPTER 44

Y ou know, I think we should just go back there now and catch that son-of-a-bitch. But I'm hungry. Aren't you?"

Looking around Boyle said, "We can't catch criminals on an empty stomach."

"I saw a diner on the way back. I'm pretty sure it said 24 hours. You want to coffee up, maybe get some breakfast. We could talk some more about strategy. It's good to brainstorm."

In a matter of minutes they were out the door and in Boyle's Charger on their way to the Pancake Diner, which was up the street a few blocks. Boyle parked close to the front door of the classic rectangular silver structure. The diner had developed a wide menu to cater to the needs of the Riverhead people.

They thought about sitting at the counter, but Victor chose a booth toward the back on the right with good sightlines of the front and parking lot. When the waitress brought the menus, they glanced through them. Then Boyle asked, "Do you have any breakfast specials?"

"Sure, honey. They're on the back." She took his menu, turned it around, and gave it back.

Victor turned over the menu as well, the waitress waited patiently, then Boyle said, "I'll have the 'Riverhead Special', american fries, eggs scrambled and sourdough toast."

"We don't have sourdough, honey. How about rye or wheat?"

"Rye," Boyle said.

"Did you want sausage with that?"

"Oh, yeah."

"Links or patties?"

"Links."

The waitress finished writing, then looked at Victor. "I'll have the same," Victor said.

"Ok. That should be right up. I'll get you guys some coffee."

"And some water please," Victor asked.

The waitress walked away.

"I don't think she liked that request," Victor said, "Why?"

"She didn't smile."

Boyle looked at his watch. "It's 2:30 in the morning. Would you smile waiting on people like us?"

"But we're nice people," Victor said. "She doesn't know that. It would help her pocket book."

"You mean tips?"

"Yeah. Even if she has to fake it, she should smile."

"What are you trying to say?"

"It doesn't cost anything to smile. Even if you don't feel like it."

"It depends on the person. Some people are just naturally bubbly. You know, perky! Like Katie Couric on the Today Show."

"I don't watch TV."

"You don't have one?"

"No. It's a waste of time."

"But you get the news in the morning."

"Yeah, fake news. They only report what they're told to report."

The waitress brought two glasses of water balanced in one hand and the coffee pot in the other. She placed the coffee pot down to set the water in front of them. Then she poured two cups of coffee glancing at the dispenser of sugar packets, sweet and low to make sure there was enough.

"Your orders will be up in a minute," the waitress said. Then she walked away.

The place was unusually busy for this time of the morning. Boyle lit a cigarette, then looked over at Victor, after sipping the coffee.

"Tell me some of your CIA stuff."

"There's not much to tell really. It's just common sense applied to the situation with a lot of room to improvise. That covert stuff you read about and see in the movies, it goes on, but not as much as you think. Take me, for instance, I just use my brain and wait for the right time. There's a crack in every defense, so I watch and observe. Then I analyze the situation."

Boyle thought for a minute, then said, "Watch, observe, analyze. Yeah, I hear you."

"You sound like you use it also."

"All the time. What else do you do?"

"That's about the size of it. But when the time's right, you have to be ready. That's the hard part." Then he spoke as if reciting from memory. "'Patience long endured."

The waitress came by and said, "Your breakfast will be right here." She poured more coffee for them. Then she moved to the next table in her section. Victor noticed she smiled while speaking this time.

"There, you see? I knew she wouldn't let me down," Victor said.

"Why's that," Boyle said, sipping his coffee.

"She smiled. It makes me feel good."

"Oh. I didn't notice."

"That's because you eat out a lot. You're so jaded that you don't recognize the smaller, everyday things in life that give it meaning."

"You just get used to it, that's all," Boyle said.

Victor pointed at him. "Don't exclude the smaller things. They can bring joy, no matter how small they may seem. That's all I'm saying here."

"Ok. I agree," Boyle said, wishing he would get off the subject.

The waitress brought the Riverhead Specials and placed them in front of the men. "Can I get you guys anything else?"

"I think we're good for now. Thank you," Boyle said. "Yeah, thanks for smiling. You're a lovely woman."

She stood frozen, as if she didn't know how to react to the statement. She smiled, tears formed in her eyes, then she just stood there speechless.

Feeling uncomfortable because she was looking at him, Victor said, "Ma'am, are you alright? I didn't mean to upset you."

"No, no," she said, her voice quivering with suppressed emotion. "I just haven't heard those words said to me for so long."

"Well, it's true! You're a very lovely woman, and you have a beautiful smile."

"Oh, thank you. You're so very kind."

With that the waitress burst into tears and ran back into the kitchen.

They went back to eating their breakfast. Finally, Boyle said in between bites, "You have a real way with women there, bud. Do you always drive them to tears?"

Victor shook his head. "I told her she was pretty. What's wrong with that?"

Boyle hiked his shoulders. They went back to eating, opening packets of strawberry jam to put on their toast. Victor spread butter on his, then the jam, using it to scoop the eggs onto his fork.

Then looking up, toward the cashier, he noticed a man that had just come inside the diner and was waiting, as if to pick up something. The man had a bald head and from the side looked familiar to Victor.

He told Henry he had to use the men's room and got up to walk toward him. He sat at the end of the counter not wanting to get too close. As the man waited, glancing at his watch, he finally looked at the rest of the diner in Victor's direction.

Through the distant retrieval method the brain spins in a pathway to memory---much like fog gradually rising in the morning---Victor recognized the face as Dr. Carl Emerson, dressed in a suit jacket with a tie loose at the collar. Victor studied the face to make sure it was him, then getting up to move closer, he stood behind him to get a better sense of who he was. Looking at the back of his head, he waited until a waitress brought out a takeout sack that she handed to the man.

"Just add it to my account, will you, hon?" the man said. As soon as he spoke, Victor was sure it was him.

Then as the waitress responded, "Alright. Thank you, Dr. Emerson." The verification was complete.

Dr. Emerson turned to leave without looking at Victor, his old patient, and exited the diner. Victor watched from inside the door and saw him enter a black Infiniti Sedan etched in chrome. As he backed out and turned to exit, Victor ran outside to get the license number. After memorizing it, he ran inside, grabbed a pencil from the register and from a blank ticket pad wrote down the number TWR-1679. Then he tore off the ticket and placed it in his pocket. He turned and yelled at Boyle.

"Henry! Come on!" he said, waving his arm with a sense of urgency.

Then turning to the girl who waited on him, he took out some money from his pocket and placed it in her hand.

"Thank you, my dear! Please keep this! And don't forget you are a lovely creature!" Boyle arrived at that time.

Victor turned to him and said, "It's him. Come on!"

They ran outside and jumped into Henry's Charger, backed it out of the parking space and onto the road.

"Are we going to Riverview?" Boyle asked. "Yeah, I got the license number. Black Infiniti."

Back inside the diner, the waitress was looking for the tickets inside her apron. When she finally found them, totaled them up, and started to ring up the check, she undid the money squeezed in her hand and found it was a hundred dollar bill. She started crying again and ran to the ladies room.

CHAPTER 45

Boyle had no problem catching up to the Infiniti that was driving at a leisurely pace on its way to Riverview Drive. He stayed a safe distance behind not wanting to be noticed at that hour of the morning.

"That was a stroke of luck that you eyeballed him like that," Boyle said, while keeping his eyes on the rear lights of the Infiniti. Then he added, "You're positive it was him?"

"I walked up and stood behind the son-of-a-bitch. I looked over his shoulder and smelled his breath. Then he turned around and looked at me. I'm positive it's him."

"Well then, it looks like tonight's the night. Now you can kill the cameras with that fancy software you got. Then we can move in and have a chat with the doctor."

"Don't forget, he won't be alone. Not in a place like that," Victor said. "I've been ready for a long time."

As they approached the turnoff for Riverview, Boyle slowed down just enough to keep the Infiniti's rear lights in sight. Then when it turned in at the gate, he cruised by at a normal speed to make sure the car was inside the gate. He drove to where they had previously been, killed his headlights, made an illegal U-turn and parked on the grassy roadside approximately in the same spot they were in earlier.

Getting out, they moved to the back of the Charger. Boyle opened the trunk, then removed the lid to the hidden compartment to remove the assault rifles and Victor's backpack. They put on their combat boots and each grabbed a Mag-Lite, then checking themselves to make sure they had everything they needed, Boyle asked, "You got your handgun?"

"Behind my back."

Boyle grabbed a wicked looking knife from the side of the hidden compartment.

It looked like a Rambo knife, only minus the teeth. Victor stared at it, as Boyle attached the knife to his belt. "It's for close encounters. I got another. You want one?"

"No. I got my own, only not as big," Victor said, smiling. The knife was long and strong. And would definitely do the job.

"Well then, I guess mine is bigger than yours...excuse the implication," Boyle said jokingly.

"In your dreams," he said, laughing.

Looking for the kevlar vests, he found only one. He stared at it for a minute, because he knew one of them would be at risk. Dan must have taken two that were fitted tightly together by mistake. He grabbed the vest and held it for Victor.

When Victor saw it, he took it and began to put it on. Then noticing Boyle, motionless, he asked, "Where's yours?"

"I don't know. It must have gotten into Dan's trunk." Then he looked at Victor. "Honest mistake. You know how it is in the dark."

"Yeah, but...it could be costly." Then he took the vest and handed it to Henry.

Boyle pushed it back. "No way. You're my suspect, and by God I'm not losing you to anyone or anything." Then he pointed at him. "Put it on."

"Henry."

"Just watch out for me if the shit goes down."

Boyle remembered to place a pre-written note underneath the windshield wiper that said they were gone to get gas and would be right back. Then they walked down the embankment and started plodding toward the wall just inside the tree line out of sight to avoid the mud. The grass was long and soft under their feet. They stepped on a few twigs that snapped, making a small echo along the bank. A car was seen coming in the distance, so they knelt down to hide until it passed. Then they continued until they came to the corner of the wall that was short enough to look over.

Taking out a pair of binoculars from his pack, Victor looked around the grounds. At the end of an asphalt drive he could see the house. Another vehicle was parked to the side of it in addition to the one Dr. Emerson was driving, a black Cadillac SUV that looked like it had one way tinted glass.

There was so much light coming from the floodlights that the stars could hardly be seen. The grounds in whole looked like a football field with all the light centered at the fifty yard line and decreasing light stretching to the edges of the field. Exterior lights lit up the house. The only light inside came from the back end, which was within walking distance from the parked Infiniti. Perhaps, the doctor was having an early breakfast before retiring.

Victor glanced at his watch and pressed the button to light up the dial. It read 3:10 A.M. He saw Dobermans behind the house secured in a kennel. He was glad that he brought the tranquilizer gun that he used quite often in his CIA service, because he hated to kill dogs, and especially innocent people that interfered with the target person, so he would use the tranquilizer gun on them. Without the tranquilizer gun, he would have to kill the dogs, but it was worth it to gain access to the house unannounced. He was glad he brought it along.

"How does it size up?" Boyle asked.

Lowering the binoculars, Victor said, "Well, it looks pretty easy from here, but I've learned never to trust that. There's only one light on in the back, two vehicles, and dogs are in the kennel."

"Do you have a tranquilizer gun?" Boyle asked. "Yes."

"Good. At least, we don't have to shoot them."

"My sentiments exactly."

Boyle paused for a moment, then asked, "What do you think? Go in the back door?"

"That would seem appropriate. The light is still on, though. Someone is still awake or maybe they just leave it on."

"We should probably check the other side. We don't know what's over there."

Victor nodded. "I'll see if I can disable the cameras, maybe some other equipment inside," Victor said, taking out his laptop to power it on.

Boyle watched him clicking the keys on his laptop. "So you can kill the cameras, and whatever else inside, right from there?"

"Yes, it's a program called DUMBO. It's still in the testing phase, but we've had good results with it so far. It was rolled out to a few lucky people like myself to test in the field. And so far, so good."

"Why do they call it DUMBO? Seems inappropriate."

Victor smiled. "I know. IBM never made sense with their naming conventions either." Victor looked over at Boyle. "Maybe they took after them."

Boyle nodded. "So how long does that take?" Boyle asked, referring to his work on the laptop.

"Well, I'm waiting for it to connect, but it just keeps spinning." Victor gestured for Boyle to lean closer, then used his finger to point on the screen. "You see when it connects to their Wifi? A dropdown list appears to indicate which operating system they use. Then I just click on that and we can shut down these cameras, and any other stuff that will give us problems. If it takes too long, we'll just have to wing it."

"You mean shoot the cameras?"

"Either that or point them in a different direction. If they have motion detection, we'll have to do something else. But shooting seems too extreme. My motto is "A bullet saved is a bullet earned.""

Boyle wrinkled his face, not getting the drift of what he meant. "Don't take it seriously. Just a joke."

Suddenly, a wave of mechanical sound accompanied by wind fell over them as a helicopter came in over the trees. They both ran back to the tree cover, watching as the helicopter, a black silhouette against the sky, maneuvered to a position over the concrete landing pad. A spotlight underneath the craft came on to light up the targeted

E. They ducked down lower to watch as the craft struggled against the wind to hold steady, as it slowly came down to land. Then the light was cut off and the high-pitched turbine was shut down.

The rotors spun free for a while, then came to a halt. The pilot's door opened and someone got out. With his binoculars Victor saw it was a male. The pilot moved to the rear door of the helicopter and opened it. Expecting someone to get out, they were surprised to see a big dog leap out to go running around the grounds. The dogs in the kennel woke up from their slumber and started barking at the new dog. It was dark and hard to tell the breed, but Boyle guessed from its size that it was a German Shepherd. Then the dog stopped, sniffed the air, turned and started running toward their position behind the wall barking loudly. Victor was ready with the tranquilizer gun in case he had to shoot the dog which would completely blow their cover. They would have to stop everything, collect their stuff, hustle back to the car.

Then the pilot shouted, "DAKOTA!"

The dog stopped and turned. The man repeated, "DAKOTA! COME BACK HERE!"

The dog immediately turned and headed back to its master, who was waiting at the back door with a briefcase in one hand to greet him cheerfully. Then they both entered the house.

"Ok," Boyle said. "Something new has been added."

"Right," Victor agreed. "Looks like a delivery of some kind. Let's give it a few minutes. See what develops."

The few minutes were short lived, as the pilot came out quickly, having dropped off what he came to deliver. He came out carrying the same briefcase, having deposited its contents inside the house. He was followed by the big dog again, who took off running at a full gallop to the same spot, where they were behind the wall. The dog was barking loudly and caused the Dobermans to join in for a dog barking chorus. Then the pilot shouted his command again.

"DAKOTA! GET BACK HERE! NOW!"

The dog stopped, turned back to the pilot, then looked at the wall where Victor and Boyle were hiding behind.

"DAKOTA! COME!" the pilot shouted, waving his hand in a frustrated gesture.

Reluctantly, giving into the override of her master's call, the dog trotted back to the helicopter. The dog stopped to take a leak, then they both got in; the engine was started and the helicopter lifted itself up from the landing pad to disappear over the trees.

"Well, we have to take care of those dogs," Boyle said.

"Yeah," Victor said. He checked his laptop again, then added, "This isn't connected yet. We'd better take out the cameras by hand." Then remembering something, he said, "Wait a minute." Victor reached into the bottom of his pack trying to locate something, then checked the rest of the zippered pockets hidden from view.

Finally, opening the last pocket he pulled out an aerosol can of flat black paint. Then he started laughing. "I almost forgot. I had to do this one other time, and I thought I would keep it in case I needed it again."

"Lucky for us," Boyle said.

"Good thing I remembered." Then focusing on the grounds. "I'm going to crawl over the wall, then stay low and take out these first two in front. After that, I'm going to work my way around to the other side. Test your scope on the house."

Boyle lowered his rifle and checked the scope leaning it on top of the wall. "Yeah, I can see it fine."

"Turn up the magnification a few clicks. I want you to cover me in the back," then looking around he said, "I wish we had another can of spray paint."

Then Boyle had an idea. "How about some mud? We got plenty back there."

Victor smiled. "Yes, we do. I didn't think of that. Now, do you see why I wanted to contact you?"

Boyle smirked. "Yeah, it's all about mud. You got a plastic bag?"

"Maybe," he said checking, then he added, "Bingo! There you go, detective."

"Be back in a minute."

Boyle disappeared into the trees with the plastic bag and Mag-Lite. He walked several feet into the wooded area until he reached a convenient place with mud that sucked at his boots that he avoided as best he could. Then he scooped with his right hand to extract the mud from the bog and placed it into the bag. When it was a little over half full, he swished his hand in the surface water, then drying his hand on his shirt, he took the bag back to the place at the wall next to Victor.

"Ok, you ready? I'll go first. Then, you follow with the others."

"Ok, go," Boyle said

Victor nodded, then moved several feet away, then rolled over the wall with as little motion as possible, letting his body go limp until his legs touched the ground. With his rifle strapped to his back, he crawled like a bug low to the ground to each camera pole and sprayed it with the black paint. He continued the process until he blacked out the three cameras closest to their position by the wall. When he was done, he waved for Boyle to take his turn with the mud, as he disappeared farther down and circled behind the garage to the other side of the house.

Boyle repeated the motions of Victor crossing the wall, but he didn't crawl because of the mud in the sack he carried. He crouched low and moved in a gliding, graceful kind of run moving from pole to pole, plastering the mud on each camera until each one was finished on this side of the house, except for the ones attached to the house itself. He would see if Victor had enough paint, when he got close enough to talk to him.

The dogs hadn't barked since the helicopter took off, so Boyle figured that Victor had shot them with the tranquilizer gun. Moving close to the house, he followed the drive to the back of the Infiniti, where he took cover to rest his knees a bit. He saw the kennel and there was no movement from the dogs. That was good. Then looking back at the work they had completed, he considered it a good example of field expediency in their improvisational use of materials to cover the cameras. But the ones attached to the house still bothered him. Checking the bag, there was still some mud left, maybe for one or two, possibly three cameras, but he wanted to use plenty to cover them completely or else it was useless. Then looking at the kennel, he saw a water faucet used to water the dogs. And there was a bare spot close by where he could make more mud to add to his present supply. Perfect!

So grabbing one of the dogs' water bowls, he opened the faucet to run water in it. Then he plunged his knife into the earth to turn it over and poured water on it to mix the mud, kneading it with his hands into a consistency that stuck together to make mud balls that when thrown would stick to the cameras. He made several and placed them in the bag. Then walking quietly around the house tossed them with a smack on each camera obliterating any outside view possible. When finished he hustled back to the faucet to wash his hands, drying them on the thighs of his pant legs and looked for Victor, who had finished with the spray can on the remaining pole cameras.

Boyle waved at him and seeing it, Victor trotted over, but seeing an electrical box by a corner of the house, he went there first, opened it, then using his light discovered all the circuits marked cameras. Boyle watched as he turned the switches off, then he walked over to him.

"Are all the cameras covered?" Victor asked.

"Everyone on this side. How about you?"

"We're good. I shut off the breakers for the cameras. Let me go in the back door first to clear that room. I think it's a kitchen. Then we can regroup and continue from there."

"Got it. What about an alarm system?"

"I just disabled it from the box."

CHAPTER 46

T hey moved to the backdoor with the stealth of two hungry cats—caution and secrecy at its highest demand. Boyle used his knife to pry the aluminum door from its hinges where they entered a storage area for shoes, coats, fishing poles, boating equipment, and boxes of various sizes with unknown contents. Shouldering their rifles, they brought out their sidearms. A light coming from one of the rooms drew them farther in.

Entering the kitchen, Victor saw the takeout bag from 'The Pancake House' was still on the table. Victor pointed to it and Boyle nodded. A jacket was draped across a chair, dishes were in the sink but not washed.

Moving into the living area, a dining table, some scattered furniture, and a corner for bookshelves populated the room. Along a wall, raised above eye level, surveillance monitors hung menacingly. All the screens were dark, except a few in front that they had overlooked.

A voice from upstairs disturbed their concentration. Someone began descending the carpeted steps while talking on a cell phone. Victor waved with a quick jerk of his arm for Boyle to get out of sight. Then he moved quickly and quietly to the shadows of the staircase, placing his back against it and pointing his handgun extended to the length of his arm ready to fire.

As the person reached the bottom step and turned to enter the room, Victor pressed his gun to the back of his head saying, with an extended hand, "Give it to me."

The person paused. Victor pushed the gun harder. "I said, give it to me!"

With the phone in his hand, Victor reached back for Boyle to take it. He had come out of the shadows to retrieve the phone with his gun pointed. Then moving to get more light, secure in knowing Victor had the man covered, he holstered his gun and began checking the contacts and recent calls.

Victor recognized Dr. Emerson as all the dark memories of what happened flashed before him. Dr. Emerson began to speak, but before he uttered a word Victor jabbed him in the throat, causing the doctor to fall to his knees clutching his throat, coughing and spitting saliva. Deciding whether he should help him, Victor moved toward him and, reluctantly, pushed him onto his back. Then standing over him, Victor thought to himself, I could let it end here and no one would know. But he knew it was too easy and some suffering needed to take place. So he grabbed the doctor's belt and lifted his torso to increase his airflow, lowering it to repeat the process.

"Breathe, you miserable bastard! Go on, breathe! Unless you want to choke to death."

Victor continued to raise and lower his torso, as dark thoughts of killing him impinged his mind. Finally, Victor stopped and dragged him over to an armchair and sat him in it. He secured one arm to the armchair, using flex cuffs. Slowly, the doctor regained his breath.

Eying his assailant, he spoke, wheezing and coughing a little.

"I never thought…we'd meet again like this." Pulling at the cuffs, he said, "Is this really necessary?" He continued to cough more until Victor thought he would cough up an organ.

Calmly, Victor replied, "After what you did to me, I don't think it matters. But I tell you what, I will not destroy your face with the butt of my gun. I just don't feel the need right now. But maybe later. I feel sorry for you, though. Your mind is so twisted that reason is gone completely from you. All you care about is your fucking experiements. You are not Tesla, doc! You could have been recognized with him, but you went the wrong way! You're evil!

Most evil men don't realize they are, and you're right there with them."

"How dare you talk to me like that? I'm a scientist! Look what I did for you. I made you into something the world has never seen."

"And they never will again. Not from you."

There was silence, then Boyle started walking toward them. "Who's your friend? Dick Tracy?"

"That's Detective Henry Boyle from the NYPD. You should be nice to him. He's here to take your confession."

"My what?" The doctor jumped up from the chair, but his tethered arm refused.

Victor paced up and down, as Dr. Emerson continued struggling, then he said, "I've thought of a million ways I could torture you, peeling your skin off inch by inch, and I've done that previously I'm sorry to say, but..." he paused, chuckling ironically. Then he continued. "I'm just not like you, doc."

"You certainly are not!" he said, coughing and wheezing. "You are the bright light that our group has been searching for—the ultimate candidate for my experiments! And you've come through with flying colors! You are unique beyond measure, my boy. Don't you realize it? So when you say you are different, good Lord, you're different from everyone! Get that into your head, will you?"

"I'm not Superman, you fuckin idiot."

"But you could be! Come back with me, Victor! I'll adjust your input to see what we can accomplish. I'll be there to fix and adjust any problem or difficulty you might have. I'll hire a team of doctors to keep you healthy. And possibly prolong your longevity."

Boyle interrupted with a pen and yellow legal pad. "I hate to interrupt this most interesting conversation, but we need to get the ball rolling." He placed the pen and paper on the table. "If you would release him, Victor, we can get started."

The doctor went crazy for a minute. "Wait a minute! Now, wait, just a doggone minute! I'm not signing anything! I want my lawyer present! Now!"

Laughing to himself, Victor said, "Do you think he's really going to come for this?"

"I do. He's been my lawyer for years!"

"Then he's a twisted cocksucker of a counselor. You just tell him what you want and he agrees? Is that how it works?"

Dr. Emerson took a deep breath and looked around. "Gentlemen, I believe we have started on the wrong foot here."

Victor laughed. "You hear that, Henry? The wrong foot."

They both laughed as Boyle took out his Rambo knife and moved toward Dr. Emerson, who dragged the chair away and threw up his free arm to stop. "Oh no! Just a minute! Wait! I said wait! Please! I'm not guilty of what you think!"

Close to him, Boyle said, "Shut up for a minute, will you?" Boyle leaned over with the knife as the doctor looked away with a hurtful face after he cut the flex cuffs.

Boyle pointed his finger at him. "Don't get any ideas, you hear me. Now, go sit at table and start writing."

Dr. Emerson turned to him and stated, "Did the both of you ever stop to think that I'm a human being? That I have choices?"

Victor rushed forward and shoved his gun underneath his jaw. "That's enough! You didn't give me a choice, did you?"

Pushing the gun away, as Boyle restrained Victor, the doctor said, "We had no choice! It was a governmental decision!"

Victor stared at him, holding in his hate, then said, "Oh, it was the government! At last we know!" Victor pointed at him. "You sit in that fuckin chair and start writing or so help me I'll disembowel you while you're still alive so you can watch yourself die!"

"Alright! That's enough!" Boyle said. "We need to focus on the task."

Almost laughing, he said, "What task? A confession? I have no idea what you want from me."

"You mean you've forgotten all the things you've done. Your crimes against humanity? Your cruel experiments."

"Do you know how long it would take to write about my experiments? And what crimes? What are you talking about?"

Victor looked tired. He leaned over, took a breath, then looked to Boyle for help.

Coming over, Boyle said, "I think I can help you out here, Dr. Emerson. We're not asking you to write a book here. Just what happened to cause you to put that thing in Victor's head?"

"What thing?"

"Oh, you've got amnesia, now?"

"I don't understand what you want me to write."

"What I said. The facts leading up to whoever operated on Victor. And what part you played in it. Alright? We'll start there and then look at it when you're done."

"But I keep telling you both. I didn't kill anyone."

"Oh, I know. I know, but–" Boyle said, sounding sympathetic.

Victor came charging at him again, saying, "you son-of-a-bitch! You put me through hell! Don't push me! I could change my mind and blow your head clean off!"

The doctor stood firm and remained calm. "No, you won't! That implant needs to be adjusted! If you kill me, you'll be killing yourself!"

Victor grew even more tense, his insides twisting with an extreme heartache. "Never once did I hear you say you're sorry. Not once! YOU MALIGNANT MAGGOT!" Grabbing his shirt Victor threw him around, banging his head on the table.

Dr. Emerson threw up his hands to cover his face and said screaming, "OK! I'M SORRY! I'M SORRY! ALRIGHT? I'M SORRY!"

The doctor started crying from the stress. Victor pulled away his gun, breathing heavily.

"Well…at least, you said it. Even though you don't mean it. You miserable fucking asshole." Then looking at the floor and being careful where he stepped, he said, "Looks like you had an accident there, doc. I'll have to side step this, so I don't get wet."

Dr. Emerson pleaded with him. "For God sake let me change. You don't have to humiliate me in front of your friend."

"You mean Detective Boyle? Yeah. He's my friend. And you…well, I think that's been established."

Thinking for a minute, Dr. Emerson stood up and said, "Let me change. Then I'll write your confession."

"No. Don't go there. It's not our confession. It's yours."

"You're forcing me to write it! Under duress!" Then pointing at Boyle, he said, "You! You're a police officer! You should be ashamed!"

Boyle looked at his feet chuckling and said, "Well, I've been ashamed. But not in this case." Then his demeanor changed to a darker side, "Now, sit your funky ass down and start writing, you limp dick son-of-a-bitch!" Boyle moved quickly to him and the doctor sat down just as quickly.

Turning to Victor, Boyle said, "Go see if you can find something dry for him to wear." They looked at each other, then Victor went upstairs. Boyle removed the rifle from his shoulder and set it on the table. Then he sat across from Dr. Emerson. "You and I are going to get to know each other a little better, doc. I'm here to help you get through this transition."

"Transition to what?"

"Well, you must understand that you'll go to prison for the crimes you've committed. That's a given. I'm not a lawyer, but it would be in your best interest to write a complete confession stating what you did, why you did it, and what the projected outcome would be."

"So you want me to write about my experiments?"

"Only the one you performed on Victor. That's not so bad, is it?"

"I didn't perform it. I just participated in the background."

"Then write about your experience leading up to the day the implant was placed in his head. Conversations, meetings including others who helped. And who was responsible. Who gave the order?"

"You want me to give you names?"

"That would be nice. Addresses also," Boyle said, tired of the conversation. Thoughts of frontier justice ran through his mind for a more efficient way to determine guilt and execution. Then he reached across and tapped the paper. "It begins by writing something, not just anything. The important facts. If they're wrong, we can fix it later."

The doctor looked at him and asked, "How did you get hooked up with Victor?"

"Well, it started at Grand Central Terminal. I was called there to investigate a murder."

"How did Victor come into the picture?"

Boyle looked hard at him. "That's going to take a long time to explain."

"I'm waiting for my dry pants," the doctor said, smiling.

"Well, it started with a series of notes left on the bodies I found, then he got ahold of my phone number and he kept telling me that he knew who the real killer was and he wanted to help me find who it was."

"Really? That's very interesting. You should try to get a book deal on it. I'm sure it would sell wonderfully."

"Yeah. Sell the idea. Have someone else write it."

"Well, you could do that. Who would be better suited to the task than you."

Boyle started to laugh. "What are you up to, doc. That confession won't write itself. We'll stay here all night, if we have to be. So get moving." He tapped the paper again.

"How should I start?"

Boyle thought for a minute, then said, "On the above date and approximate time, I, Dr. Carl Emerson…" Stopping, Boyle said, "There you go. That's your beginning."

"Oh, that was good. Give me some more."

Victor came down the stairs and tossed a pair of pants to Dr. Emerson. "See if those fit. I just had to guess. I brought some underwear, too."

The doctor got up, stripped off his wet trousers and underwear without any shyness or embarrassment, while Boyle and Victor looked away. Then he put on the dry clothes and discarded the wet ones in the kitchen as Victor followed him. Then coming back to the table, he turned to Victor and said, "That feels so much better. Thank you so much. You're a good friend."

"I'm not your fucking friend, you sick bastard. Not after what you did to me."

"Oh," he said, with a flip of his hand. "It's water under the bridge now. Time to start over. We have lots to do."

Victor moved forward and pointed the gun straight at his face, only a few inches away. The doctor threw up his hands to cover his face and bent forward in a childish effort to hide. He was shaking with fear. The doctor had fallen to his knees with his hands clasped, pleading for his life. "Please, don't kill me, Victor! I am so sorry!"

Victor relaxed, lowered his gun and said, "You're not sorry. That's one thing I know about you. You've never been sorry for anything you've done in your whole miserable fucking life!" Then thinking for a moment, he said, "Come on. Get up. I don't want you to pee all over yourself." Victor helped him into the chair. "Start writing."

Dr. Emerson paused, looking at the paper, then stood up and looked directly at him in a strange way. "All I know at the moment, Victor, is that you can't kill me. You'd be endangering your own life. You need me to keep you going. That implant has been inside your head way too long. It needs to be checkered, cleaned, and updated…even repaired, perhaps."

"What…what do you mean?"

"You'll die… eventually, if I'm not allowed to go in and check it…to make sure it's operating properly."

There was silence in the room. The ruffling sound of wind searching the exterior for a way inside was the only sound heard.

Shaking his head, Victor said, "It's just amazing to me how you talk about what you've done to me like it was nothing. Just another day at the office."

"Well, in a way, it was. But I'm telling you the truth."

A hidden sense of fear rose inside Victor that came out with, "Good God, doc. I'm a human being, not a guinea pig. Do you ever stop to think about that?"

"Victor, that's why you were chosen. You're an elite human being with exceptional skills beyond what we've seen. We've gone this far. We can't go back now." The doctor stepped toward him.

"That's far enough!" Victor said, giving him a straight arm in his chest. "I should have just killed you long ago and been done with it."

"And then you'd be dead."

"I mean before the implant you dumbass! When you guys suckered me into it!"

"Victor, you agreed to it. You signed a document to let us proceed. Don't you remember?"

"I remember you guys manipulating me. Forcing me to sign."

"But you signed. We didn't."

Victor rubbed at his head, as if trying to work out thoughts from long ago. "I just don't understand people like you!"

"You don't need to understand. I can do that for you," he said, pointing his finger at him. Victor stood there speechless.

Exasperated, Dr. Emerson asked, "Detective, could you go into the kitchen and make some coffee please? I don't think any of us are going to get any sleep tonight."

Dr. Emerson looked at them both hoping his request would be answered.

Boyle thought for a moment, then said, "Sure. No problem. Where do you keep it?"

Happy that Boyle responded, he said, "Above the coffee maker. You'll see it. Filters are there, too. And help yourself to anything else you see, if you're hungry."

Boyle looked at Victor, their eyes met. He nodded, then went into the kitchen. There was a prolonged silence as Victor and Dr. Emerson played the waiting game.

The ticking of an antique clock was heard in the other room. It became louder the longer the silence lasted.

Finally, Victor said, "That confession isn't going to write itself."

The doctor paused, looking at his watch. He remembered some things he had to do. "I have to sign in to my computer to check the system updates and downloads."

"Those can wait. Get to writing."

"Actually, they can't. They must be checked on a daily basis, otherwise the system here goes into a complete shutdown. It's to safeguard against hackers. You can understand that, surely."

"Where do the updates come from?"

"Brookhaven, but DARPA mostly. I'm one of their chief engineers. I'm on call 24/7. That's why I'm usually up at this bewitching hour. It's amazing how the body adapts to lack of sleep."

"You're preaching to the choir, doc. Do what you've got to do, then get to writing."

"Thank you, Victor. Regardless of what happens here, I don't want to lose this system.

It holds practically my entire life's work."

Victor nodded. "I'm sure you're a good scientist, doc, but there's one question I feel compelled to ask you?"

The doctor paused, turning to him. "Ask away."

"Do you have a conscience?"

"Of course, everyone does."

"Then why did you agree to have that thing put in my head? Did you dislike me that much?"

Dr. Emerson leaned back in the chair, searching for the most meaningful answer.

"Oh, no Victor! Of course not! But, like I said, you were the prime candidate! That's why I agreed to it. And no one person gave the order. It was a committee agreement done for science and the advancement of mankind."

Victor leaned forward in the chair. "Did it ever enter your mind that it might kill me?"

The doctor's expression changed to a cold glare. "Is this one of those truth questions?"

Victor nodded, then said, "I could shoot you right now you miserable fuck...watch you bleed a little, and enjoy watching you die, the last flicker of light leaving your eyes. No one would ever know or find me. But just for shits and giggles, I'd like to hear what your answer is."

"What difference does it make?"

"Let's say...for the sake of science. Or maybe I want to tell my grandkids someday."

"You won't live that long, Victor. I don't mean to upset you, but in your line of work, it's just a matter of time. Your work is based on living dangerously."

He got up and moved into his space. "And yours is running short! Get to writing! Now!"

"Alright, alright!" The doctor said, raising his hands in defense. "I just need to finish one final thing."

"Good! And keep your mouth shut!"

The doctor had his back to Victor as he typed away on the keys. He kept looking over his shoulder to see where Victor was. When he was finished, he rubbed the bridge of his nose. Then turning in the swivel chair, he looked at the clock on the wall, then over at Victor,

"I want you to take your gun... and kill Detective Boyle...when he comes back in the room."

Victor laughed at the doctor, thinking he was delirious. He looked like a mess, holding his arms in close, because he hurt so much. Blood dried on his face. Victor could smell its foul stench. "You really are fuckin nuts. You know that? But you're time's up, doctor. No more human experiments."

Dr. Emerson eyed him carefully watching his movements. Then, as Victor turned, something foreign stirred deep inside his brain, a movement through pathways that normal thoughts seldom took, like a worm finding its way underground until it reached the light. Turning back, he knew the reason he was there. Dr. Emerson smiled.

Boyle returned carrying three coffees with his fingers laced tightly through the mug handles. In his other hand was a bottle of whisky. He sat them down carefully at the far end of the table, then raised the bottle of MacAlisters, a single malt Scotch whiskey and said, "This is too good of a whisky to waste in coffee, but that's all I could find. If anybody wants any, go get a glass from the kitchen." He stood facing Victor and said, "So, did you guys make up yet?"

Dr. Emerson watched Victor with no result, then he repeated the command. "Victor...shoot Detective Boyle."

Boyle looked at Dr. Emerson like he was nuts.

Dr. Emerson repeated his command. "Victor! I told you to shoot Detective Boyle!" Boyle started laughing and said, "I think that beating he gave you affected your brain.

You're talking out of your ass, doc," he said, reaching for the bottle of MacAlisters, squeezing out the cork. Then he started to pour his drink.

The doctor struggled to his feet and shouted, sometimes spitting the words through the blood in his mouth, "VICTOR! SHOOT HIM NOW! KILL DETECTIVE BOYLE!"

This time Victor calmly drew his gun and fired three rapid shots into Boyle's chest and torso. Boyle hardly moved, feeling only the jolt of the bullets entering him. His mouth dropped open and his eyes widened, caused by the utter disbelief and contorted surprise that Victor would do such a thing. Then he experienced an unfathomable, surreal sense of surprise that Victor would do such a thing. He didn't move, while the light slowly dimmed---then he dropped his drink and faded out, crumpling to the floor.

CHAPTER 47

Victor stood as a soldier at attention. Dr. Emerson waited and studied him. Then getting up slowly, he maneuvered his way to the body. His vision somewhat blurred, he turned and said, "Good, Victor! It appears the implant is still operational. Sporadic, but operational."

"Thank you, sir."

The doctor turned to him with a hurt look. "Victor, relax. Don't be so rigid. And please. After all we've been through. Call me, Carl."

"Yes, Carl," he said, standing at ease.

"There. That's much, much better," he said. Looking at the body, he said, "So, Detective Boyle is finally dead." Then turning back to Victor, he said, "There's a plastic tarp near the doorway as you come in the back. Also, a blue nylon cord. Would you mind bringing them in, please?"

"Yes, Carl."

Victor went out through the kitchen to get the items. After a few minutes he brought them back.

"Thank you, Victor. Now, unroll the tarp next to him here by the table," the doctor said, indicating the area off the carpet on the hardwood floor.

Victor obeyed his command.

"Good. Now, go through his pockets to see if he has a set of car keys and hand his badge and ID to me."

Victor went through the pockets of his jacket and pants, then finding the keys and also his badge and ID, he gave them to the doctor.

"Very good. Now, I want you to put the body onto the tarp. Pick him up or drag him, whichever you prefer. Then roll it up tightly."

"Yes, Carl."

"Try to keep the body level. We don't want any blood spillage."

Victor obeyed his command, then rolled up the tarp with the body inside. The doctor checked the hardwood floor and the area rug where Boyle had fallen.

"Good! No drainage. Now, take the cord and wrap it around the tarp, then tie it securely." The doctor waited for Victor to perform the task, then when he was finished, he walked over to pull on the cord to test the tightness. "Very good, very good, Victor! Now, I would like you to carry the body outside to a wheelbarrow, which is…," he stopped to think. "…yes, I remember now… next to the garage. I'll hold the door as you exit. When you have the body in the wheelbarrow, wait there for my next instruction."

"Yes, Carl."

Victor picked up the rolled tarp, now heavy with the weight of the body and carried it with both arms in front of him into the kitchen, angling sideways through the door, while Dr. Emerson held the outside door open. When they were outside, Dr. Emerson used the flashlight to light the path, as Victor followed. Then reaching the wheelbarrow, Victor sat the body inside of it.

Dr. Emerson was feeling slightly better, because he was up and moving around. He ran some cold water and splashed it on his face from the faucet by the dog kennel, noticing the dogs were sleeping which seemed unusual.

"Victor, did you tranquilize the dogs before you came into the house?"

"Yes, Carl. They'll be fine."

Dr. Emerson nodded, then dried his face using the arms of his robe.

"Alright," he said, observing Victor. "How are you doing? I'm sure it was heavy carrying that tarp."

"I'm fine, Carl. What do you want me to do?"

"Let's move to the dock. If you follow me with the wheelbarrow, I will tell you when to stop."

The doctor began walking the path to the dock shining the flashlight across it for Victor to see. It was a small dock, but large enough to tie up boats on either side. It stretched into the river a good thirty feet. The channel was deep at the end of the dock with a swift current capable of whisking anything away that was dumped into it.

When they reached the end of it, Dr Emerson said, "Alright, Victor. Push the wheelbarrow to the end of the dock." He waited for Victor to do it. "Now, I want you to raise your end of the wheelbarrow and dump the body into the river."

"Yes, Carl." Victor raised his end of the wheel barrow, and the blue tarp was dumped in the river with a splash, submerging, then rising to the surface bobbing like a buoy to be swept away by the swift current.

Dr. Emerson had been rubbing his forehead. Blood still oozed from cuts on his face. He removed a handkerchief from the pocket of his robe and wiped away some blood from his eyes.

"Are you alright, doctor?" Victor asked.

"I'm fine, Victor," then he looked at him and smiled. "Thank you for asking."

He reached out and touched his face. "I have such plans for you, my boy! Such plans! You and a host of others!"

Looking out across the river, a few lights were visible. A soft dome of higher light converged from other towns. Above it a low ceiling of bright stars closed in on the dock as if wanting to be touched.

"I suppose, that's it for now," the doctor said, looking around with the flashlight. "Something ends for something new to begin. Oh, I have such a headache. You pack a good wallop there, my boy," the doctor said, rubbing his jaw and the side of his face.

Then looking back at the house, he said, "Let's go back inside."

CHAPTER 48

Once inside the house, Dr. Emerson took some painkillers and gave attention to the cuts and bruises on his face, applying a cold compress to help keep the swelling down, but the bruising he could do nothing about. Then eyeing the whisky, he poured himself a healthy glass to help alleviate his pain. In the living room, they sat to converse about some things that needed to be discussed.

Dr. Emerson kept touching his face with the cold compress and he sipped the whisky.

Then they heard some commotion in the other room. Dr. Emerson told Victor to see what it was. Walking into the room just off the staircase, Victor discovered that the man he had subdued and silenced was now waking up and struggling to get loose. He was the personal bodyguard for Dr. Emerson, who in Victor's opinion was not that good.

Looking down at him with his hands resting on his knees, Victor said, "If I remove the handkerchief and then release you, do you promise to behave?"

The man spoke in a muffled fury still trying to get loose. At that time Dr. Emerson walked into the room and noticed his man on the floor gagged with his hands secured behind his back.

"Oh, no! No! Victor, cut him loose! Please! He's my bodyguard!"

Victor stared at him again thinking, and not a very good one. Then leaning over he yanked the handkerchief from his mouth. And taking out a folding knife from his pocket, he cut the flex cuffs, then helped him to his feet.

Breathing easier, he glared at Victor who offered his hand, saying, "No hard feelings? It was just business."

Suspiciously the bodyguard, Leo Balfour, accepted his handshake, while rubbing his head with the other. He was middle aged, older than Victor with gray hair around his temples and spots on top where his scalp showed through.

Then looking at Dr. Emerson, Leo asked, "So, he's back with us?"

"Yes, Leo. Victor has returned to the fold. Isn't it great?" Then, taking Leo by the arm, he said, "Come. Let's all sit down and have a drink to celebrate this occasion."

They walked into the other room to sit comfortably and talk. Dr. Emerson poured drinks for everyone, but Victor still declined.

After situating himself across from Victor, he said, "So tell me. What have you been doing since we've been apart?"

Leo sipped his drink and sat quietly in a chair by the doorway. "I've been looking for you, Carl."

"Yes, and you found me, not that I was trying to hide. I've never hidden from anything, but protection is necessary. I'm on the verge of something great, my boy. And if it works out you can help achieve it."

"Achieve what?"

Looking at Leo who was listening intently, he said, "Dominion." No one said anything. They just sat there perplexed, thinking the doctor was nuts. Then the doctor continued. "The way it was in the beginning. In the garden."

"The garden of what?"

"Victor, please. I've asked you to call me Carl. We've been through so much together. I feel as if you're my reborn son."

"How do you mean, reborn?"

"Well, you don't have to concern yourself with that now. You're more a messenger, a courier," then raising his finger, the doctor said, " and an enforcer when need be."

"What am I enforcing, Carl?"

The doctor paused, then began, "That's a big question with a long answer. At this moment, you're still in a testing mode. And I must say you have come through with flying colors! I am so proud of you and excited that I can barely contain it! But to answer your question, you are a messenger of this new order whose purpose is...well, to control."

"Control what?"

"The earth, of course. It's way too overcrowded. If we keep populating it there won't be enough food for everyone. Starvation has already begun in Africa, Ethiopia and other places abroad. It's been that way for quite some time. People are dying before our eyes, and we are so callous to allow it to continue. It's inhumane. But it's also important to control the News Media to show people only what we want them to know...to keep them from finding out about the horrors of the world." They looked at him, as if he were a mad man.

"The population is controlled by major corporations-- conglomerates whose sole purpose is domination. It's actually the same thing Hitler tried to install without the gas chambers and concentration camps. And its a much more humane exercise of population control, I must say." Then pausing, for a more comfortable sitting position.

"Don't you think that's a bit much?" Victor asked. "Yes, it's a huge endeavor."

"You're going to need a lot of help from people who won't agree with your plan."

"Exactly. That's why we need to control them, until they come aboard."

"How are you going to do that?" Victor asked.

Changing his seating position, Dr. Emerson continued. "Let me explain this first. After World War II, this country scrambled to attract the knowledge of the Nazi scientists. They brought thousands of them over here to continue their work that we are now doing. We have the greatest minds in the world working on it. We're going to fix the world, my boy! Yes, we are!"

There was a silence large enough and heavy enough to slice. Victor and Leo exchanged glances. Then Victor spoke first. "How can you do that? How does it include me?"

The doctor reached over and patted him on the knee. "You just keep doing what you are doing. You've been a good soldier, but listen for my voice when I call you."

"Call me? What do you mean?"

"That voice that you hear in your mind that eventually becomes your own. You've heard it."

Thinking then remembering, Victor said, "That's you?"

"Yes! That's me! Isn't it exciting? I've been able to communicate my thoughts directly into your mind for you to carry out my orders, all from the convenience of my laptop computer! It's fantastic! Forget about AI! We have a scientific breakthrough! "

No one said anything. They sat there looking at each other in an icy silence. Then Dr. Emerson, moving forward in his seat to pat Victor on his knee, said, "I know it's a lot to take in, but there is something we must do in order to carry this out. You came with Detective Boyle. Is that correct?"

"Yes."

"Where did you park his car?"

"On Riverview Drive," Victor said, then turned to point, "...about a hundred yards down."

He gave the keys to Victor and said, "Ok, I want you to go back to the car and dispose of it. Do you understand?"

"Yes, Carl."

"Did you have a motel or hotel room in town?"

"Yes, Carl."

"Good. Then just leave the car there, but make sure you wipe it down to remove any prints. Did you meet at any place prior to that?"

"I met Boyle and Dan Kearney at Sam's Bar and Grill."

"And what did you discuss?"

"We talked to Mr. Jacobs about how to get a hold of you?"

"And he suggested the house?"

"Yes, Carl. Then we came here to investigate."

The doctor thought for a minute. "And that was you that ran into me at the Pancake Diner?"

"That's correct."

"Alright," the doctor said thinking. "Now, listen to me carefully. I want you to remember nothing after leaving the Pancake Diner. Everything concerning me from that point forward is erased from your memory. Do you understand?"

"I understand."

Leo Balfour stared at Dr. Emerson with a wrinkled brow.

"Later, I will key in those instructions, so that you will hear my voice. So be listening."

"After you pick up the Charger, I'll have Leo meet you at the gate. He will follow you to the motel. Then after you're finished he will bring you back here."

"Why?" Victor asked.

"I need to observe you for a while, Victor. Just to make sure that everything is working properly. We've come so far we don't want to regress," he said, putting his hand on his shoulder."

"Where would I sleep?" Victor asked, looking confused.

Chuckling, the doctor said, "It's a big house, Victor. But we may have to vacate, because of tonight's actions. Wherever I go, you'll come with me, until I feel it's safe to release you."

"Yes, Carl."

"Good! That's all we need to do for now. So collect what you need and I'll walk you out the back way."

They both got up and collected the weapons that Victor and Boyle had brought, placing the hand guns inside Victor's pack; the rifles slung over his shoulder. The doctor walked with him to the backdoor and out into the yard. He was still a little shaky but managed to point in the direction that Victor came.

"I assume you came through the woods. I believe it is best that you return the same way. I will have the surveillance cameras cleaned and adjusted." Then he smiled. "That was very ingenious of you to obscure them that way."

"That was Detective Boyle's idea. Not mine."

"Well, as good as he was, he'is no longer a threat to us. Don't forget to watch for Leo at the gate, and I'll see you when you get back."

Victor began walking toward the wall. Once on the other side of it, he walked through the tall grass in the same way that he came, only now with the addition of Boyle's weapons. He began walking just inside the tree cover until he reached the Charger.

Clicking the remote, he unlocked the trunk. Opening it, he removed the cover for the hidden compartment. He wiped his prints off the rifle and put it back in its place, then closed the trunk lid. As he began to get in the car he saw the note that Boyle had left under the wiper blade. He removed it, crumpled it up, and placed it in his pocket. He got in the car, started it up and drove to the gate where he met Leo, who had his window down smoking a cigarette. Victor parked beside him and lowered the window on the passenger side.

"You go ahead. I'll follow you," Leo said, flicking his cigarette away. Victor nodded, raised the window, and drove to the Star-Lite Motel.

CHAPTER 49

Arriving at the motel Victor parked by the Ranger, got out, and began wiping down everything he had touched in the Charger with a handkerchief. When he was finished, he took the keys and rubbed them clean. Then he placed them far enough under the seat that you needed a light to locate them.

He went inside the motel, made the beds and cleaned up the bathroom wiping down everything he could think of that he touched. Then giving the room one final check, he closed the door, being careful not to leave prints. He turned in the key at the office. He had paid the bill. When he got back to the Ranger, Leo was standing outside of it.

"Did you drive this here?"

"Yes."

"Is it in your name?"

Victor paused, then answered, "No. It belongs to a friend of mine."

Looking at the truck carefully, Leo said, "We need to dispose of it then."

Victor jumped in. "No, Leo." Then remembering that they really weren't acquainted, he asked, "Is it alright if I call you Leo?"

Their eyes locked for a moment. Then Leo said, "Sure."

"How about we take it back to the owner. It's not far. He lives on a farm with his sister. It's early in the morning and they'll be asleep. I'll just leave the keys in it. Ok?"

Leo considered what could go wrong, then asked, "Is there a road leading up to the farmhouse?"

"Yes, it's off of 27. Close by. Surrounded by cornfields."

Leo thought about it some more. He didn't like it. Victor spoke up again. "He's a good friend. He knows I worked for the CIA. He won't say anything."

"What about Dr. Emerson?"

"He knows nothing about him."

Their eyes locked again for a tense moment. "You're sure?"

"Yes."

Leo still didn't like it.

"Ok, but when we come down that road, turn off the lights. Understood?"

"Silent like a lamb."

Then he got in the Ranger, followed by Leo in the Infiniti, and drove in the direction of Manorville.

After traveling about ten miles, Victor felt a returning headache that he remembered from previous encounters with the implant at Grand Central Terminal. He hadn't experienced it since then, but now that it was returning he recognized it for what it was, swarming through his brain to interfere with his vision, as if his brain was fighting to regain control.

Seeing an upraised sign for gas, he turned off and pulled up to the door of the convenience center. Leo pulled in beside him and rolled down his window. Victor rolled down his also.

"Everything alright?" Leo asked.

"I haven't eaten all day. I was getting light headed. Thought I'd stop and grab a takeout sandwich."

Leo nodded, then motioned for him to go ahead. Victor did well to disguise the intense headache he had, and it began to cease as he walked in the door with his memory coming back in full. He remembered what he had done to Boyle. The thought of it caused him to bend over to rest his hands on his knees. And he realized where they were going and the danger in doing that. He stood there by the potato chip section frozen like a post, overcome with the emotions related to what he had been ordered to do. He hoped that his plans were not dead, and he didn't want to complicate the matter any more by exposing Leo to the Taylor farm. It must be kept a secret.

So looking around, he saw Leo at the cashier's counter purchasing gum. He walked to the cooler that housed the pre-packaged sandwiches and took out a turkey sandwich on wheat bread. As he turned around Leo was there looking at the various choices.

"I think I'll have one myself."

Victor stepped aside as Leo reached over to remove a tuna fish sandwich on a roll. They walked back to the counter where Victor offered to pay for it all. Leo agreed. When it was over they turned left outside the door and sat the sandwiches on the hood of Leo's car. They unwrapped the sandwiches and ate them quickly. Leo grabbed the napkins and left over wrappers and took them to a trash barrel at the end of the walk.

When he turned around to walk back to where Victor was standing, Victor said, "You're not going any farther."

"What do you mean?"

"I mean this is it. You can turn around and go back now."

Leo looked at him shocked. "I thought you were just going to drop off the Ranger, then go back with me. That was the agreement."

"Change of plans. Now you can go."

"I have to bring you back."

"That's not going to happen."

"Then we've got a problem."

"No. You have a problem. You can go by choice or I can persuade you to go. Which do you prefer?"

Victor waited, eying him closely as Leo looked to the parking lot. They were positioned away from the view of the counter to the building.

Then Victor spoke, smiling. "Do you want to see if you can take me? Is that what you're deciding? I don't advise that. I used to kill for a living, cleanly and efficiently. You don't want any part of that, Leo. You're a good guy. You want to retire healthy. So get in your car and go. It's that easy. And I won't say a thing."

Leo paused, looking at him. Then he nodded, as his expression changed to a smile. "Hit me."

"Why?"

"You have to make it look good."

"Are you kidding me? I could hurt you."

"I have to show them that you got away. Here," he said, changing places with Victor so that he was against the wall. "Now. Go ahead. Make it a good one."

Reluctantly, Victor smacked him across the face with his right hand hard, knocking Leo partially off his feet but he fell against the wall as planned. Victor backed away as Leo spat blood and regrouped himself. Victor checked to make sure Leo was alright.

Leo said, "Ok, go. And thank you."

"For what?"

"For being straight with me. Good luck."

"Give me your gun."

Leo gave him his automatic. Victor withdrew the magazine, then gave the gun back to him. "I'll leave it on top of the pumps," he said, pointing to them.

"Always careful," Leo said, with a smile of admiration. "You bet."

Leo nodded. Victor walked to the pump, looked toward the cashier's window, he wasn't watching so he put the magazine on top. Then he walked back to the Ranger, got in and drove to Manorville. Leo watched him drive away and thought about chasing him. But after thinking more about it, he walked to the pump to pick up his magazine. Then he returned to the Infiniti.

When he arrived there at Riverview, he got out to give Dr. Emerson the news, who was not happy, but took it, surprisingly, in a good stride. Leo explained that they were headed to Manorville to drop off the Ranger for his friend.

"And Victor overpowered you?"

"Yes. He said he was hungry. We pulled over to a gas station and it happened there."

Dr. Emerson placed his hand on Leo's shoulder and said, "Well, old friend, I'm glad you're alright. And don't worry, I'm not angry. Victor is a very formidable opponent."

Then he shook his head and said while walking away, "We'll just have to keep plugging away.

CHAPTER 50

The cold water of the Peconic River and the tarp wrapped around Boyle enabled it to float somewhat like a raft. Boyle was not dead, when he was dumped in the river. The shots taken in his chest and torso had missed any vital organs. The trauma from the impact of the bullets rendered him so significantly unconscious that he appeared to be dead. That, along with the battered state of Dr. Emerson was what kept them from firing additional bullets into his brain to make sure he was. The tarp served, along with the cold river water as a therapeutic blanket to lessen his pain and inhibit his bleeding. The current carried him along to enter Flanders Bay, past the town of South Jamesport, where the waterway opened up into the Great Peconic Bay.

As Boyle slowly regained consciousness, his vision came and went much like a flickering light, as he squirmed and twisted with the little strength he had to see out ahead of him through an opening in the tarp. He reasoned in his clouded mind that this was probably it for him, but as his instinct was to go down fighting, he struggled with everything he had to lift to see where he was, even if he had no idea of the location.

He saw an island or a piece of one up ahead, but lost his vision as a wave washed the opening of the tarp closed. The water choked him, and he struggled to regain his breath, as he had no idea that he was sailing past Robins Island, where the Bay opened up even more. The sun was beginning to rise, and Boyle, occasionally, could see the glow up ahead through the tarp's opening. He was thankful to see it, the only thing he could do, except wait for the end.

And as the sun rose higher to peek above the horizon, he knew by instinct he was sailing out to sea. He thought to himself, why not? What better way to go than to sail out to the ocean, beautiful and free, except for what bound him. He wished he had the use of his arms. Then he could paddle awkwardly to the shore, but he was restrained and tired in his bones. He had lost his strength to try and break free.

Then the thought that maybe the blood from his wounds released in the water would attract a shark who could have a nice meal to start it's day overtook his mind. At least, that way his body would be consumed to leave no trace for someone to clean up or examine the evidence. His death would be a mystery! How astonishing! But then he knew that was all rubbish and his mind was playing tricks.

With his last ounce of strength, he struggled to put words together that formed the semblance of a prayer, as he asked his unknown God to forgive him for not completing the mission. He asked for one more chance, but knew it was useless. His eyes were heavy and started to close, as he began to drift into a long, extended, and restful sleep. Then stirring, he strained to look through the opening of the tarp one last time, and thought he could see a glimmer of the sun.

***

News that Boyle was missing traveled fast throughout the station house, becoming the major topic of conversation in the break room, the stairwell, the bathrooms especially---or any other place where ear raising conversations took place. Those that cared about Boyle were genuine with their inquiries, but those who held a grudge or who just plain didn't like him spread obnoxious rumors about the quirk in his nature that was the reason for him not coming to work---that he was a closet alcoholic and was seen cruising the lowlife bars of Lower Manhattan on an extended bender sleeping it off in the company of hookers.

One ridiculous rumor was that he had stolen a sizable portion of Mafia money, having been given a tip on the location of one of their warehouses, and had disappeared to start a new life under an assumed name in another country or tropical paradise where no one would ever find him.

And the most ridiculous rumor of all was that he had gone undercover to try and infiltrate a religious cult upstate, known as 'The New Way of Life', whose charismatic leader was a Jim Jones type of doomsday preacher, who proclaimed the end of the world was coming soon.

Eddie decided that he was through with all the nonsense, the good wishers and the bad, and wanted to take charge of the situation. He sat at his desk and called Dan Kearney who answered on the third ring.

"This is Dan."

"Dan, it's Eddie. Have you heard anything from Henry?"

"No. He hasn't contacted me."

"It's been about a week. No one has heard from him."

"What about the girlfriend...what's her name?"

"Natalie. No. She was just here asking about him."

Dan paused. "Well, that's not good. But don't get your underwear in a twist. Henry is resourceful. There's a reason for this. Where did he call from the last time you heard from him?"

"He was still in Riverhead. I'm worried, Dan. Should I call the police there? Maybe they know something?"

"No, don't do that! Cops out there get lazy with second hand call-ins, especially when it's from the bigshots of NYPD. I'll go out there myself and ask around. You want to join me? You're one of us now."

"Let me clear it with Langley. Then I'll call you back."

"Ok."

Eddie disconnected the call and walked into Lt. Langley's office. He sat in the chair across from his desk. Langley was on the phone and raised his finger to indicate he would be off the call in a moment.

Eddie grew impatient, as it turned out to be more than a minute, so he took out his notepad and scribbled a note that he tore off and gave to Langley, who read it quickly, then he told whoever he was talking to that he would call them back.

When he hung up the phone, he looked at Eddie, who had a sense of urgency on his face, and asked, "Haven't you heard from him yet?"

"No, sir! I need to go look for him! Now! He may be in trouble!"

Langley gave him a hard look. "Jesus Christ! Detective, what the fuck is going on?" Eddie raised his voice for the first time. "I don't know! But I need to find out!"

Langley pointed at him. "You've known all along! I'm not stupid!" Langley leaned on his forehead and rubbed it. "Where was he at again?"

"Riverhead."

Langley looked up. "Where the hell is that?"

"Long Island... between the Forks."

"Between the what?" Langley got up and moved to the wall map. He spoke while moving his finger to find Long Island. "I'm not familiar with that. Is it near the Hamptons?"

"Yes, the East Hamptons!" Eddie said, moving over to the wall to point at the map. "Here...in the notch of the two forks, North and South," Eddie said, tapping his finger on the map again, "This is the mouth of the Peconic River, and that's Riverhead."

Langley nodded, still not understanding completely. "That's where he was last seen?"

"That's where he called me from," he said, moving closer to demonstrate on the map.

"Just follow 495 straight across and you'll come to it."

"Ok," Langley said, running his hands on top of his head, then pointing his finger at him, he said, "I'm going to the Captain and insist we start a manhunt. What county is Riverhead?"

"Suffolk County, sir."

"Good. I'll call Nassau County to see if they'll help us. There's a lot of ground to cover out there. We need to find him."

Then he looked directly at Eddie. "I want daily reports! You hear me? Starting today! Now, go see what you can find out, and keep your radio close because everyone's going to be calling you. Start thinking of where to set up a report station," Langley said, dismissing him with a wave of his hand, but then shouting after him, "And when you find Boyle, ask him what the hell he's been doing!"

"Yes, sir," Eddie shouted over his shoulder.

CHAPTER 51

Driving through the Midtown Tunnel, Eddie remembered to call Dan to tell him he was on the way. Dan said rather than meeting him in Hicksville to go on to Riverhead and he would meet him at the Starlite Motel. Having never been there, Eddie asked if it was hard to find. Dan said that he'd probably run into it and that the town was easy to maneuver in.

After an uneventful ride of an hour, Eddie found the Starlite Motel right away, and cruised into its parking lot to find Dan sitting there in his silver Cherokee waiting for him. Dan lowered his window, and Eddie lowered the passenger window of his cruiser.

"Have you checked the Charger yet?" Eddie asked.

"It's been wiped clean. His assault rifle is still in the trunk, though."

"He had an assault rifle?"

"There's a hidden compartment. He keeps it there for occasions like this."

"What about his Glock?" Eddie asked.

Dan shook his head, then said, "It's good to see you, Eddie. How's the job treating you?"

"No complaints, except for those better left unsaid."

"Right," Dan said, nodding his head.

"Do you have the key?"

Dan thought a minute, then said, "Forget the room. The maid service has already cleaned it. There's nothing in there."

Eddie paused, looking at the Charger. "Did you meet any other place than here?"

"Sam's Bar and Grill."

"Have you been back there?"

"No."

"We should probably go there then," Eddie said, looking at the Charger. Dan nodded. "Yeah."

"Should I just leave it?" Eddie asked, referring to the Charger.

Dan looked at him. "You can decide later. But if it belongs to the department. It should be returned there."

Eddie nodded. "I'll tell them to pick it up." Then he motioned with his hand. "I'll follow you."

They arrived at Sam's Bar and Grill in just a few minutes. Eddie said, as he got out of the cruiser, "I must have seen a bar on every block on the way over here."

Dan smiled, "What are you trying to say?"

"That people in Riverhead drink a lot."

"That and they go fishing," Dan said, slapping him on the shoulder, trying to keep things light. But he was more concerned about his missing friend.

They sat at the bar and waited to be served. Dan waved at Ralph, who was pouring a beer. When Ralph saw who it was, he finished pouring the beer and placed it in front of the customer and came down to greet them.

"Long time no see," he said, shaking hands with Dan. "Who's this guy with you?"

"This is Detective Genesco."

"Glad to meet you, detective. Ralph Jacobs. Welcome to Sam's Bar and Grill."

"What happened to Sam?" Eddie said.

"It's a long story. I'll tell you another time," he said laughing. Then back at Dan, he asked, "I guess you made it to Riverside?"

"Actually, it was Riverview."

"That's right, Riverview," Jacobs said, snapping his fingers. "I told you wrong. Sorry about that."

"No problem. We found it."

"What can I get you guys?" he asked, moving his finger back and forth between them. Dan thought for a second, looking at Eddie who shook his head.

"Two cokes. We're on the clock looking for someone."

Ralph nodded. "Hold that thought." He poured the two cokes from a fountain machine. He tapped the glass a few times against the button to cut down on the fizz, then brought them back to be placed on coasters.

"Ok. So you found the house?"

"Yes, but then I had to go back, because I have a bum knee."

"What's wrong with your knee?"

"I had it replaced. I got shot on the job, had to retire, but I still do contract work."

"So that's what this is?"

"Yeah," Dan avoided the real reason.

"You got shot in the knee?" Ralph asked with a painful look.

"Afraid so, Ralph. But I don't want to get into that now. We're on the trail of that guy I was with, the last time I was here."

"The detective?" Dan nodded. "What's up with him?"

"We can't find him. He's not calling in to anyone."

Ralph looked concerned. "You know, I remember that guy you're talking about. Kind of quiet, but his eyes were always moving. I would have remembered him if he came in here."

"I'm sure you would have. He's hard to forget, but I wanted to check with you. I remember you said you used to be a cop."

"Yeah. All I do now is hustle drunks out of here."

"Free beer, though," Eddie said.

Ralph lowered his head. "Something like that, but you know...I still miss it, just the routine. Everyday something different happens to spice things up." He looked down the bar. "Now, I'll just grow old like the rest of these bums." He looked back at Dan. "That's what they are. Bums! Who in their right mind would sit in a bar and waste away their life?

So fuck 'em! If they're that stupid, I'll take their money and laugh at their stupidity! It's been a good addition to my pension. Someday, Boca Raton, here I come!"

Everyone laughed. Then Ralph continued. "So your guy is MIA, huh?"

"Yeah," Dan said. "It's not like him at all. We don't know what to make of it."

"Did you go by the house? Push the call button, ask to speak to Dr. Emerson?"

"I guess that's the next thing to do."

"If you go by the police department, they'll just file a report and that'll be it. But, at least, you'll have done that. It's a point of reference."

"I think we both know how that'll go," Dan said.

"So your guy just disappeared. Wow," Jacobs said, shaking his head. "Yeah. He was an outstanding detective."

They paused. Finally, Ralph said, not because he knew Boyle, but like all cops there was a brotherhood between them that went beyond normal boundaries of explanation, so he said, "That's one of the hardest things about the job. But you have to do what you have to do. Fellows, my heart goes out to you! And I hope to God he turns up! What was his name again?"

"Boyle. Henry Boyle."

"I'd still go out to the Riverside address," he said looking down the bar. "Riverview."

"Yeah, you're right."

"I think we'll find Mr. Murphy's been there."

"Murphy?" Eddie asked, turning to him. Dan looked at Ralph. They both smiled.

"It's called Murphy's Law. If something can go wrong, it will." Eddie nodded, soaking it in.

"Well, you never know. And I'll make sure I include him in my prayers."

Then leaning forward and lifting his hand for emphasis, he said, "You know, it seems like we don't ever hear from God anymore, but believe me fellows, he's still around. You guys keep the faith." Then Ralph wrapped his knuckles on the bar and stood up.

They finished their cokes and got up to leave, appreciating Ralph's kind words of encouragement. They shook hands with each other.

"Good luck to you, my friends. I wish you all the best. Come back anytime. It's on me."

CHAPTER 52

Eddie followed Dan to Riverview Drive to check out the house. They pulled into the paved area to turn around and parked side by side in front of the gate. Dan got out and pushed the call box button, waited for a response, but no one answered. He pushed it a few more times, thinking someone was either on break or using the bathroom, but the same thing occurred.

He walked over to the gate and looked at the house. No cars were parked at the side. He examined the wall a few feet away, then he turned to Eddie, and asked, "You have any boots?"

"In the trunk of the cruiser. Why?"

Dan walked over to him, then looked over at the wall again.

"Feel like taking a walk?"

"I guess. Why?"

"I'm going to climb over the wall and walk down to the house. Why don't you come along?"

Eddie looked around, unsure, then said, "Yeah," Eddie remembered something and he added, "I didn't tell you that when I talked to Langley. He was going to go to the Captain about launching a manhunt, and the checkpoint will probably be somewhere in Riverhead. I need to locate that when we're finished."

Dan nodded. "Then we'd better do this now."

Dan opened the back of his SUV and put on his boots. Eddie did the same at the cruiser. Then they walked a little way up the road and found a place suitable with natural footholds to climb over the wall; first Eddie, who assisted Dan because of his knee.

After both were over it, they walked through the overgrown grass to the asphalt drive. Their feet sunk slightly in the asphalt, as they continued at a leisurely pace to the house. Dan unfastened the snap that held his gun in place. Eddie noticed and did the same.

There were no cars visible. Dan noticed tire marks on the asphalt drive that became heavier on the turnaround in front. The marks of the tread were larger than normal which told him a truck had been brought to the house. Examining the front porch and the front door, he found faint evidence of moving things in and out---scratches on the frame, and on the hardwood porch in front of the door. He knew what that meant, but he wanted to look inside to make sure.

Looking at Eddie, who was at the bottom of the steps, he said, "Let's check the back." They walked around to the side of the house until they reached the back walkway.

The kennel was now empty of dogs, and walking over to it, Eddie witnessed something. He looked back at Dan and said, "There used to be dogs here. I think they've been moved recently."

"Why's that?" Dan asked who was trying to get in the door. "Fresh poop."

Dan thought more about trying to open the back door but didn't want to break the lock. After all they were trespassing, and he didn't want to add breaking and entering to that, but he could always use his FBI identification to validate his presence and reason for entry. But he didn't like doing that unless it was necessary.

"Walk around and see if you can look in the windows. Ok?" Eddie nodded, then disappeared around the corner of the house.

Dan walked over to the garage. He found more tire marks in the asphalt to indicate moving. The door was secure. He looked around at the grounds with the scattered surveillance poles. It looked like a small vehicle of some sort had driven to each pole, evidenced by the indentations in the grass that formed a trail to each one. Curious, he thought. Perhaps, it was a maintenance vehicle making adjustments on a service call.

Eddie came back in a few minutes and said, "I climbed up on the AC unit and looked inside. It looks bare."

"I was afraid of that. It looks like Dr. Emerson has moved on to somewhere else." Eddie nodded. "I think so."

Looking around, Dan said, "Let's walk down by the dock."

They walked down to the dock, on the path laid with bricks, and looked out onto the river. The sun was out, scattered clouds in the sky. Some fish were jumping. A few ospreys were flying above the water eyeing the surface for activity to satisfy their hunger.

Looking to their left, they thought they could see the ocean that was really the Great Bay that was followed by connecting bays that led to the Atlantic. They looked at the river and the surrounding elements feeling empty, helpless...and profoundly sad.

Eddie looked over at Dan and asked, "What should we do?" Dan took a deep breath and let it out.

"There's not much we can do, Eddie...except wait for the manhunt. It hurts like hell, I know...like we've lost a brother...a valued friend."

Eddie paused slightly. "Do you think he's—"

"I don't think anything. And what I know is that I don't know. We may never know. That's what's so fucking hard! A man like Henry...his talents, his instincts...he was a Marine! He would have found a way to call, if he could. We would have heard by now." He turned to Eddie. "I'm not trying to be gloomy, but I've been doing this for a long time. Don't get your hopes up, detective. You run into this every now and then, and it never gets easier. When you confront the death of one of your own, the best thing to do is walk away...if you can. And you never forget. Not trying to be cold, but that's how death is...cold! You just handle it the best way you can."

They paused looking at the river, absorbing its mysterious melody rising to encircle them with a soft, continuous murmuring—narrating a heart song of past secrets on its journey to the sea. The wind rustled the trees playing its leaves as strings in a violin or cello to assist the river's song. Seagulls overhead cried out, resting on wind currents to search the water for fish to eat. No one said anything for a long time as they bled inwardly with the river's eulogy. A squirrel ran up onto the dock, looked at them, then took off like a shot.

"What do you think happened?" Eddie asked.

"Something bigger got him. It could be another Jimmy Hoffa...nobody ever finds him. And it can happen to you and me." Then turning to him he said, "That's why you always...." He looked away, then back. "...well, it's not important now. We'll go over that some other time."

Eddie looked around, not knowing what to do. Then he fixed his eyes on the river. "You know, I really hated him at first. I thought, who the hell is this son-of-a- bitch? Then, he grew on me...the things he said. They made sense after a while. And when I put them into practice ...they worked! He was the best, no doubt about it."

"And people hated him for it. Can you imagine? That goes along with being that good. And if you asked him, he'd just slough it off like it was nothing. And it probably was to him. It's just who he was."

"The best damned detective I've ever seen." Dan looked at him. "Yeah, me too."

They walked back to the front of the house, Dan stopped, and looked at the front door. He walked up to it and wanting to make sure that no stone was left unturned, he took out a lock pick set from his pocket. After fiddling with it for a minute, he got it open and walked inside followed by Eddie.

They walked to the huge area where the struggle took place, where the surveillance monitors had been removed, but it looked clean. From the looks of it, Dan was sure it was wiped down by professionals and it was useless to inquire any further. They checked the rest of the house, upstairs and down, including the kitchen and back room by the door.

He looked at Eddie, who was still looking around like he was lost. Eddie's phone rang. He watched him answer it, take the information, and then hang up.

"You ready?"

Eddie nodded while walking over and said, "That was Langley. The manhunt isn't approved yet, but we're going to go ahead with it anyway. He's sending the K9 Unit. They're on their way now."

"How many officers?"

"I didn't ask. He said Suffolk County is going to help, still waiting on Nassau, and I'm supposed to report to the Riverhead Police Department to secure a room for Check-in."

"I'll call Westhouse. Maybe he can round up some agents."

"Are you going to come?"

"Hell, yes!"

They walked out the front door; Dan locked it from the inside, then shut it. Tried it from there to make sure it was secure. They followed the asphalt driveway back to the wall not saying a word to each other. They climbed over it. Eddie first, who then helped Dan.

Stopping in front of their cars, Eddie asked, "What happens now?"

"We do the search and hope for the best."

"I mean...after that."

Dan saw the concern on the young detective's face. He shook his head and tried his best to be as truthful as he could. "It's hard to say. This hasn't happened for a while...a long time, as I remember. I do know that the mayor doesn't like negative headlines. If a cop shows up missing or believed captured, they want to sit on it, keep it quiet, because it shows weakness in the department. But if a cop gets killed…" Dan said, turning his jaw back and forth, "that's a different story. Front page news! And those wearing suits come down to stand in front of the cameras to tell the people... the ignorant people, that this is one example of how much the police force is fighting to protect them."

Then he turned to Eddie and said, "You know the ones I'm talking about, the political animals that don't give a fuck about you and me. But they smile and tell you how much they love you and need you, and then they lie right through their fuckin teeth." Then raising his finger, he added, "And given the right opportunity, they'll promise you the world, then stick a knife between your ribs much like what happened to Julius Caesar. It hasn't changed much since then."

Then he took a breath. "So be alert, detective! Beware!" Then turning back to Eddie, he surprisingly said, "If I were you, I'd start looking for a good lawyer, not that you have to hire one, but just in case. I've got some numbers at home. I'll give them to you."

"You've got to be kidding me?" Eddie said, completely surprised.

"They'll use whatever they have to glorify themselves. Even use you as a scapegoat if it fits the scheme."

"No! They couldn't do that."

"I'm just saying, so don't get bent out of shape. Just don't trust them is what I mean for now."

Eddie nodded. Then an ironic smile crossed Dan's face.

"Here's one for you. I knew a guy who worked Corrections. He worked up in the towers with a rifle, high powered scope, trained to shoot center mass if an inmate was trying to escape. He told me, cold sober, that it's an unwritten rule between officers that if you shoot---and you have to shoot or else it's your ass---that they miss intentionally. Because if you hit the escaping inmate, even if he lives or dies, a lawsuit will come from his family. And the state will not back you up. What do you think about that? Isn't that some bullshit?"

"Unfucking believable!"

"This is the world we live in, and the job we've chosen." There was an incredibly long silence, then Dan asked, "So...after all that...are you going to stay with me?"

"Yes, of course."

"You know, I loved him like a brother." He paused, tears forming in his eyes. "And it's going to take me a while to get over it. Hell, I may never get over it! Guys like Henry are few and far between." He paused, thinking of what to say. "I can pump twenty years of FBI knowledge into you at no charge, detective. Then, you can use it how you want. What do you say to that?"

Eddie paused, eyes to the ground, then he looked up and said, "I'm in."

They shook hands, then Dan pulled him into a tight embrace. They didn't let go, overcome by the emotion of the day, and they both let go and cried for Boyle. Two grown men crying for their lost friend.

After releasing each other, Eddie walked up to the gate to look through it. The house, and the surrounding grounds, now looked empty and desolate.

After a minute Dan asked, "You want to follow me?" Eddie turned and nodded.

He walked back to the cruiser, as Dan backed up and turned around. Eddie did the same and followed him to the Riverhead Police Department.

CHAPTER 53

Lieutenant Langley urged Captain Pelasio to push the approval of the manhunt as quickly as possible. Therefore the Captain contacted Commissioner Kendall, who in turn called Mayor William Rosenthal, who after listening to the request, summoned him for a sit down at his office located at City Hall Park in Lower Manhattan. The mayor leaned back in his custom chair as John Kendall sat across from him looking out at the sweeping views of New York Harbor, the Statue of Liberty, Ellis Island, the Verrazano Bridge, and One World Trade Center. He had been there before and it always took him a while to adjust his eyes away from the captivating view.

The mayor took a deep breath and let it out.

"John, this couldn't come at a worse time. I don't mean anything against Detective Boyle. God, if we had the funds I'd call the

President to summon the Joint Chiefs and utilize all their forces, but the fact is we just don't have the money right now."

"Bill, I urge you to reconsider. And just indulge me for a minute...I'm the head of the oldest and largest, most versatile, and powerful police force in the world. I get requests all the time from other agencies around the globe about law enforcement training. We are the top, the elite, the gradient by which all other police forces measure their capabilities."

Then he leaned forward and said, "Do you want it to leak out to the press that you declined this for lack of funds? How would that make you appear to the public? What would my police force think of you? Do you want them to turn their backs on you?"

Then he paused and came back with, "You know, your election is coming up soon. So please...consider this."

****

As the officers came in the back door to volunteer, Dan and Eddie gave them sign-in sheets, and as soon as one sheet was full they were dispatched to comb that area. The areas that needed searching were woodlands, marshes, bogs, swamps and lake areas, as well as the beaches, which were quite extensive. Riverhead Police Officers helped direct the volunteers to where their search areas were located. They were extremely helpful and most of them worked overtime without pay.

Officers from the NYPD took it upon themselves to take time off from work to help in the search. Surprisingly, some FBI agents reported to Riverhead to assist in the search. NYFD and firemen on the island showed up eager to help. Dog teams were dispatched, helicopter surveillance was utilized, and the East Hampton Marine Patrol boats were to be used to search the wide area of beaches.

As many as 1,000 officers from state, federal and local law enforcement formed a dragnet, creating a 5-square-mile noose that began to tighten as the search continued. Roughly 300 officers were on the manhunt daily, working 12-hour shifts of 150 officers each, seven days per week. But after that week, when their efforts had turned up nothing, the searches were cut back and gradually, much to the disappointment of those involved, it was called off.

The only indicator of where the body might be came from the Suffolk County K9 Unit, when they were directed to search the Emerson House on Riverview Drive. The dogs knew the right scent from smelling the inside of Boyle's Charger---the trunk, glove box and console compartment. They started at the gate that led to the wooded area where nothing was found. Boyle's scent was picked up along the road again, then into the woods and to the rock wall, but again, nothing was discovered. Climbing over the wall and through the grass to the backdoor, they entered the house where the dogs were hot on the scent which was very strong. Then leading outside to the garage and the wheelbarrow, where the dogs paused, they continued to the dock where the scent ended at the water.

A BOLO was put out to the East Hampton Marine Patrol in case the body was found washed up on one of the many beaches encompassing their 500 mile jurisdiction. The following day the New York Post ran an article concerning the manhunt:

> "After fruitless searching for NYPD Detective Henry Boyle the search was called off to focus on more immediate police activities. The sprawling search followed reports that Boyle had not shown up for work, or called in for several days. Officers were seen combing wooded areas of Riverhead, through sand and thick brush. His car discovered at the StarLite Motel was untouched.

> A high-ranking NYPD source said, "The detective was working on a lead in the Grand Central Killer case that led him to Riverhead in Suffolk County, Long Island. No indication of foul play. But there's obviously more to this story."

CIA HEADQUARTERS LANGLEY, VIRGINIA

Dr. Carl Emerson pulled up to the visitor's parking area in his Black Infiniti and parked in the nearest vacant spot closest to the walkway. He got out with his briefcase, closed the door, clicked it locked and continued walking under the sun canopy to the front door. Once inside, after emptying his pockets, removing his watch, ring, and glasses, he placed his briefcase on the conveyor belt for it to be run through the electronic scanner, while the TSA Officer carried the tray of his personal items to the other side of the electronic arch that he walked through without setting it off.

Smiling at the officer, who passed his personal item tray to him, he said, "So how are you this morning?"

"Pretty good, sir," the one closest to him said. "And you?"

"Oh, it's a fine day! A fine day indeed! Thank you very much!"

He continued walking across the great circular seal of the Central Intelligence Agency embedded in the floor, past the wall of honor for the unnamed killed in the line of duty, until he came to the elevators, where he took one to the seventh floor.

He had an appointment with Deputy Director Richard Benzinger. The secretary smiled as he got off the elevator and welcomed him. "Hello, Dr. Emerson. How are you this morning?"

"You know, I'm just wonderful, because it invigorates me each time I come here to see that you're lovelier than the previous time I came."

"Well, aren't you the charmer! Go right on in, doctor. He's expecting you."

"Thank you, my dear. And that reminds me of a song I've heard, 'Love is Lovelier the Second Time Around.' I believe Frank Sinatra recorded it. Have you heard of it?"

"I don't believe I have," she said, turning to him.

"Oh, it's a beautiful song, but with you it's not only the second time, but the third, the fourth, and then it just keeps on rolling."

"Would you like to come home with me?" she said, laughing.

"I'd have to take a rain check my dear, because I'm just too damn busy. But we'll keep that thought in mind. Ok?" he said, pointing at her as he backed through the door.

The secretary went back to work chuckling to herself.

Deputy Director Benzinger rose to his feet and came around his desk to greet Dr. Emerson.

"Hello Carl. How are you doing? Glad you could make it. Have a seat," he said after shaking his hand, then walking around his desk, he asked, "Could I get you some coffee?"

"Only if you are. I don't like to be a bother, Richard. So don't go out of your way for me, please," he said, with a wave of his hand.

Then he got comfortable in the chair and placed his briefcase on the floor to the side.

Benzinger, leaning back in his chair said, "I understand you have some good news for me."

"Yes, Richard, I most certainly do. You can call off your dogs from chasing Victor. I have successfully retrieved him for our purposes."

"Wonderful! That's exciting news, Carl! How did you manage that in your bag of tricks?"

"Oh, it's no trick, Richard, I assure you. Strictly nanotechnology with knowledge of the human brain."

"Awesome! Fantastic! It makes me proud to be an American!"

Dr. Emerson looked out through the windows above the trees that stretched as far as he could see. "I had feared that he was lost, because my updates had not been taking hold with him. But I kept working at it, refusing to give up, because as you know, Richard, I am not a quitter," the doctor said, raising his finger for emphasis. Benzinger smiled and nodded.

"And then one day he showed up at my door fully operational." Then changing to a more reflective tone.

"In retrospect, it was probably good to give his brain a rest. There is such a thing as information overload, and my God, who knows what he could have done if that happened. Those killings at

Grand Central were…," he paused, searching for the right words. "How should I put it? Above and beyond the call of duty." Shaking his head, he stated, "We learn from our mistakes."

"So what's the future plan? A cyborg soldier, or what?"

"No, no! No cyborg! That gives off the connotation of a synthetic human. God forbid!"

"So what is it then?"

"Just as we're doing now. A completely human entity controlled under a government contract to do what we say." Then leaning forward, he said, "I'm considering using stem cell injections to prolong the life expectancy, the all around physical health of the subject. I've read the research and it looks good. But I'll need to inject myself first to test the stem cells.

I'm not getting any younger. So I'll need all the help I can get." Then he sat back. "That's it in a nutshell. Then it's up to you guys to get the laws passed. Then we're good to go."

Benzinger nodded. "Ok." He paused, then said, "You've read Orwell and Huxley, I assume?"

"Yes, back in school, I believe."

"Those men seem to have a prophetic voice from what you're telling me here."

"Yes, they were exceptional writers with a real grasp of the future."

Scratching his head, Benzinger leaned forward. "Are you telling me that the technology they spoke of is here today...with the experiments you've undertaken?"

"Yes, that's the exciting part, but I've only touched the surface! I need more time and money! That's why I need to do the stem cell injections."

"On yourself."

"Yes, to begin with."

Benzinger spoke by taking his hand away from his chin and gesturing with it. "Well, money isn't the problem, ever since we went off the gold standard. We can simply make as much as you need."

He paused and looked coldly at Dr, Emerson. "If the American people ever find out what we're planning, they'd lynch us in the streets. There would be complete bedlam! We'd have to issue martial law! We'd have no choice but to become a complete military government!"

Dr. Emerson nodded, then, he said, "We've heard for several years this phrase, 'The New World Order', or Huxley's, 'The Brave New World'...this will be the 'Brave New Order.'

Think of it! It's mind-boggling! But when you take it apart to examine the pieces...it's completely doable. Praise God for scientific research," he said, with a brush of his hands.

There was a long pause with no sounds of any kind, as if their conversation was locked in a vacuum.

"Well...just don't let the cat out of the bag. That's all I have to say." Chuckling with a sarcastic edge, he said, "I understand. I do understand."

"What do you need?"

"Well, money of course. Lots of it. And I need a new place of residence where I can experiment uninterrupted. I had to vacate the address in Riverhead."

"Yes, I heard that." Then thinking, he said, "So, a mountain retreat...something like that?"

"That sounds ideal, but when I deploy my experiments I like to be close so I can examine them."

Benzinger nodded.

Looking off and beyond, Benzinger said, "Perhaps an old army or air force base?" he said with a gesture of his hand. "We could have them remodeled to fit your needs. You don't mind relocating?"

"I go where the work is, Richard. And yes, that sounds better all the way around. Plus security."

"Yes, of course. I'll go to work on it and let you know soon."

"Good. But before I forget, those two operatives you had following Victor---"

"Carpenter and Johnson. Yes. I replaced them with Billings and Caldwell."

"I believe you could let them off the hook now, since I've retrieved Victor. He was a little out of their league anyway. And, of course, the Detective Henry Boyle. He was a thorn in our side, let me tell you, but we don't have to worry about him any more."

Benzinger looked at him questioningly. Then he asked, "Collateral damage?"

"Unfortunately. Too bad. We could have used him." Benzinger nodded.

"Is there anything else we need to discuss?"

"No. I believe we've covered it for now. But I do want to say that I'm thankful to you, the CIA, and God almighty for being given the opportunity to work on something as monumental as this. It's given me a new sense of hope that the world can be right again."

"Again? You mean it used to be right and now it's wrong?"

"Well, a long time ago…before man appeared…God had a problem. He created us and gave dominion of the earth to man. It all went downhill from there. And now, we're going to right that wrong."

Benzinger's eyes brightened. "I like the way you think, Carl. Keep me posted. And if you have a problem or need something just let me know."

They shook hands, said goodbye, and on the way out Dr. Emerson winked at the secretary before getting on the elevator.

Deputy Director Benzinger walked back to his desk, tried to focus on his work, then he got up and walked to the window behind him. He stood with his hands clasped behind his back like a soldier at ease, and he looked down and out across the forest of trees surrounding the complex. And he tried to imagine the earth before God created man.

CHAPTER 54

THE NEXT DAY...
at GARDINER'S ISLAND

As the Peconic river flows through the various bays and around smaller islands on its journey to the sea, Gardiner's Island is the last stop before the Atlantic Ocean. It's caretaker, Malcolm Parks was cruising the beach area of the island's eastern curve in his three-wheeler accompanied by his red-haired labrador, appropriately named Red. From aerial photographs the island looked much like a stingray with its tail stretching south. The curve of the island's eastern side was a deposit, a 'catch all' for most anything the current sent its way.

It was a habit of Malcolm's to collect driftwood, and much to his dislike, an occasional can or plastic bottle, a supermarket grocery bag discarded by an unsympathetic boater. He stayed on the island, hired by the owner to maintain the property and keep away unwanted visitors. It was a paradise with influences that stretched back to the Revolutionary War with only a few modern conveniences. No boats were allowed to the island unless by invitation, or authorized ahead of time. He was ex-military with medical training. He was licensed to carry firearms and to police the island, one of the larger, privately owned islands in the country.

Having collected a supply of driftwood and a few sacks of garbage, he was on his way back to the inner part of the island to relax and have lunch. Before doing that, he stopped to let Red have a run and to relieve his bladder. It was beautiful to watch him sprint along the beach kicking up sand behind him, his red coat against the white beach. The dog was truly happy in this unspoiled environment. And Malcolm, along with the island's owner, was fighting hard to keep it as pristine as possible despite the rising costs of property taxes and the cost of maintaining it.

Red brought back a piece of driftwood for Malcolm to take and throw so he could fetch it in a never ending, enthusiastic retrieval. Malcolm took the driftwood from his mouth as the dog tugged back on it, finally releasing its grip. Red watched the flight of the wood as Malcolm flung it, end over end, until it reached the treeline as Red almost grabbed it from the air before it landed. He brought it back to Malcolm who took it from his jaws and this time he sailed it down the beach for Red to chase.

Malcolm picked up his military surplus magazine and sat in the driver's seat of the three wheeler. He flipped through the pages for a minute, but not hearing the playful barking of Red, he looked farther down the beach and saw him paused at something that looked like a log that had floated this far out. The dog was sniffing it up and down, and then nudging it with its nose. Then he started to bark, as if something was not quite right.

Malcolm put down his magazine and started the three wheeler to drive toward the log. As he neared it, the color blue came to his eyes that he thought quite strange for something that large to drift out this far. Red was barking the entire time and he was yet to be silent.

Stopping his three wheeler, then turning off the ignition, he got out and said, "Red! Stop it! Quiet down!" The dog backed up and whimpered, but never took its eyes off the object.

Malcolm saw a blue rolled up tarp tied with a nylon cord. Kneeling down, he touched it pushing with his hand; it was firm and somewhat solid. Moving to the end, he tried lifting it to feel the weight. Then coming to the head, he repeated the lift, noticing the heavier weight, then lowered it to the sand.

Red started barking again. "Red! Shut up! Dammit! Be good!"

The dog immediately stopped barking and lowered itself resting on its haunches. Malcolm's curiosity caused him to open the flap on the end, and when he looked inside, he saw the hair on a man's head.

He jumped back.

Quickly, he moved to the nylon cord, searching for the knot that secured it, but unable to find it, he pulled a knife from his belt and cut the cord, unraveling the tarp to reveal a man's body with blood stains. Standing back, Malcolm surveyed the body, fully dressed with shoes wearing a light jacket. Kneeling down, he felt the pockets looking for identification, but loose change and a disposable lighter was all he found. When he searched the inside pockets of the jacket, he found a soaked pack of Camel cigarettes, which he discarded.

Then moving to the face, he felt it. It was cold yet not discolored the way he associated someone being in the water for God knows how long. He put his fingers under the nostrils and thought he felt a faint trace of air coming from them. But then, he thought it might be just his imagination. This man was dead no doubt. Looking at the bloodstains, it was obvious to him that they came from gunshots. Who knows what illegal activity he had been involved in.

Red came over to him wanting affection, so he rubbed his ears and said, "Well Red, it looks like we have an unexpected guest." Then looking back at the body, he added, "What should we do with him?"

It was at that moment out of the corner of his eye, he thought he saw the head move, but thinking it was just a twitch in his left eye, he looked away at the waves lapping onto the shore. Then he heard a groan, and in turning quickly to view the head, he saw movement in the face and lips in an effort to breathe.

"My God, he's still alive! He must have the constitution of a freight train," he said to Red. Quickly, he ripped open the man's shirt to inspect his torso to find three wounds that he knew came from a gun. Turning him slightly, he tried to feel for the exit holes. He thought he could feel them, but he didn't want to move him any more."

He looked at Red and gave an order. "Red, go get my bag! In the vehicle! Go get it boy!"

The dog took off like a shot tossing up sand from its paws. Locating the medical bag in the back of the three wheeler, he clamped its teeth around the two leather handles, then pulling it out brought it back to Malcolm, who was on his phone waiting for the East Hampton Marine Patrol to answer.

"Come on, come on," he said. "Answer the fucking phone!"

Finally, dispatch answered, and he said in a fury, "This is Malcolm on Gardiner's Island. I have a male body here with three bullet holes that washed up on shore. I just checked him. He's still alive. I need air medical services and a rescue boat here pronto!" He waited a minute, frustrated by the person on the other end asking too many questions, then he screamed into his phone with his face growing redder by the second.

"I SAID HE'S ALIVE, YOU IDIOT! HE'S STILL FUCKING ALIVE! STOP TALKING AND GET YOUR ASS OVER HERE, NOW!!!"

Malcolm snapped his phone closed, frustrated by his lack of ability to help the man. Looking at the poor soul struggling to breathe, wondering what else he could do for him, he untangled his arms and legs to free his body more. He knelt beside him to rub his hands, his arms and legs to increase their circulation. Then stopping, he sat back on his haunches and just looked at him, wondering who he was, why he was there, struggling with himself to believe his efforts were not futile. He checked his nostrils to make sure his breathing was consistent.

Then standing, he looked at the thin water line for a glimpse of the Rescue Boat, wondering why they were not on their way yet. Red brushed against his pant leg. He looked down and rubbed his head.

The End

www.ingramcontent.com/pod-product-compliance
Lightning Source LLC
Chambersburg PA
CBHW040329020826
48978CB00013BC/964